Praise for Eric Jerome Dickey

The Other Woman

"Dickey offers plenty of straight-on sex and violence, but also probes questions of contemporary morals and the psychology of betrayal, writing compellingly and believably from his heroine's point of view. . . . Another crowd pleaser."
—*Publishers Weekly*

"The prediction here is that *The Other Woman* will show up on beaches all over the country this summer."
—*Fort Worth Star-Telegram*

"One of the hottest African-American male writers out there."
—*The News & Observer* (Raleigh, NC)

"Dickey shows an uncanny ability to develop sympathetic female characters."
—*Ebony*

"Good and gritty storytelling."
—*Kirkus Reviews*

Thieves' Paradise

"Smartly paced . . . heart-pumping . . . electrifying. . . . In his compelling picture of another world, Dickey believably shows how even in the underbelly of society, loyalty, respect, and love have their place."
—*Publishers Weekly*

"Dickey delves deep and brings light into a world where crime has its own set of rules."
—*The Baltimore Afro-American*

"Passionate, sensual, rhythmic, comical. . . . If Eric's previous novels are food for the soul, *Thieves' Paradise* is the nectar and ambrosia of life."
—*The Chicago Defender*

continued . . .

D0092325

Friends and Lovers

"Fluid as a rap song. Dickey can stand alone among modern novelists in capturing the flavor, rhythm, and pace of African-American speak." —*Fort Lauderdale Sun-Sentinel*

"Dickey uses humor, poignancy, and a fresh, creative writing style." —*USA Today*

"A colorful, sexy tale." —*Marie Claire*

Milk in My Coffee

"Rich *Coffee* steams away clichés of interracial romance . . . a true-to-life, complex story of relationships." —*USA Today*

"Heartwarming and hilarious." —*The Cincinnati Enquirer*

"Dickey scores with characters who come to feel like old friends." —*Essence*

Sister, Sister

"Genuine emotional depth." —*The Boston Globe*

"Vibrant . . . marks the debut of a true talent." —*The Atlanta Journal-Constitution*

"Bold and sassy . . . brims with humor, outrageousness, and the generosity of affection." —*Publishers Weekly*

ERIC JEROME DICKEY

THE OTHER WOMAN

NEW AMERICAN LIBRARY

New American Library
Published by New American Library, a division of
Penguin Group (USA) Inc., 375 Hudson Street,
New York, New York 10014, U.S.A.
Penguin Books Ltd, 80 Strand,
London WC2R 0RL, England
Penguin Books Australia Ltd, 250 Camberwell Road,
Camberwell, Victoria 3124, Australia
Penguin Books Canada Ltd, 10 Alcorn Avenue,
Toronto, Ontario, Canada M4V 3B2
Penguin Books (NZ), cnr Airborne and Rosedale Roads,
Albany, Auckland 1310, New Zealand

Penguin Books Ltd, Registered Offices:
80 Strand, London WC2R 0RL, England

Published by New American Library, a division of Penguin Group (USA) Inc.
Previously published in a Dutton edition.

First New American Library Printing, July 2004
10 9 8 7 6 5 4

 REGISTERED TRADEMARK—MARCA REGISTRADA

New American Library trade paperback ISBN: 0-451-21193-6

LIBRARY OF CONGRESS CATALOGING-IN-PUBLICATION DATA:
Dickey, Eric Jerome.
The other woman / Eric Jerome Dickey.
p. cm.
ISBN 0-525-94724-8
1. African American television producers and directors—Fiction.   2. African American
women—Fiction.   3. Los Angeles (Calif.)—Fiction.   4. Married women—Fiction.
I. Title.
PS3554.I319 086 2003
813'.54—dc21   2002153861

Set in Sabon

Printed in the United States of America

PUBLISHER'S NOTE
This is a work of fiction. Names, characters, places, and incidents either are the product of
the author's imagination or are used fictitiously, and any resemblance to actual persons,
living or dead, business establishments, events, or locales is entirely coincidental.

BOOKS ARE AVAILABLE AT QUANTITY DISCOUNTS WHEN USED TO PROMOTE PRODUCTS OR SER-
VICES. FOR INFORMATION PLEASE WRITE TO PREMIUM MARKETING DIVISION, PENGUIN GROUP
(USA) INC., 375 HUDSON STREET, NEW YORK, NEW YORK 10014.

for Dr. Melanie J. Richburg,
Clark-Atlanta University,
my "baby sis"

1

shouldn't have been surprised when I met my husband's lover, but I was.

This is the face of the woman in the mirror, the wholesome face of a woman who has been married for four years: I have brown skin and cinnamon freckles that come alive in the sun, delicate freckles that all of my former lovers loved to play connect the dots with, or pretend that my face was the sky and the freckles were the stars and find as many constellations as they could. I'm in my early thirties, but on a good day, with the right makeup and the right clothes, I can pass for early twenties. Men in their twenties are the ones who ignore the ring and flirt with me the most. I think it's the locks. Ever since I lost the perm, people say I look younger.

This is the life of the woman in the mirror, the life of a woman balancing her marriage and career as a news producer: I drive an hour and fifteen minutes in traffic every day—and that's in one direction—to the 10 westbound so I can drive La Brea into the edges of Hollywood, trying to get to a job that stresses me out to the nth degree. Some days the Freeway God shines down on me and I only have to deal with traffic for an hour, but if it's a rainy day, it could take two and a half. If somebody has lost it and killed somebody on the freeway, make it closer to four. Pretty irritating, spending that much time in traffic, either alone or looking for somebody to call on the cell phone and talk with to help take the edge off the road rage.

Before I bounce to work, I rush to cook dinner and leave it in the microwave or oven—ready for my husband. If not a full dinner, then at least sandwiches. Just like my mother always did for us, there is always food in the house. When I get home at night, after working on stories on all the freeway chases, and the murder coverage, and the child abuse segments, and earthquake reports, I leave the pessimism at the door; refuse to bring negative energy into my household. I stop being a news producer and focus on being a wife. That's the Pisces in me. The emotional and sexual part of me that believes in love and is ruled by spirit.

Charles is from Slidell, Louisiana, a small country community east of New Orleans. He's a Libra, well balanced, has a high sex drive, is emotional at times, and hates drama. He has eight brothers and sisters back home, all by the same parents, all with the same black curly hair, the kind that looks wavy when it's brushed, but Charles and his mother are the only ones with hazel eyes. Very family oriented. Alligator meat, crawfish, and gumbo—that's what he was raised eating, and he can make some hellified beignets, and can throw down some thigh-fattening bread pudding with enough whiskey sauce to make you feel like you're DUI. And don't let him get his hands on some catfish. He'll fry the hell out of that bottom feeder.

My husband has a solid build, broad shoulders, and a great smile. He has a few scars here and there from being in so many fights as a boy, and boxing as a teenager and young adult, the kind of marks that make him look more rugged than pretty. His soft hair makes me wanna run my fingers through it all night. And I love his Southern accent; it's mild, not too much twang. The kind that tells you he'll treat you like a lady, open doors, and defend your honor. When he smiles with one side of his face, I know he's thinking of the position he wants to get me in. Sex is communication. Sex is food. I believe in feeding my man. And I believe in being fed. Feed him or he'll eat somewhere else. That wisdom came from Momma. She told us that a woman has to be a woman to her man, or some other woman will be.

Charles goes to bed by ten, nine if there's not a game on and he can manage to be done grading papers. He has to get up by six so he can drive thirty miles east on the 60 freeway to get to West Covina and teach social studies to middle-school rugrats. My post-show meeting runs over some nights because we have to go over what was good about the late night broadcast, what sucked, what could've been better, and if something was hot, have it ready for the next day. That can have me at the station until almost midnight, maybe damn near one in the morning.

By the time I make the drive home, Charles is dead to the world. I come in through the garage and drag myself upstairs to a dark bedroom and silence. Sometimes I just stay downstairs, massage my temples, undress, then tiptoe up to the guest bedroom and just have some "me" time. Give myself a facial and take a long bath by candlelight. With his early schedule, Charles hates to have his sleep interrupted. But I'm wired and up until two, maybe three in the morning, trying not to make too much noise. Those are lonely hours, when the world is asleep and I'm wide awake, no one to talk to, feeling like Tom Hanks in that movie *Cast Away*.

All they have on Showtime are erotic movies—some pretty bad fucking, but fucking all the same. When the moon is high and my hormones are on fire, voyeurism is nothing but damn torture. In those bewitching hours, I creep into the bedroom, touch Charles, try to get his penis to rise, and he pats my hand, asking me to let him sleep.

Then it's me, loving a capella. Or me, myself, and my little rabbit; *ménage à trois.*

Sometimes Charles drinks a little too much ginseng mixed with Noni juice and wakes up at the crack of dawn with the energy of a sixteen-year-old, rubbing against me with a raging boner, kissing that sensitive spot on my neck, his morning breath uneven and wanting.

After three hours of sleep, I'm a rag doll. My nipples don't rise, but I don't push his hand away, never have, not since we stood before God and made promises. He rubs against me and my hand drifts down, takes his girth and hardness and guides it toward my hollow. He moves inside with gentleness, but the dryness stings. Seldom do I come like that, being half-awake and barely aware, because by the time my back starts to arch and moans begin crawling from my mouth, he's holding my ass with a firm grip, his strokes strong, deep, and steady, shuddering because he's trying to keep from letting his orgasm get the best of him, and letting out that pre-orgasmic groan that sounds like an apology for being premature.

He jerks inside me, fills me with pain and pleasure, with hot liquid, heat that excites me into consciousness, and I hold him, move up against him and watch him. I love to watch him come. He has the most amazing, intense look. And it's tender at the same time. He slows down, but I keep grinding against him, contracting the muscles of my vagina around his softening penis, and try to orgasm as he catches his breath.

He runs his hands over my locks, swallows, then whispers, "You okay?"

I sing, "Good morning."

I rub his back, feel his solidness and strength over me, run my fingers through his soft hair, kiss his face. Then I tell him how good that felt, how wonderful he is, how much I love the way his dick feels inside me, and ask him to chill out with me for a moment.

"Freeway time, baby. Can't be late."

I put on a schoolgirl pout. "Thirty seconds?"

I feel him, unfocused and on edge, glancing at the red numbers on the digital clock. In less time than I've asked for, he pulls himself out of my vagina, breaks our Siamese-ness, leaves my emptiness tingling to be filled, legs ready to open wide for another ride.

His feet hit the carpet and he's a silhouette moving away from me at a fast pace.

I say, "Maybe we can finish tonight."

No answer.

I hate it when he hops right up and runs to the shower. But he can't be late for work, has to beat traffic so he can get across the freeway at least thirty minutes before the bell rings for first period, even earlier on Tuesday because of the teachers' staff meeting.

Sometimes I sit up, fight the sandman, and watch Charles shower. He knows I'm watching, enjoying the way the water runs over his body, but he's rushing, doesn't look my way. I think he's ashamed when he comes that fast, or takes me like that, invading my dryness with his hardness, all without warning. I like to think that he finds me so irresistible that he can't help himself, that he has no control when it comes to wanting me. That makes me feel as if I am the master, that he is the slave to his desires for me, and only me.

That's what I pretend.

He throws on his jeans, a nice polo shirt, grabs a jacket if it's cool, then kisses my lips.

He says, "The remote is right here."

"Have a good day. Love you. Call me."

He leaves me, some mornings his honey drying between my legs, the smell of our sex on my skin, the remote at my side. He always leaves the remote within arm's reach because he knows that I go to sleep with the news and I wake up in search of Katie Couric.

My morning is pretty much the same day after day: get up, start a load of laundry, a four-mile run around Cal State University at Dominguez Hills, come back and lift some light weights to tone my upper body, then a few hundred sit-ups. I'm no Janet Jackson, but I do want my body and tummy as tight as possible before I get pregnant and have our two-point-five kids; only God and Miss Cleo know what will happen to my figure afterward. Then I'm throwing clothes in the dryer, rushing to make myself a low- to nonfat breakfast while I figure out what I'm going to make for dinner, pulling my locks into a ponytail and taking a quick shower, then throwing on some jeans and tennis shoes and heading back to do battle with the congestion on both the 110 North and the 10 westbound, blowing my horn at people who cut me off or refuse to let me merge, losing my religion and becoming one of the heathens, changing lanes like a maniac, listening to the "all news and traffic" station, KFWB.

"What year is that Mustang?" A man in an overpriced

sports car rolls down his window, breaks his neck trying to get my attention when I get caught at a light at La Brea and Washington, the edges of the urban and Hispanic area that leads into Hollyweird.

I answer, "Sixty-four and a half."

"And a half? That's the one they introduced at the World's Fair."

"Sure is." That chunk of knowledge about my Baby Blue makes me smile. My car is very rare. Before Shelby, before fastbacks, this was the ultimate pony car. The grandfather of all muscle cars. "Fully restored from the ground up. Every nut and bolt and clip replaced."

"How much you put into it?"

"Close to ten thousand."

"Wow."

"New paint, brakes, belts, radiator—it's all new."

"Baby blue with white interior. Awesome."

"Thanks."

"You look good topless." With the double meaning comes the devilish smile. "Wanna gimme your number?"

I wave my wedding ring.

He waves his own wedding band, then shrugs as if that symbol has no value.

I adjust my shades, the light changes, and I speed away, top down, laughing the way a woman laughs at an idiot, the cool wind blowing over the top of my locks. He tries to race with me, tries to keep up, but I move in and out of three lanes of traffic like butter and lose him at Olympic when he gets caught by the light. I wave good-bye with my middle finger.

* * *

Soon as I get into the station, it's pandemonium. Little Miss Executive Producer is on a rampage, screaming so loud that I hear her before I get inside the building.

"Who the fuck missed that story?" Our EP is running up and down the halls, ranting and raving, her mules slapping against her feet. "Why am I looking at that breaking news on Channel 9? Get off your fucking asses, dammit."

We call our EP "Tyra the Tyrant." Our green-eyed queen of the type-A peeps runs around like she's on some genetically supercharged coffee. A friggin' Leo with a diva mentality. Aggressive and lacking tact. Has about as much emotional control as a two-year-old.

"Who the fuck missed that story? If I wanted to see the news on Channel 9, I'd be working at Channel 9, dammit."

Tyra has an auburn weave that looks better than real hair, cleavage showing off the best boobs that money can buy, and a high waistline that makes her legs look like stilts. She always wears pin-striped suits in earth tones, and radical colors on her face: winterberry eye shadow, juicy lipstick and lip gloss, bronze blush, and light brown lip liner. Today her store-bought hair is pulled back into a bun so tight she looks like Cruella De Vil in *101 Dalmatians*.

"Why don't we have a fucking live remote at the scene?"

A crew rushes out to the news van as another one of the writers hurries in. Tyra snaps her finger at him and he follows her to her office; every step of the way she's ripping him a new orifice because of factual errors that were in a story of his that aired two days ago.

We all can hear the rumble and thunder as she curses him, threatens to take his job.

The writer snaps back at her, "I'm in the Writers Guild."

Now she's offended, and her anger echoes throughout the building.

"I don't care about the Guild or a friggin' union. I can still fire your ass."

"Do it."

It's like listening to a battle between a mortal and a god.

"Or better yet, I won't give you the satisfaction of being fired. Until you're up to standard, I'll deny every vacation you ask for, change your schedule."

"You can't fuck with me like that."

"I will until you either get it right or quit."

She also blames him for another show that crashed last week, one that literally fell apart on the air; the anchors read the wrong scores, the boxes were wrong, graphics were jacked. His ego tries to outdo hers. Two chess players trying to checkmate the other. Tyra goes apeshit and suspends him for three days without pay, tells him to get out of her office and off the lot.

He rants, "You can't do that."

"I just did. Now get out of my office."

"You can't suspend me."

"Do I need to call security?"

The writer trembles as he comes back out of Tyra's office, sees a lot of us moving up and down the hallway, most trying to pretend we didn't hear, others looking stunned. He lumbers away, anger up and shoulders down, hating Tyra, but no doubt thinking about his high mortgage up in Sherman Oaks, and new car note, about the high cost of having a new baby at home, wanting to quit, but he knows that this is L.A., that other stations are laying off, being consolidated, and there aren't many things an unemployment check can cover.

She stands behind him, watches him walk away and cross

the open area to get to his desk. Keeps her eyes on him and checks the clock as he gets a few things and heads out the door. He grumbles and curses, but never looks back.

Tyra's frown goes away; this glow comes over her face. I've seen that expression a thousand times. It's the tingly look a woman has after a series of multiple orgasms, before the twitches die and she finds the wind and strength to reach for a cigarette. She digs in her jacket pocket, pulls out and opens a piece of Nicorette—eases the gum into her mouth, chews at a methodical pace, and that air of satisfaction deepens.

Our EP walks away, at first her rhythm lazy and diva-ish, as if she's having flashbacks from being on a runway, then picking up, her mules slapping against her heels, and she's off to oversee the rest of her kingdom, leaving the strong mint scent from her breath behind.

Classic Tyra the Tyrant. When she was twenty years old—which was at least twenty years ago—she was a singer-actress-model who couldn't sing, act, or model. She tanked out in three fields and had to settle for a real job. So she went into journalism and eventually slithered her way into news. She was an anchor in Detroit a decade ago, and now she's divorced with two kids, away from her old life back on Eight Mile Road, and menacing Los Angeles.

This is where I work, a place where fingers are snapping and curse words are flying in every direction. I rarely cursed before I started here, but now I'm a card-carrying member of both the Four-Letter- and Twelve-Letter-Word Club. That's why I pop two aspirins to start my day, have to desensitize and become a demon in tennis shoes to get any respect. A job where I have to prove myself every day. Can't cry and take it personal when one of the control freaks throws a temper tantrum and calls me a bitch, or talks to me like I'm a slave at their daddy's plantation, because at some point, I'll be doing the same to them. That's the way the business is.

So, every afternoon around two, I step in the door, cell phone at my ear, checking messages, returning calls, scrambling to read the wires to find out what's going on in the country, state, and locally, then running in to a planning meeting to decide which overnight tragedy is newsworthy, wondering if we should cover Robert Downey, Jr.'s latest court appearance or the abused illegal immigrants being treated like slaves in a sweatshop in downtown L.A. Most of the time, in this narcissistic and aesthetic part of the world, Robert Downey, Jr., is more important—more important because stories like that generate better ratings. And Downey'll get bumped if we find another R. Kelly sex tape.

Damn humanity and give us ratings, especially during sweeps.

All the while I'm multitasking, sipping on a smoothie, cruising in a very confident and high-strung, can-be-a-serious-bitch-if-your-shit-ain't-together news mode, making sure all of my packages are together, and before I know it, it's after four. By then, Charles is on the way home. Today, like most days, he calls me while he's fighting rush hour on the 60 westbound, and at the same time I'm running to find a quiet spot to have a private conversation with my man, which ends up sounding a lot like another business tête-à-tête, being mostly talk about things we need to take care of around the house: paying the bills, dropping clothes off at the dry cleaners, reminding him that there are clothes in the washer that need to get tossed in the dryer, or him telling me how his day went, what twelve-year-old got caught with LSD, or what preteen kids got caught fucking in the bathroom, how the Asian kids continue to be much smarter than the blacks and Hispanics, what some stupid asshole parent said at a parent-teacher meeting.

But all of that's on the phone with freeway noise in the background on his end, and the craziness of the newsroom on mine, stress riding both of our backs. We hardly have any soft words that stir each other from within, not the tender conversation that makes a woman moist and want to get off work early. Not the kind of sensual talk that makes a man stay up past his bedtime and wait for his wife to get home and finish what was started at sunrise.

At sunset, I sneak outside and sit on the side of the building, imagine that I'm down on the beach, on the rocks, the ocean breeze in my face, watching the sun get swallowed by the ocean. I love those colors at the end of the day, the deep blues at the top of the skies, the orange hues at the horizon, and all the fascinating colors in between, that array of colors caused by the poisonous smog. Beauty is so bittersweet. Sunset is my moment, when the world is ready to rest, when bodies that have been in motion all day are yearning to be still.

Sometimes I take my sax and sit outside on the steps, do that at the dimming of the day, pretend I'm Coltrane, play a couple of his timeless songs.

Most of the time, like today, I just sit alone and think about my life.

Time to time I think about my father. The man who left my mother. And my two sisters. The first man who left me. Left us all back in North Carolina, in that Southern wilderness to fend for ourselves. Every day I try to prove to myself that I'm strong. I grew up wanting to live in a big city, have a better job, wanting a bigger house, a family and a man who wouldn't abandon me, because I would choose not to abandon him, but to love him unconditionally.

Sometimes I think about all I do, how I'm trying to be a career woman, a good wife, trying to be everything to everybody and nothing to myself, and I feel overwhelmed, scared, sadness covers me, makes me want to cry. But I don't, not with tears.

This isn't a world for the weak.

Based on my experiences, a lot of women look down on weak men, and just as many men despise weak women. This guy I used to date back in North Carolina used to always say that the strong always despise the pathetic, and the pathetic always worship and follow the strong.

A lot of the time I think about Charles. About the way our lives have become. He wants kids. I do too. But we're both so busy. And some days I hear that clock inside me ticking away. I'm not where I wanna be career-wise. Wonder if I'll be able to handle being a mommy and having a career. Wonder if we're ever going to get to the next level. Some days it feels like Charles and I have become the echo of two heartbeats when we should only hear one.

My cell phone rings. A number from inside the studio. An editor, a producer, somebody wants to yank me away from my ten minutes of peace and call me back inside Stressville.

I answer; it's my girl, Yvette, the hottest videotape editor at the station. She's from Birmingham, but this business has changed her, made her one of us, has stolen her life, has even stolen most of her sweet Southern accent.

She says, "Freckles, they have an APB out on you."

She tells me that Tyra the Tyrant is about to have a stroke trying to find me.

I snap, "Can't I leave for five fucking minutes?"

She laughs. "A'ight, don't make me cut off your goodies."

"You brought me back something from Atlanta?"

"Did some nice shopping down in Little Five Points, brought you something, and since you tripping out on me, you ain't getting it."

"Don't even think about it. I'll tell your husband that you're getting flowers delivered here once a week from your little boyfriend over at BET."

"So, it's like that? Why you gonna tell my old vibrator on my new vibrator?"

We laugh. She has no husband, no man, and no true boyfriend on the horizon.

My threat is as empty as a drum. Most of my threats are. She gets on my nerves every night, and she is my friend. I have other friends, but Yvette is the one I see five, sometimes six days a week. For the last few years, she's become my best friend by default. Yvette's off day is Wednesday, just like mine, midweek when the rest of the world is working. We both work every weekend, all holidays. Every day is a news day. Hard to meet and maintain a steady lover on the schedule she has. I know how it is. Been there, done that for years. Hard for a man to take you for more than a booty call when you can't get to him before midnight, if that soon.

She gets back to her work tone. "Pregnant woman in Encino got bit by a pit bull."

"Black, white . . . ?"

"Hispanic. An illegal."

"Mauled?"

"Leg messed up. Husband beat the dog off her with a baseball bat."

"How pregnant?"

"Six months or so."

"She die or . . . ?"

"Nah. But the dog did. He beat the shit out that dog."

"What we have?"

"Baby, we have enough video to piss off the INS, animal activists, and the people who make Louisville Sluggers. We could start three riots with this shit."

She sounds orgasmic. I'm coming too. We all do when we have a good package. A live high-speed chase can have us coming all night; an Andrea Yates story can give us multiple orgasms all year; but on a slow news night, we settle for whatever gratification we can get.

Yvette says, "Stop slacking and get this shit hooked up."

We hang up without real good-byes, very abrupt. To an outsider, that sharpness would ring as bona fide cruelty, just like everything else in this snapshot of our world.

I take off in a hurry, then something hits me, and I stare at the sunset.

Instead of running, this time I walk.

2

I barely get a foot in the door before people call my name, reminding me about stories that need to be written ASAP, about missing video footage, about making changes in the rundown, and before I can complete a sentence, my cell phone rings again.

It's my husband.

I answer with abruptness, "Can I call you back?"

He snaps, "Whatever. Bye."

"Wait, wait," I say with urgency. His voice matched mine, was laced with irritation. Already I feel bad for talking to him like he was a coworker. I try to readjust. I look at the time and try to slow my pace, tender my tone and ask, "What's going on, sweetie?"

He falls silent. I know he's annoyed and wants to hang up, and I know that he hates it when I talk to him with that curtness, but it's so hard to switch from one mode to another.

He says, "Look . . . nothing . . . just had an accident today."

"What kind of accident?"

He stalls. "Was breaking up a fight between two kids, a black kid and a Mexican—"

"Gangbangers?"

"Twelve-year-old wanna-bes. And I stepped in and caught a good blow to my left eye."

"*What?* Are you okay?"

"No biggie. Just a bruise."

"You sure?"

"Yeah, icing it and taking a couple aspirin will be enough."

In that moment, I feel helpless, useless in his life.

He sounds deflated. "Get back to work. I gotta grade papers anyway."

"Are you sure you're okay? Anything I can—"

"Just calling to hear your voice. Didn't mean to bother you. See ya when you get in."

"You gonna stay up?"

"Long day. I'll try."

"If you stay up, watch the news. Let me know what you think about the pit bull story."

I hang up, again without a real good-bye, knowing that he won't be up that late watching the news, watching my hard work. I'm worried about Charles, but as soon as I put the phone down, my assistant is in my face saying, "Somebody was at the gate looking for you."

"Who?"

"David somebody. Security said he was acting weirded out."

"Great. God. Hope I don't have another stalker."

When I check my messages, there is one from a man who identifies himself as David Lawrence and leaves me his cell phone number. His voice is troubled, chills me, and the message is too vague. Sounds like someone has read the credits at the end of the broadcast, jotting down the names of producers, and is in search of someone in news to tell or sell his story to. Could be a whistleblower, or somebody who witnessed a crime. It wouldn't be the first time we've had a murderer who wants to turn himself in to the media. Or it could just be a man with a crush on a woman who has helped the station win an Emmy.

I don't return David Lawrence's call. I'm worrying about my husband, but that worry gets swallowed up by other things. Tired of all the running and screaming. Don't need no mo' drama tonight; have had my share of negativity for the day. If it's important, David Lawrence'll call back. And he'll learn to leave a detailed message, like the recording asks. Vagueness is one of my pet peeves. An idiot who can't follow directions is another. He just got a two-fer.

Mango Jamba Juice in hand, I go back to Yvette's editing world. She's working on a package for tonight, clicks and whirs from the tape spinning, that sound piercing the air. She has a bootleg Maxwell CD on, creating her own mood. She's beautiful enough to be a model, long legs, plenty of breasts, and a heart-shaped ass, an earthy woman who dresses down, wears no makeup, sports thrift-shop jeans, T-shirts that have seen better days, and colorful bandanas most of the time. Almost as if she tries not to look too pretty so she can be taken seriously.

I rush into her world and check to make sure she has all the video she needs to make me look good, and before I can rush back out, she stops me with her words. She says, "And oh . . ."

"What what what?"

She has an angular face with light brown eyes under well-defined eyebrows. She gives me a slick, one-sided smile. "Guess where I went."

A curious smile comes across my face and I rush back into the room. "You didn't go."

"Yes, I did."

"You went to . . . that . . . that . . . sex house thing?"

"I went."

My voice is an excited whisper. "You're lying."

"Me and my cousin rolled up in there." She glances at me, evaluates my clothes, does that on purpose to slow me down. "Cute sweatshirt, Freckles. Yellow is your color."

"Whatever." I have on a UCLA Bruins hooded sweatshirt, a blue UCLA baseball cap with large golden letters fit for a billboard. "You have a problem with my clothes?"

"As Samuel Jackson would say, that sweatshirt is fucking repugnant."

I flip her off. "And you need to stop dressing in the dark."

"So original. You *needs* to be advertising for HBCU."

UCLA is my husband's alma mater; she knows that. I pull up my sweatshirt and show her my blue and white Tau Beta Sigma T-shirt from my alma mater back at Johnson C. Smith.

She grunts. "Like that's a real sorority. That's an organization for wanna-be musicians."

"Hater in the house." Sometimes that stings, that acknowledgment that I didn't make it in music, but I never let that show. I move away from that memory and get back to what I want to know. "Was that . . . was the freak show . . . was it buck wild?"

She mocks me, "What what what?"

"You know what I'm talking about. Stop playing me like that."

"It was wild." Her thin eyebrows dance. "Damn, about to mess up this tape."

She leaves me hanging, my mouth open wide, curiosity on high.

I ask, "You did the *ménage à trois*?"

She laughs. That's her fantasy. A thick line she'll stare at, but may never cross.

I go on, "Did you?"

She laughs.

I'm getting impatient, right where she wants me. "Come on, tell me, did you?"

Her continuous laugh tells me that she's not telling me anything, not yet. Next to her escapades, I'm Snow White, the one who runs straight home after work, no time to stop and get a drink and wind down with the rest of the crew. The one who runs in here from church on Sundays. I live through her tales from the wild side, through her freedom. She teases me to keep me coming back for more. I never judge her and I'm the keeper of her secrets.

I ask, "Well?"

Yvette edits at the speed of light, an ambidextrous queen, the master of multitasking.

She says, "I didn't. Just watched. It was okay."

"Were people doing it?"

"All over the place."

"And it was just okay?"

"People can't throw down as good as you think."

"You do anything?"

"Just sipped a beer and watched. Saw a cutie up in there."

"Really? Exchange numbers with anybody?"

"Nah. Went with my cousin and we acted like lesbos to keep the men away."

"How you keep the lesbos away?"

"Said we were strictly dickly."

"How many rooms of sex?"

"You're sounding like a journalist."

"We are journalists. How many?"

"About seven rooms, no furniture, just large beds."

"Pretty big house?"

"Pretty big. At least three thousand square feet and a maid's quarters."

"Damn. Sure you didn't indulge?"

"No, I did not. I'm not a freak. I just get freaky sometimes."

"Sounds . . . interesting."

"Ask your husband to take you. They have couples' night."

I push the side of her head. "Are you crazy? Charles'd never do anything like that. "

"Maybe you can leave him grading papers and upgrade for a couple of hours." She laughs at her own joke. "We should go one Friday night after work. For the hell of it."

I ask her what she saw people doing, and she tells me without shame. She tells me she saw one woman take seven men orally, back to back with no break in between, in front of a crowd of at least twenty people who were sipping on wine, people who looked like schoolteachers and attorneys. Then that insatiable woman stripped and made love to just as many, two at a time, right there on a mattress in the middle of the room, lights on and the fireplace blazing in the background. When she was done, she took a shy-but-curious woman into a private room, didn't come out from educating her timid lover for two hours.

Yvette said, "And peep this, that girl was up there with her husband. He brought her up there to get her fantasy on. He helped pick out the girl for her."

She talks fast, her tone almost nonchalant, still working on a tape as she tells me about another petite girl who came in and went into a private room with three black men, three strangers built like football players; came out some time later, skin glowing, and left.

I make the yuck face. "White women do anything."

"She was blacker than a VHS tape."

"Damn, have we crossed over or have we crossed over?"

"You don't watch much porn, do you?"

She tells me of others she saw, of how they stood outside doors that had two or three couples inside, listening to the sounds of people making love to people they had just met.

My face is decorated with fascination. All the sounds in this building fall away, all but her voice, and all I see in front of me is the picture she paints with her words, a powerful movie of sin and seduction that makes me feel as if I'm on opium, drifting, and I'm speechless.

My imagination is in overdrive. I think about my own fantasies. Lately I've been having the desire to give my husband head in a public place, somewhere people can see me, but not in a sexual place like the one where Yvette goes to get her fill of voyeurism. Someplace where no one else will be doing that and everyone will be staring at me, but no one will ever know who I am. I'll never do that though. Too conservative in public to expose that side of me.

Yvette laughs again.

I ask, "What?"

"That look on your face. Freckles, your face be *screaming* what you be thinking."

My chuckle can't mask my thoughts. I become a sixteen-year-old, exposed and naughty.

She shakes her head. "Unbelievable."

"What, the swingers' place?"

"Hell no." Frustration covers her face as she zips through the video from the pit bull story. She rants, "I have a degree in African studies, a degree in journalism, ten years' experience in news, eight in editing, and am I doing something meaningful like putting together a documentary geared toward recognizing East Africans? Do we do spots on the Eritrean situation?"

"Run that by your friends over at BET."

"Please. If it ain't comedy or a damn rap video, you know it ain't happening."

"We're local news, not CNN."

"Yeah, yeah. We're one rung below the Us Po' Niggas station."

"Stop saying that."

"Whatever."

"People on Crenshaw haven't heard of Eritrea and people on Wilshire don't care."

"We need to raise consciousness."

"You need to do something on why there are more black men in prisons than in college, if anything. We have enough shit in our own backyard."

"That's the point; we have the power to educate them and make them care, the way we make them care what J.Lo or Janet or Julia Roberts or Halle Berry is wearing to a friggin' award show. We could be groundbreaking with a special report on the Habesha people."

"What the hell does habesha mean?"

"Duh."

"Don't 'duh' me."

"That's my point, Freckles. Do I get to work on that? No, I break my neck to do a spot on a non–English-speaking woman who snuck across the border in the back of a melon truck and got bit by a damn rabid dog on Ventura Boulevard."

"We're all whores."

"This job should come with a keg of Vaseline."

Another producer comes in looking for me. "A guy was at the gate asking for you."

"Just now?"

"Not five minutes ago."

"Still there?"

"Gone. Couldn't find you. Paged you twice."

"You did?" I look at my pager. "Great. Batteries are dead."

"Security said they paged you too."

I ask, "At the gate, same guy or different guy?"

"Dunno. Missing some video and gotta edit three stories in the next hour."

The frazzled producer rushes away. I go to my desk and call the front gate. They report that the guy came three times tonight, asking for me, but left no message.

David Lawrence calls back and leaves another message, right after the broadcast, almost as if he were watching the news and timing when I might be free. Desperation is in his voice.

That scares me.

At the end of the night, after the post-show meeting, way after midnight, I'm riding in Baby Blue with the top down. Cal

Trans has shut down two lanes, so I'm stuck in never-ending and barely moving traffic on the Santa Monica Freeway. I'm feeling frustrated and need to talk to keep from screaming into the wind, so I call Yvette to laugh and bitch away my road rage.

She's in her SUV, jamming Remy Shand's CD, music on high. She mutes the volume and says, "Freckles, you forgot the goodies I brought ya back from the four-oh-four."

"Damn. Where are you?"

"Antsy. Might barhop. Wanna hang a bit?"

"Rain check? I'm hoping for an Altoids night."

"You and those Altoids."

"Don't hate."

"Not hating."

"Just work that magic and get you a good man like I have."

She tells me, "It would be easier trying to find a parking space in New York."

We laugh and chitchat about things only a woman understands.

I ask, "Think you'll ever get married again?"

"I'm struggling with that concept. Not now. Maybe when I'm forty or so."

The conversation breaks when she has to curse somebody out; sounds like somebody cut her off. Horns are blaring on that end. She dares somebody to get out of their car and repeat whatever they said to her. Screeches as the other car zooms away.

"Cockeyed bastard." She screams that, then comes back to me. "What was I saying?"

"Why you wanna wait until forty?"

"Maybe forty-five. Maybe I won't be as gun shy. Dunno. Maybe because I don't know one person who is faithful in their marriage. I want more than that. I want what my parents have."

"I feel ya."

"It's hard to find a man like my dad. They don't make niggas like they used to."

We laugh.

I ask, "What kinda man you want?"

She says, "I'm a bold black woman from the Bible Belt. I want a man who can make me scream for Jesus on a Saturday night, then take me to see Him on Sunday morning."

I scream. "You are a fool."

She talks on, "Living the single life is fun right now."

"But that gets old."

She's tells me that she's under the bright lights and billboards on Sunset Boulevard, near the House of Blues, cruising down a jam-packed street in search of a bar to stop and blow time.

"Yvette, you're so pretty, I don't see why you have a hard time."

"Freckles, you know men are so insecure. If you're pretty, they don't want you to leave the house. If you're ugly, they don't want you to leave the basement."

That one gets me deep; makes me laugh so hard the muscles in my stomach tighten up in knots. I swerve a bit, ride the reflectors on the freeway and almost leave my lane.

I get control of myself and say, "You're crrrrrrrr-azy."

"Being crrrrrrrr-azy keeps me from going insane."

I let her go and that lonely feeling creeps up on me, so I call to see if any messages are on my service. David Lawrence

has called again, leaving a message that I can't make out because of bad reception. My heartbeat speeds up. A headache
comes on. I freak because somehow my stalker has gotten my
pager number. Then I remember that it's on the voice mail at
my job.

3

I end up getting home close to two a.m. Music is playing in the bedroom, low and soft, the sounds of Gabriela Anders singing the song about Ipanema. I sit on the bed, reach for the remote to turn off the CD player. Charles sits up. A plastic bowl is next to the bed, and in that bowl is a bag of ice. Aspirin and a glass of water are on the nightstand as well.

I say, "Hey, baby."

"Was waiting for you."

"Traffic was a bitch."

"You shoulda called or something."

His voice isn't groggy. I'm worried and I want to see his eye. Charles won't let me turn on the light, doesn't want to have to let his eyes adjust. The shutters are open and the moon is high. Charles moves the covers away, stands up, lets me see the swelling.

"Unbelievable."

"Calm down."

Charles can barely open his left eye. It's surrounded by puffy flesh that will have shades of blues and blackness, a left eye that will turn red because of the broken vessels, or veins, or whatever it is that makes it turn bloodshot.

"We need to get you to the emergency room."

"Already went."

"What did they say?"

He winces. "Calm down."

"Stop trying to be so macho, will you?"

"Will you please calm down?"

He tells me he had his eye X-rayed and there was no retina damage. The doctor gave him an ice pack and ibuprofen.

He says, "My eye is sensitive to light. Gonna have to wear sunglasses with dark lenses for a few days. They gave me an eye patch to wear around the house."

I'm scared and mad; very pissed off at the person who hit him, and I'm pissed off at Charles for playing the injury down. He tells me how the boys were going at each other, swinging wild, trying to kill each other, and he stepped in and halted the battle.

My mother-lover instinct takes over. I want to protect my man, want to do something. At the least, I'm ready to call that kid's parents right now and go ballistic. Or go down to his job in the morning and meet with the principal, make sure that rugrat is kicked to the educational curb.

Charles pulls me to him. "You can't go running down there acting like Mike Tyson."

I say, "I'm gonna bite that bastard's ear off. Turn his ass into a baby Picasso."

"Van Gogh was the one Mike Tyson had for lunch."

We laugh.

We stare at each other, so much concern and caring, and the climate changes.

"Damn. You got hit pretty hard."

"Shhhh. Let it go."

"It's gonna be bloodshot for a few days."

"C'mon, I said let it go."

"Okay, okay."

"We have some unfinished business."

He kisses me on my neck and my shoulders, kisses me as my clothes are coming down, his tongue on my shoulders, my breasts, my stomach, my hips, the edges of my vagina. I fall against the wall and his tongue stays between my legs. Heated sounds escape my mouth. His warm tongue makes me drip like honey. Then he stands, lets me kiss him and rub him as he takes his boxers and T-shirt off. We're naked. Adam and Eve. He touches my face, stares at me in a way that excites and scares me. Tells me how beautiful I am in the moon's light; says that over and over as if this were the first time he's seen me this way. Charles lays me down, climbs on top of me, slides himself inside, and strokes me, and strokes me, and strokes me.

He says, "I love you."

I haven't heard him say it this way in a while. It's so passionate.

I ask, "Where did all of this come from?"

"Am I the love of your life?"

I'm moaning, quivering, holding on to my husband for dear life, another orgasm rising.

I catch my breath, kiss him with fervor, voice trembling when I answer him, "Yes."

"Can you imagine your life without me?"

"Never." My left leg starts to shake. "Was worried about you all evening."

He strokes and strokes and strokes. Turns me over, loves me that way, my face in the softness of the pillow, his hands on my hips, on my ass, our moans turned up high.

I tell him, "Take it easy, baby."

"Sorry, baby."

"No, I like it like that. Just worried about your eye."

"How is sex going to hurt my eye?"

"Then don't take it easy."

We laugh a little. Then he turns me back over. We fall into a crazy kiss, the kind where we are so hungry for each other, sucking tongues, nibbling lips, deep kisses. And he strokes.

He asks what he already knows, "You like this?"

"Loving it." My breathing is ragged. "You . . . you need to be inside me every night."

I throw my head back, arch my back, come so hard that my moans scare me.

He strokes me and strokes me and strokes me. Orgasms roll in waves, back to back, and even when I tell him I've come enough to last me a lifetime, he makes me come again. We're newlyweds again. Feel like it's the first time, when our bodies were so new to each other.

He says, "Maybe we can sneak up to Palos Verdes like we used to."

"Oh, God, I'd love that."

We used to ride up those rolling hills that stand over the Pacific Ocean, then take a blanket and sneak down by the water, make love until we were almost too tired to walk back to the car. I feel so good now that I begin to cry. Cry like Halle Berry did when she won her Oscar. I feel just that good right now. He's my Denzel and he holds me like I'm his most cherished award. My cries become soft whimpers. He asks me if I'm okay. My voice drowns in my tears; I nod, tell him to keep stroking me and stroking me and stroking me.

Tears roll from my face into the sheets. Over and over I tell him, "I love you so much."

He kisses me and holds me tight when we're done. Music covers us; Gabriela Anders singing with Eric Benet. I sing along, massaging my husband's penis, the penis I own.

"You're still pretty hard."

"Yeah."

"And you're wide awake."

"Yeah."

"You drink too much Noni juice?"

He chuckles. I get up, go to the bathroom, and come back. I'm feeling dead tired and euphoric. His eyes are wide open. Usually in the time it takes me to go potty, he's snoring. He's staring at the ceiling, doesn't hear me walking across the carpet, his mind somewhere else.

I say, "Let me make you an ice pack."

He jerks out of his trance. "Wait a few. Come get next to me."

"It's almost three." I get next to him, my cool skin against his warmth. "Get some rest."

"Not working tomorrow. Don't know how sensitive my eye will be to light."

"You don't need to find out on the freeway."

"My lesson plan is on my desk."

"You hate subs."

"They're nothing but baby-sitters. Kids deserve more."

He reaches up and touches his swollen eye. He makes a sound of anger.

I put my head on his chest. He's a weekend warrior, downgraded from being a Golden Gloves boxer, and I can see that he's taking getting caught with his guard down pretty hard.

Silence, his fingers rubbing me in a disturbed rhythm. His mind is working overtime.

He says, "We can spend some time before you go to work."

"Cool."

He smiles. "Love you."

He talks like a teenager who has just discovered love. Tonight feels like Christmas.

Then he makes a pained sound.

I ask, "Your eye—?"

"It's okay. Bastard just got in a lucky blow."

"Don't tell me that the rugrat meant to hit you?"

"Nah, was just saying. I should've been paying attention."

I sit up and ask him to tell me about the brawl; he shakes his head. I press him for more info, that journalistic side of me on the rise, and he shushes me with a thousand kisses, doesn't want to talk about that, wants to enjoy me, wants to live inside this moment.

Silence and touching; more tender kissing and caressing.

He didn't come; despite my own wetness, I know that.

I ask, "What you need me to do, sweetie?"

"I'm cool." His fingers play in my locks. "Your hair is getting long. Looking good."

I relax and get ready to sleep in my husband's arms, but I can't rest because I feel satisfied and selfish, like a bad lover. I know what he likes, that's why I keep Altoids in our nightstand. I pop one, chew it, and before it dissolves, walk my tongue down his skin, roll my face over his penis, and tease his soft hairs against my cheeks. His aroma turns me on. I pull his foreskin back and admire the texture. It's beautiful. I move my hair from my face, suck him soft and easy, all mouth and no teeth, and do that first with no hands, then with hands. Altoids are strong, create a wonderful heat, take what I'm giving him to a new level. He jerks, grips the sheets, moans, growls, writhes and cries out like he's never had an orgasm before. I feed on his honey. I'm drunk with passion.

I crawl back into his arms. We kiss. Cuddle. We sleep, holding each other, closer than Siamese twins. So close that I can't hear the lies that have been told in this room.

4

This is where my life changes. Today is the day I meet the truth.

It starts hours after I leave my husband at home. Hours after we shower and make love again. Hours after he cooks us breakfast.

Today, not even bad traffic can jack with my damn good mood. I drive Baby Blue up the 110 to the 10, take the bumper-to-bumper route through downtown L.A. toward the urban sects that lead into Hollywood, turn off La Brea and drive up Willoughby just as my girl Yvette's SUV is pulling into the lot. I'm behind her, waving and laughing. Her bumper stickers read SOME WOMEN ARE BORN LEADERS—YOU'RE FOLLOWING ONE and DOING MY PART TO PISS OFF THE RADICAL RIGHT. We park next to each other. She has on funky, clog-style tennis shoes the color of pink bubble gum, low-cut jeans that show off the edges of her purple thong, a bright yellow T-shirt that reads WILD WOMEN DON'T GET THE BLUES, a wrinkled jean jacket. A purple scarf is on her head. Oversized shades with pink lenses give her that movie-star-diva look.

She smiles. "Damn, Freckles. Ain't you dressed for the prom."

I smile back at my girl. "Gimme a stick of that gum."

She stops and digs in her backpack. "You got dem bow legs in a tight skirt."

"Is it too tight?"

"Your backside giving J.Lo a run for her money."

This is the face of the woman in the mirror. Happy. I feel pretty so I have on my "feel pretty" clothes: a long, tan skirt with a double-split, up both thighs, a hip and hippie-style peasant blouse, suede jacket, and boss-ass boots I paid too much for. I look like a rich pauper. My perfume is on and popping, skin glowing like a virgin the morning after.

I ask, "How did the hunt go last night?"

"All I can say is ugly men are not shy. But they stopped being ugly after a while."

"After how long?"

"After two or three drinks, everybody started looking cute."

We head up the steps. I'm chewing on the gum she gave me like I'm a teenager.

She says, "Ain't your ass a li'l bit perky-perky today. How was your night?"

"Altoids."

She frowns. "Stop bragging about your high-protein diet, bitch."

I laugh. "Hater in the house. Get off the Hater-Ade."

She says, "I have one more word to say to you."

"What?"

"Eritrean."

I groan. "Don't start with that again."

"If you're not outraged, you're not paying attention. Don't sleep on it."

I get compliments all afternoon. My skin is glowing and my face is a big smile. I'm singing and prancing all over the place because my world is supercalifragilisticexpialidocious.

Another producer comes up to me, laughing his ass off. "You hear about the lady who's suing airport security for making her drink her own breast milk to make sure it wasn't a dangerous substance?"

"You're kidding, right?"

"It's on the wire."

I say, "Good thing she wasn't shipping product for a sperm bank."

We laugh so damn hard.

Around five p.m., all hell breaks loose. Breaking news all over the city.

A four-point-six earthquake hits the high desert in Palmdale, an hour outside of L.A. in no traffic. Not a large quake, but enough to make us have to rush a crew out to the site.

Charles calls me as soon as the quake hits. "Everything okay out there, sweetie?"

"We be cool, baby. Didn't feel it out here. What's all that noise in the background?"

"I'm out getting my prescription filled."

By six p.m., an immigrant kills his wife and shoots her lover, then parks his car on a freeway overpass, gun in hand, and puts one in his temple. His body falls down on the 110 South in the middle of rush hour, lands on the roof of a car going about eighty, kills the driver, and causes numerous injuries.

Everyone is scrambling to get that story together, looking

for witnesses, relatives, anybody who can give us an exclusive and a one-up on the other stations.

Before we can get coverage on that, a plane crashes on Hollywood Way and almost takes out a gas station. Then we get word that an old-school Hollywood celebrity is on his deathbed, dying like a vaudeville act, and we have to rush to cover that as well.

With all the bad news, Tyra is having multiple orgasms.

We're short on staff as it is, sending helicopters to fly over scenes, struggling to verify sources on other news, and we have an "all page" in effect, meaning Tyra is demanding that everyone get their asses in gear and get to the station pronto, whether they're on vacation or not. I'm running from place to place and time is crucial.

The news station has the feel of a warehouse, lots of openness, low-cost desks side by side. We're not in fancy offices, or situated in private cubicles. It's shared space with zero privacy. Tonight I'm so busy I can't treat myself to a calm moment at sunset. I'd wanted to call Charles then, talk to him a hot minute, at least try to share the day's end via Verizon and Pac Bell, kick back and flirt like we used to when we were new to each other. But instead, I'm lost in this world, bumping by floor directors, camera operators, and other people racing toward the studio.

By nine p.m., I make it to my desk and pull my boots off. With all this drama, it's not the best day for sexy boots. I rest my feet, grab a PowerBar, and check my messages. Hunger headache is creeping up on me. We have an hour before the late news comes on and everyone is still in panic mode. We're trying to get interviews with friends and family of the distraught immigrant, getting footage on earthquake damage, and I need verification on the dying or dead celebrity so we can finish the graphics on that package. I'm sitting in my aged swivel chair, legs crossed, gulping bottled water, operating in full work mode, when my phone rings.

I jump to answer and say my name.

He clears his throat. "This is David Lawrence."

Then there is a pause, like he's expecting me to react to his name.

I take charge, speak in a clear and aggressive tone. "I understand you came by here several times and called just as many yesterday."

"I was hoping you'd call me back, so we could talk about it."

My voice is rushed, curt, no time for bullshit. I say, "Sorry . . . do I know you?"

He hesitates, heaviness and anger in his voice. "You don't know, do you?"

"No, I don't know who you are."

"No . . . I mean . . . it sounds like . . . unless . . . You don't know, do you?"

"What am I supposed to know?"

He hesitates. I'm about ready to hang up.

He says, "My wife . . . do you know about Jessica Lawrence?"

Now I'm a little concerned. Too much news is swimming in my brain. My mind goes through all the people I've met, from elementary school to graduate school, wondering if someone I know named Jessica Lawrence has died; maybe she's one of the people from church, or somebody in the world of journalism, and this is the phone call telling me the bad news.

"I'm sorry . . . Maybe it's been a while . . . Where do I know Jessica from?"

Silence on his end for a few seconds, then he laughs. Not a funny laugh, but a laugh filled with angst and irony.

He speaks with difficulty. "She left . . . She's been hooking up with your husband for a while . . . months . . . hotels . . . evenings after she left work . . . some nights after she finished teaching aerobics at the gym . . . Jessica . . . and Charles . . . She left me to be with your husband."

Again, silence.

Then I manage to say, "What was that, one mo' again?"

He repeats the news.

I laugh.

I say, "Okay, who the fuck is this?"

He repeats his name.

I ask, "Yvette put you up to this crazy shit?"

He holds on until my laughter wanes.

He says, "Your husband is a middle school teacher."

That slows me. I ask, "What's your point?"

He says, "My wife and your husband are . . . They ran off together."

"When was this?"

"Thursday night."

"Thursday as in last Thursday?"

"Yeah."

"My husband . . . sorry to burst your bubble—" I say that as I feel a sudden wave of relief. I chuckle and shake my head. "My husband is at home. Wait, hold on."

I laugh again, spin away from my PC, and look around the newsroom to see who is in on this idiotic prank. Writers, production assistants, and assignment editors are all around. No one is paying attention to me; everyone is busy with death and destruction. Not a smirk in site.

He says, "Me and Jessica got into a big fight when I confronted her. Charles, that's your husband's name, right? I haven't been able to find her since she left, and I know she's with him. I went looking for her. I know she freaked out and ran to him. I couldn't get to him over the weekend, but I knew they worked together. She's a P.E. teacher."

I'm listening, waiting for someone to laugh.

He says, "Her emotions got the best of her and she got pissed off, and when she's pissed off, she talks. She lied about it at first, then I confronted her with the e-mails. She broke down and threw the affair in my face, told me she was leaving me, that Charles was in a lousy marriage, and she was in a lousy marriage . . . some bullshit like that. Said that he was the motherfucker who made her happy."

No one is laughing.

My voice trembles. "Look, this has been fun, but you've wasted enough of my time."

He says, "He tell you about our fight?"

"What fight?"

He chuckles. "I fucked him up."

No one here knows about that incident, not even Yvette. I swallow, get light-headed just that quick, begin to feel sick in my stomach.

I ask, "The fight . . . where was this fight?"

"Parking lot at Rowland Heights Middle School."

"When?"

"Yesterday morning."

I whisper, "Yesterday morning."

"Went looking for him. Had my gun. Was going to kill that motherfucker. But you know"—he pauses—"thought about my momma. Told myself it wasn't worth all that."

I'm standing. No one in the shop is looking at me. I need someone to start laughing.

He says, "Thought you knew all about them."

Not even a chuckle, or a smile, in sight.

A headache attacks me; the sudden burst of pain shuts me down. I struggle to think but my thoughts are swallowed by blackness. Everything goes out of focus until the room vanishes.

"What's your name again?"

"David Lawrence."

"And your wife is . . ."

"Fucking your husband."

I hang up.

5

call home. No answer. I call Charles's cell phone. No answer. I call home again. I call his cell phone again. He's vanished from the face of the earth. I call and I call. I don't leave messages because I need to hear his reaction to these accusations.

My body has become heavy; head is easing down, being supported by my hand. Leg bouncing. All of a sudden, there is no air in the room, only heat. I have to regroup.

Five minutes later, I'm standing in Yvette's editing world. Stunned. Trying to repeat the conversation I had with David Lawrence.

Yvette asks, "He says he was fucking your husband?"

"No, his wife . . . somebody named Jessica."

"Go home." Yvette stops her work, gives me that stern woman expression, the one that takes no shit. "Get out of here and handle your business."

I have to go to Tyra the Tyrant, and that's hard to do.

I tell her I have a family emergency.

She tells me I can't leave.

I tell her that it's late, the broadcast is set, and I really have to go.

I say, "I'm damn near begging you, Tyra. This will never happen again."

She stares at me and walks away shaking her head.

I take that look of disgust to mean I can go home early. This time.

Fucking your husband.

Those words echo inside my head. Tonight Baby Blue makes that hour drive in forty-five minutes, zooms me across the freeways before the end of the broadcast, at the time that Charles is usually already dead to the world. All the way home I'm having an internal battle.

The garage door goes up and Charles's car isn't inside.

My insides feel hollow. I park the car on my side of the garage and step inside. The house is quiet. No lights are on. No music is playing. My headache doubles as I hurry from room to room, moving across hardwood floors and carpet, hurrying by wedding pictures, family pictures, turning on lights and calling his name in vain. All of my husband's clothes are on his side of the closet, at least as far as I can tell.

I dial his cell phone number again. No answer.

I hear the garage door going up again and I rush back downstairs.

I'm standing at the base of the stairs when Charles walks in from the garage with three big bags, two of them from California Pizza Kitchen. He's looking rugged, needs to shave.

My face is stuck on "smile." He smiles back, gives me that one-sided smile that lights up a room. In my eyes, both of our expressions are awkward.

He says, "Hey, you're home early."

"Yeah. Surprise."

Fucking your husband.

I say, "Called you a few times. Was worried about your eye."

"Went to a movie."

"This late?"

"Got bored."

I say, "You don't stay awake at movies that start after nine."

"Think the pain pills I took have me wired."

"Who you go with?"

"Nobody. Went by the South Bay Galleria to pick you up something to eat, stopped in just when something was coming on, decided to blow some time."

"Where's your cellular?"

He motions toward the kitchen counter. There it sits, next to his laptop.

He has on a pair of worn black sweats, same color baseball cap. He knows that something is wrong, but he's not asking. First, I'm never home before the news ends. Second, he's never out this late, not that I know of.

A smile rises on my face as I take slow steps toward him. I ask him the same thing he asked me last night, "Am I the love of your life?"

"Yeah."

"Can you imagine your life without me?"

"Not a day."

"Have you ever tried to imagine your life without me?"

He puts the bags of food down on the island, puts his hand around my waist, pulls me to him, and kisses me. Charles holds me and tongues me long and deep, his hands rubbing up and down my back. I try not to get lost in his tongue, but I do.

I believe him. I want to believe. Have to.

While I kiss him I tell myself that that phone conversation with David Lawrence was a lie. That's the emotional side of me, the side that is so afraid of pain. But there is more to me than that. The journalistic side of me rises, pushes me to question the things David Lawrence said to me, reminds me that they weren't verified, and until proven the truth, all accusations were lies.

Charles says, "Glad you got in early for a change."

He kisses my cheek, then that sensitive spot on my neck. Then my eyes. I feel his hard penis pressing against me. I reach down, rub it, then back up a step.

I ask, "Working tomorrow?"

He chuckles. "You don't expect me to go in looking like this, do you?"

He takes the food out of the bags. Chicken pizza, pasta, and shrimp rolls, two kinds of dessert. Wine and a candle are in another bag. Enough things to have a late-night picnic. These are the things a man does when he loves a woman, not when he is leaving a woman.

I repeat, "You really don't want to go in with your eye jacked up, huh?"

"You're off tomorrow."

"I'm always off on Wednesdays."

"Not always. Sometimes you end up going in."

"I'm off."

"Thought we could spend some time, maybe drive up the coast."

"Cool."

He grabs two plates from the cabinet.

Fucking your husband. That voice won't go away.

I run my hand over my locks and chuckle. "Strange thing happened tonight."

"What?"

"Guy calls in with a news tip."

"That happens every night, right?"

"This breaking news was different."

"How so?"

"Weird guy. Distraught. On edge. I'm talking scary-weird."

"You think that all of them are weird."

"He called to tell me somebody was fucking his wife, that his wife and her lover, some guy who works with her, were supposed to be running away, some shit like that."

His posture changes, not a lot, but enough to make my heart stutter, to make me swallow.

I go on, "This guy . . . he had been calling all day yesterday and today, trying to reach me. Ringing my phone off the hook. Coming by the station and leaving before they could find me."

He shifts again. His eyes change.

I say, "You want to know why he was distraught?"

Charles looks at me, but gives me no reply. My tone moves from that of a loving wife, loses its raw emotion and becomes professional, my defense mechanism in times of fear.

I say, "First, I have a question."

"Okay."

"Sit down please."

"Let me fix the food."

"No, sit down."

He sits on a bar stool. I'm on the other. I turn mine to face him. Charles leaves his facing the island and the stove and the refrigerator, his eyes moving all over the kitchen.

I massage my neck for a while, my leg bouncing the way it

does when I'm upset, fingers pulling at my hair. My headache is growing, feels as if my brain is swelling.

I say, "You know, I can't remember exactly what you said yesterday, so much was going on at the shop, so could you, again, tell me what happened to your eye?"

"Why are you still asking me about my eye?"

"That's scary."

"What?"

"All of a sudden you're getting defensive."

"Don't like it when you come at me like that."

"Like what?"

"Like *that*. That reporter's voice you use."

"Answer my simple question and I can stop sounding like *that*."

He can't look at me.

He says, "It was an accident. It never should've happened. Let's leave it at that and move on."

I refuse to stop staring him down.

I ask, "What was the student's name who hit you?"

"What are you doing?"

I chuckle at myself, despite myself. "Fact checking."

"I don't know his name. He wasn't one of my students."

"Somebody hit you in the eye yesterday, and you can't remember his name?"

"Didn't I just say that he wasn't my student?"

"Somebody hit me in my eye in the third grade; this girl named Inda jacked me because I got into it with her little sister, this girl Valerie. Inda popped me in my left eye. Inda. We always called her 'Linda without the L.' That was back in the third grade and I remember that like it was yesterday. Yours happened yesterday, and you forgot the kid's name already?"

"I'll let the school handle the kid."

"Please, sweetie, work with me on this. Just give me a name so I can call the school in the morning and clear up this . . . this . . . this blatant lie that someone has told me."

"Leave it alone."

"Okay, fine. Skip the bullshit. You know anyone named Jessica?"

"Where is this going?"

"Do you know anyone named Jessica? Was she the cause of the fight?"

He takes his hat off and rubs his Creole mane. His eyes close tight, then he winces, as if his head is throbbing, or maybe a sharp pain reminded him about his damaged left eye; lines rise in his neck, in his arms, as if he is on the verge of exploding.

"What about David Lawrence?" I press on. "You know anybody by that name?"

"Where are you going with this?"

"He knows you. Knows your name, where you work, about your eye, everything. He tells me he's the one who hit you in the eye. Says there was a fight at your job yesterday."

Nothing from Charles.

"You hear me, Charles? The man said you and him were fighting over his wife."

"That's not what happened."

"He says he's losing his damn mind because *his* wife was running off with *my* husband. Told me that my husband was fucking his wife. And those are *his* words."

Still, he can't look at me. He can hardly blink, eyes held open by his own fear.

My voice is right above a whisper. "What happened to your eye, Charles?"

No response.

"Who is Jessica?"

Nothing.

"Motherfucker."

I get up and push my bar stool back. It tilts and falls over, bangs on the tile floor.

He says, "It was a mistake."

I say, "What was?"

"It was a mistake."

"What mistake? David Lawrence calling me, or . . . What was the mistake, Charles?"

"Jessica."

My head hurts so bad I can't move.

I snap, "Tell me what is going on. Seems like everybody knows but me."

"Jessie, she took the whole thing wrong."

"Jessie? Oh, her name is Jessie. What is that, a pet name?"

"Don't . . . Her name is Jessica."

"You were intimate with this Jessie-Jessica woman?"

"Look, we haven't been . . ."

"Did you sleep with her?"

"Lately . . . for the last two years—"

"You've been seeing her for two years?"

"No. Let me . . . Let me finish saying what I'm saying. I'm talking about us, the way we've been, how we . . . we just pass each other in the hallway, how you're never available . . ."

"Yes or no, Charles, did you put your dick inside that man's wife?"

He goes on, "It's been almost like we're roommates. You work every holiday, Valentine's Day, run out on Christmas, New Year's Eve; you're down at the station on Saturdays and Sundays; even your off days, you end up driving down there."

"That is my job. That is what I do. I wasn't out having an affair."

Silence.

I say, "I take that as a yes. You fucked her."

All of a sudden I feel rejected.

I ask, "Why?"

And incompetent.

"Was it something I did?" I ask, falling into that Stupid Woman Syndrome. "Or didn't do? Have I not been holding up my end of this marriage?"

"It wasn't you. It was . . . It was stupid. That's all."

Feels like everything I've done is wrong. I'm the victim, victimizing myself even more.

I'm not incompetent. And I haven't done anything wrong. I'm nobody's victim.

I say, "Your biggest complaint is that I'm successful. That's my crime."

He says nada. The wedding pictures on our walls stare at us.

I ask, "How long has this been going on?"

"Not long."

"What's not long—a month, a day, a year—what's not long?"

"Not long."

"Long enough for Jessica to become Jessie."

He rubs his neck, and then reaches for my hand. I pull away.

I ask, "Were you going to leave me?"

"You're the best thing in my life. I'd never leave you."

"Why can't you answer my question?"

"What question?"

"Did you ever make plans to leave this marriage?"

"No. I'm sorry for what—"

"How many times did you . . . How many times were you with her?"

"Don't—"

"How many times?"

"It wasn't serious."

"I don't know if that makes it better or makes it worse."

"I'm sorry. It's done."

"Is it?"

"It's done."

"If it's done, why does this David Lawrence think that you and his wife were running off together? Why did he come to your job and kick your ass?"

"He didn't . . ." His words stop. "Look, I have no idea what she told him."

"Why would she think that? Why would she tell her husband that?"

"I have no idea."

"Just like you have no idea who hit you in the eye."

Silence.

"How many times, Charles?"

"I don't know."

"Okay, let me help you out. Was it once? Was it a one-night stand?"

His look tells me that it wasn't.

I ask, "More than five? More than ten? Let me know when I'm getting warm. Twenty?"

"Look, we hooked up a couple of times."

"What's a couple? Twice?"

"A couple means a couple."

"Then you came home to me."

Silence.

"So now you remember who she is." My voice is dream-like, drifting away from this room, from this relationship. "You know who he is. Your memory is getting better."

He says my name and I don't answer him. I've been sleeping like a child, unaware and naive. My eyes keep taking in the wedding pictures on the walls.

I ask, "Do you love her?"

He says, "I love you."

"Yes or no, were you or are you in love with her? Or was it just a physical thing?"

"I love you. Nobody but you. I'd never leave you, no matter what."

He says that as if he needs to hear the same. No reply from me.

I say, "You still didn't answer my question."

He says, "It was something that happened, something that was about nothing."

His words are awkward and filled with shame, each sentence twice as desperate as the one before. He struggles to justify the unjustifiable, tries to find the words to calm me, to make me let this go, as if it were some minor thing that happens in a marriage.

He asks, "How you feel?"

"How do I feel?" Rage takes over and I don't recognize my own voice; don't know the woman who is screaming like a wounded animal. "How do you think I feel?"

"I'd never leave you."

"You left me when you stuck your dick in that woman." My voice overflows with emotion, saying all the graphic things that are running through my mind. "I'll tell you how the fuck I feel. You probably ate her pussy, then came home and kissed me. You stuck your dick in her, then came home and let me suck her pussy off your dick. How would that feel to you? If I went out and sucked some motherfucker's dick, then came home and put that in your mouth? How would you feel if you were eating my pussy and sucking some nigga's come out of me? How in the fuck would you like that shit, motherfucker? Tell me, how would you feel, nigga?"

Terror and anger are hemorrhaging my insides. I need to escape, have to flee while I can move. I grab my keys, my purse, wipe my eyes, and head to my car. He tries to stop me, but knows better than to touch me. He calls my name over and over, pleading, his face becoming lined with his own fears of being abandoned. I've been abandoned and didn't notice. He's had an affair, left me, and come back before I ever noticed a thing.

I get in my Baby Blue, slam the door, and rev up my engine over Charles's voice. Now he wants to talk, wants me to stay, loves me, loves me, loves me. I rush and put the car in reverse, not knowing where I'm going, just that I have to get there as fast as I can.

There is a loud crash, an earthquake, an explosion, like the world is caving in on me.

I've rammed the garage door so hard the metal has bent off the frame. My mind is gone. I didn't let the damn thing up. Sounds like the roof is falling in. The mountain bike that hangs from the ceiling falls from its hook and crashes on the hood of my car with a thud, taking off layers of paint as it rolls to the ground. Charles is freaking out and all I want to do is get away from him. Through my clouded eyes, I panic, put Baby Blue in drive, press the accelerator too hard and I smash into the workbench. My face bumps into the steering wheel and it feels like the car jerks around, lifts in the air as I ram that cabinet and workbench into the wall that's on this side of the family room. Again I back up too fast. The garage door wants to fall in.

All of Charles's tools and pictures are falling off the wall, crashing to the gray concrete.

I'm tearing up my car.

I'm crying.

Charles is screaming.

6

He answers before the first ring is done.

I say, "May I speak with David Lawrence."

"Sorry, lots of static on the line. Who's calling?"

My face aches from where it hit my steering wheel. My neck hurts. Numbness is in my voice as I whisper who I am.

I ask, "I wake you up?"

"I'm a . . . I work in my studio pretty late, sometimes all night."

"A night person."

"When I'm working. When shit is on my mind."

I wanted to wake his ass up. Wanted to disturb him the way he has disturbed me.

There is a pause. He's waiting. He's nervous.

I ask, "Guess you didn't find your wife."

"Haven't talked to her since Thursday. Thought you might've been her."

"She's not with my husband. At least she wasn't thirty minutes ago."

My teeth move back and forth, grit across each other.

I say, "Three hours ago, my life was fine. Thanks for calling and fucking it up."

I hang up; let my cell phone drop in my lap.

This is where I am. I'm a wounded, embarrassed, and angry passenger in Yvette's SUV.

After the Laurel and Hardy routine, Charles had to help me get out of the car. That took forever and a day. We live in a close-knit bedroom community south of Los Angeles and north of Long Beach, one where we all live behind a concrete wall and everybody is in everybody's business, so half a dozen neighbors came running over because they heard the commotion.

They saw I was a wreck, saw Charles's disposition, and did the math. Tseday, the Ethiopian sister who lives across the street, came over and tried to console me while her husband talked to Charles and tried to fix the garage door.

Baby Blue was scratched and dented beyond forgiveness. Our garage looked like the epicenter of an earthquake.

Sometime after that, while I was putting ice on my head, my cellular phone rang and it was Yvette, calling to check on my situation. She heard the anger and I told her what the scenario was on my home front. Yvette said she was leaving the news plantation, and the next thing I knew she was tapping at my door. She came in with attitude and silence, the way we do it when they have fucked up in a major way. Charles didn't say a word to Yvette or Tseday. Guess their looks and the mode they were in was a deterrent.

Yvette told me to grab some clothes, to come with her.

Now here we are. Here I am, a pissed-off passenger in an SUV, flying north on the 110.

Yvette says, "You really should go to the emergency room."

I shake my head. That simple movement aches. "Tore up my damn car."

Yvette says, "We'll check on that tomorrow."

"And the garage. And the wall to the house."

It's close to midnight and the world is passing me by at ninety miles an hour.

"A damn P.E. teacher?" Yvette frowns like she remembers what her gym teacher looked like when she was in middle school.

"Can you believe that shit?"

"That's one rung above a waitress at Denny's."

My cellular phone rings. It's my home number. I don't answer.

Then it rings again.

I look at the number. David Lawrence is calling me again. I'm pissed to a new level because now he has my personal number. Stupid me. My cellular number must've shown on his caller ID and now he's worming his way into my life a little more. I detest him. A strong, undeniable, faceless hate that has no other focus. I don't know him, and I loathe him without condition. My mind is wishing him dead.

I turn my cell phone off.

Yvette's upset, as if this pain reminds her of pains from her own past. The memories of bad relationships and broken promises are glowing in her eyes as she makes that transition from the Pasadena Freeway to the Hollywood Freeway. She rants, goes on and on, her words fluctuating between anger and tenderness, saying all the standard things a woman-friend says to another woman-friend in the middle of a crisis like this.

I'm staring straight ahead at nothing. Yvette's words fade into the sound of traffic. I can't feel anything, just my heart. Guess you always feel the injured parts of your body.

She exits the freeway early, gets off in Hollywood and

takes Sunset Boulevard past Roscoe's Chicken & Waffles and drives deeper into the part of the city down near the Laugh Factory and the Comedy Store, the tract that's filled with bright lights and thousands of people in motion, people who can't be still, people who are never satisfied.

I keep seeing her face. That Jessica person. I don't know what she looks like, and I keep imagining a thousand versions of her, from slim and sexy, to not so slim and not so sexy, but attractive in her own way. Maybe smarter than I am. Or better in bed.

I ask Yvette, "Where you going?"

"House of Blues."

"Clubbing?"

"For drinks."

"Don't wanna be around a crowd."

"Okay."

"What you got at the ponderosa?"

"Zinfandel. Rum. Dunno. I'll check my cabinets when I get in."

"Anything medicinal to take the edge off?"

"Medicinal as in over-the-counter?"

I say, "I'm not talking Advil."

"One hit chronic, something exotic from Hawaii, or something less—"

"Just surprise me."

She hops on her cellular, pushes one of her single-digit, preprogrammed numbers, and talks to her hookup. I tune her out. I look out the window at all the people, all ages and races, lost and in search of. They all look like pleasure seekers in an aquarium, swimming from place to place, like scavengers, in search of carnal and euphoric food. They are looking for something to make them feel good. Right now it feels as if I have no place in this world. Yvette is comfortable up here. I used to be, but I've slowed my roll. Touching my wedding ring reminds me of that transformation from strobe lights to a white picket fence. Yvette remains part of that surreptitious group. Part of the nightwalkers in pursuit of orgasm.

I turn my cellular phone back on. I want Charles to call. I don't want to talk to him. If he keeps calling, he's just as fucked up inside as I am right now. If he calls, then I know he's not with some middle school P.E.–teaching bitch named Jessica.

Yvette has the sofa to end all sofas in her living room. Beige and brown with a paisley pattern, large and comfortable, the kind you want to fall asleep on. Since this is a one-bedroom, that's where I'll be trying to avoid sleep tonight. Sleep will make me have nightmares, and being awake will cause me to think too much, so it's gonna be a lose-lose for me. She has stacks of books in a corner, underneath a coffee table made of unfinished wood. *Women Who Run with Wolves*. Essays on the African American experience. *Men Who Can't Love*. *Women and Madness*. *The Bell Jar*. At least a hundred other books. I think about trying to get lost in a book, but I know I won't be able to focus, especially after I have a few drinks.

Awards from her work in news are all over her white walls; very few family pictures are up. She has lots of scented candles in different kinds of candleholders, enough for her small living room to look cozy and spiritual. A plaque from her sorority is in the mix as well, right over her computer station. Photos of her and celebrities that she's met over the last few years are in the place too. Those have a dedicated wall next to her bistro-style dining room table. A Hollywood shrine to look at while she dines. Those photos are framed and posted as if she and Chante Moore, she and Ja Rule, she and Nelly, she and Angie Stone, she and Musiq, she and Ashanti, she and Hill Harper and Diahann Carroll, she and actors and actresses at the Black Grammys, she and other B-list actors and actresses in the black movies of the week, as if she and about a hundred other people, who will never put pictures of her up on their walls or in their photo albums, were the best of friends.

I toss my overnight bag at the foot of her sofa, get settled, and she goes to the kitchen, opens a cabinet filled top to bottom with a zillion brands of alcohol.

She says, "Wanna try Bacardi Limon and Mountain Dew?"

"Sounds interesting."

"Or we can spice up Skyy vodka with some Red Bull."

"Mix it all and give me a glass."

"You'll be sick as a dog."

"Mix it."

She gets a short glass.

I say, "A tall glass."

"Let's start short and work our way up, okay?"

"Sure. Whatever."

Her cellular phone goes off and she answers.

"You're outside? Be right out."

Her connection delivers medicinal products like Domino's Pizza. She gets twenty bucks from me so she can have the fifty it'll cost her for her little package of magical vegetation, leaves, and comes back within a minute. She tosses a small Ziploc sandwich bag on the counter.

I say, "Wow."

"Changing your mind?"

"Fire it up before I realize what I'm about to do."

She tells me she has cognac-dipped blunt papers, regular one-point-five rolling papers, or a pipe. None of that techno-cannabis lingo means a thing to me because I haven't smoked a joint in ten years, not since I used to date this bad boy from the east side, so I'm out of the loop. Right now, I'm so stressed that it wouldn't surprise me if Bacardi 151 went down with the ease of strawberry Kool-Aid. I tell her I don't give a shit, just get the damn herb and use whatever she usually uses when she does the do. If she wants to stuff the ganja in my mouth and light it with a candle, that'll work for me.

She goes into her bedroom, talking to me the whole time, and comes back with a cute little pipe, the kind that's discreet, made for people who get high on the down low. She puts a little screen in, puts the weed in with her hand, packs it down a bit, closes the top, and lights it.

We drink.

We smoke.

We live inside a thick ganja cloud and talk about men.

We curse and talk about niggas.

Yvette keeps a thick photo album in her living room, right at the foot of her coffee table. Going front to back, you get a chronological picture of all of her lovers from the last eight or nine years, a couple of those tenures overlapping. On beaches in the Bahamas. In San Diego. Overseas in France. On ski trips to Canada. You see everywhere she's been, all the places she's made love with men whose love didn't last. You see all that and some pretty outlandish hairstyles. Her hair speaks of her personal growth and personality transitions; from a conservative press-and-curl, to a perm, to short and natural hair, to twists, to locks. Page after page, relationship after relationship, her hair changes colors the way leaves turn in different seasons, go from being dark brown to rust to blond to black, and many colors in between. From makeup to none, the way she rolls now, all natural with colorful scarves on her mane.

We talk about heartaches. About her engagements that never became marriages. Models. Actors. Comedians. Engineers. They've all come and gone over the years. Some still call; want to hook up on some level. Yet, at the end of the day, she still sleeps alone.

Yvette says, "It's easy to fuck. Loving is hard."

"Hard for me to let a man be all up inside me and not feel something."

"That's why a lot of peeps keep it at the booty call."

"I'm not good at that level."

"I'm just saying how it is out there. Hard to find a man who ain't operating at that level."

I say, "If you ask me—and you did—the problem isn't finding somebody to love you."

"Uh huh. So what, you think you Dr. Phil now?"

I flip her off. "So many types and degrees of love. It's hard finding somebody to love you in the right way, for the right reasons. Not for money, house, car, sex, security, but they adore you simply because you're you. They accept you as you are, faults and all."

"Like I said, it's hard."

"But it ain't impossible."

She sighs. "I ain't never been treasured like that."

"Some people go through their whole lives and never fall in love."

"Been there, done that, and I've recovered. I'm fine the way I am."

"Don't you wanna have kids?"

"Nope. Can't imagine myself being pregnant."

"Adopt?"

"I'll adopt a highway before I adopt a kid. Less maintenance."

"I can't imagine not being in love. Can't imagine being that . . . that . . . that empty."

"You calling me empty? You trying to make me feel bad."

"Oh, please. Not even."

"Maybe I'll get back there. But right now, keeping it at the level that works for me."

"Sex without love is violence."

"I've had some good violence this year. Some damn good violence."

"Wish I could handle it like you."

"Nah, wish I was like you. It ain't easy being me. I just roll with the punches and make the best of it. I've never dealt with rejection too good. That's the only emotion I can't handle. So I'd rather sex and go than stick around and wait for crap to fall apart."

Talking about her keeps me from talking about my situation, and I'm all for that.

Yvette tells me, "This is why I go with the flow, move from man to man, from love to love. Love is wonderful when it's new. When it's new, it has strength."

"Uh-huh."

"I don't want to stay until love goes cold, when you need to pull away but you can't. When you want that new love to return and make it better, but you know it never will be. I chase the newness; follow that feeling wherever it takes me."

I say, "You chase the newness, right, playa?"

"And run away from the fear. Anybody says love doesn't bring fear ain't been in love."

"What about that one great love we all dream about?"

"The one that makes you a prisoner?"

Sometimes my girl sounds like a woman who is able to detach herself from the emotions that come with sex. I know I can't. I've wanted to, many times I've tried, but my system isn't made that way. I'm always attached to the men I've been sexually active with. That's why I've chosen to lose contact with all of my exes. We break up and I change numbers, change e-mail addresses, and a few times one of us had to leave town to keep it from becoming too ugly. Hormones rule my heart, and when scorned, I can become evil.

But maybe she hasn't gotten beyond that curse either; maybe she chooses one-night stands and zipless fucks as quick fixes for her desires, a placebo for loneliness. That's her style, her defense mechanism, her way to avoid being attached, her way to keep from becoming too detached, to keep away from that love thang and all that it brings, both the good and the bad.

I hit the pipe too hard and fall into a coughing fit. Yvette freaks out because I'm coughing so hard, then while I wipe the tears from my eyes, we have a laughing fit.

Her phone rings and interrupts our little powwow.

She checks the caller ID before she answers. She says a few words, then surprise covers her face. She says, "You're here in the valley? Outside? You were supposed to come over tonight . . . Snap . . . I forgot. One of my girls is over. No, no, it's cool. Find somewhere to park and come on up to the gate."

She hangs up.

She smacks her forehead over and over and says, "Shit."

"What?"

"Had invited a friend over. Forgot all about it."

"Need me to . . . Damn, I can't leave. I rode with you. My

car is trapped in a broke-down garage forty-five minutes from here."

"Don't sweat it. We're supposed to go to the swingers' house."

"You're too wild for me."

"Just to watch. I told him about it and he wants to check out the freaks."

I imitate her subtle accent. "Y'all so nasty."

She laughs. "Roll with us."

"I ain't swinging like that."

"C'mon. He'll keep us safe from the rest of the wild bunch."

I don't answer. My mind is on other things.

She heads to the door, jogs down the narrow hallway. I try to fix myself up and hope I don't look like a lush. Yvette comes back before I can pull myself together. I hear them talking and laughing before the door opens. He's holding her hand when they come inside. He has smooth brown skin and thick arms. His midnight locks come down to the top of his back. Her friend wears a simple black sweater and jeans, colorful and trendy boots. He has a nice smile and reminds me of Ricky Williams, the running back for the Miami Dolphins, only he's not as big, and has a goatee. He looks ten years younger than Yvette, five years younger than me.

She introduces us and we shake hands. He goes by the name of TJ. He's from Eritrea.

I say, "So, you're the reason she's so big on Eritrea."

He says, "I've been schooling her on my country, yes."

"And hopefully she's schooling you on the black man's issues over here."

We laugh, but his eyes tell me that this was not the evening he had in mind. He relaxes on the sofa next to Yvette, and I sit on the love seat next to her sliding glass door, the door that leads to her balcony and barbeque grill. TJ drinks a little rum, not much, but he loves the herbs.

Yvette tells him we work together, that I'm a producer.

He has an accent, the kind that reeks of both elegance and intelligence.

With a man in the room, our little pity party is set aside, and I pretend that all is fine in my life. I don't really want to talk about me, so I get into interview mode, the way a sister does when she wants to know if a man is decent enough to be taking up her girlfriend's time. I ask him where he's from and how he ended up in this country.

He says he was born in Asmara, but his family had to flee Africa because of the war. Lots of his people went to Kenya or Somalia. But his family ended up in Europe, bouncing from Germany to Italy, from Greece to Sweden, and eventually made it to America and settled in D.C. Some of his family left D.C. and moved to Dallas and San Diego, cities close to a coast.

I ask him what he does, hoping to get a simpler answer this time.

He tells me that he's into neuropharmacology and neuro-science. I think I have a blank look on my face because he breaks it down, tells me he's into learning about the nervous system function, dysfunction, and treatment. I don't really understand what the hell he's talking about, especially since the herb and brew are kicking in. And all those SAT words ain't helping. He says something about getting ready to go to Albany Medical College for its graduate program.

I'm so not even there and all I can say is, "Really?"

"I'll be studying neuronal and glial cell development, substance abuse, schizophrenia, brain and hormone interactions, stroke, and dynamics of neurotransmitter systems—"

"You'll be studying me, 'cause my nervous system is shot and all three of me think that the substance in that pipe is off the hook. My hormones need some interaction and are transmitting for me to abuse that li'l pipe some more, some more."

We laugh.

First chance TJ gets, now that he knows I'm a producer, he tries to sell me his country's plight. Point blank, I tell him I know nothing about his country, my subtle way of saying that in this moment, in the midst of my crisis, with my life unraveling, I couldn't care less.

TJ tells me, "I'm going to give you the real deal."

"As long as you do it Hollywood style."

"Hollywood style?"

My vision blurs. "Pretend we're in Hollywood on an elevator, and I'm Spielberg. Pitch your idea before I get to my floor, so you have to sell me this idea in less than one minute."

His look becomes incredulous. "The *Reader's Digest* version of a thirty-year war?"

"You just lost five seconds."

Yvette laughs.

I ask, "How long ago was this?"

He frowns. "Weren't you aware of this in the late nineties?"

"Aw, man." I throw my free hand up. "You giving me some last-millennium news?"

Yvette says, "No one ever says that when they talk about the Jewish Holocaust, so why does our news, our ongoing African Holocaust, have to be played out?"

I raise my hands. "My bad. TJ, my brother, you have the floor."

TJ gets serious. "Eritrea was colonized by Italy. Then the Italians gave us to Ethiopia as a gift. We were annexed against our will. From there, war broke out and lasted for thirty years."

"Uh-huh. Pass me that cute little pipe, please?"

"Ethiopians destroyed everything."

"Uh-huh. Where my drink go?"

Yvette says, "It's in your hand, Freckles."

"My bad. Keep talking, TJ. I'm listening."

He goes on, "They caused drought, famine—"

"They caused drought? So you're accusing them of controlling the weather."

"I'm talking about violence, destruction, economic corruption. Kids couldn't attend school. People starved. They tried to control the media. Murdered my people without mercy. They would lock large groups in a church and set it on fire, or drag mutilated bodies through our streets to instill fear. Once Russia withdrew its support from Ethiopia, we overthrew them in 1991."

"Da-ammmmmn, can't we all get along? First it was that mess over in Rwanda, now you people too? Why can't y'all do like regular black people and fight white people? Y'all got some Mississippi Burning, Hatfield and McCoy, Crips and Bloods crap going on over there that cannot be good for tourism. I mean, y'all are taking that black-on-black shit to a new level."

Yvette is on her back, laughing her ass off.

TJ says, "Just trying to give you the Eritrean side of the story."

I tell him, "Look, my brother, we need some Ethiopians in

the room to balance some of this shit out. My neighbor is Ethiopian and we jog together from time to time, and I really like her. Smart as hell. Hell, she thinks I kinda sorta look Ethiopian, so I might have some Ethiopian blood, you know? We need to verify some of those accusations against my might-be people."

TJ laughs a very polite laugh, one that masks whether he's offended or not, moves his locks from his eyes, shakes his head, sips his poison, hits the pipe, the smoke rising into his hair.

He inhales and says, "Didn't want you to get the distorted view that is often told."

"Thanks for the enlightenment. Now please puff-puff-pass the pipe."

"I'm glad you've been exposed to my world, but your next step is to try some of the food."

"Now you're talking. I could use a Twinkie or Ding Dong right about now. Y'all got those over there in Eureka, or Croatia, or Rosacea, or . . . what's the name of that colony again?"

Yvette says, "Freckles, you are fucked up."

I say, "Damn shame. We love dogs better than we do each other."

Yvette says, "You think?"

"When was the last time we started a war against a dog? Or a cat?"

Both of them are laughing at me.

I say, "That's who we need to be fighting. All them dogs and cats out there ho'ing around like . . . like . . . people. Hmmm. Do dogs ever try to do it people style?"

Yvette laughs the loudest. "Freckles, you are so fucked up."

"Whoa. Did this room get bigger?"

"No, you're taking baby steps and just taking forever to get across the room."

"This room did get bigger."

"What are you looking for now?"

"Phone."

"For what?"

"To call Charles. Time to tell that motherfucker a thing or two."

"No, let him suffer. First one to call loses; you know how the game goes."

Me and Yvette get back to bitching about Charles and Jessica, trying to figure out why Charles would do some shit like that when I cook, clean, pretty much sex on demand, swallow, give him backrubs, foot rubs, manicures, pedicures, do pretty much every erotic and exotic thing that comes to mind. I give him minimal drama. We both know how men hate Drama Queens, because we hate Drama Queens—our boss, Tyra the Tyrant, being at the top of that list.

I say, "I keep a clean house. And I can cook, dammit. I cook my ass off. I used to be in that hot-ass kitchen with my momma and my grandmomma, and we were some all-day-sweating and fried-chicken-cooking and cake-baking heifers. You hear me?"

I'm slurring and crying.

I say, "He left me, came back, and I didn't know he ever left."

She holds me like I'm her child.

I say, "It is not a good feeling when you feel like everything in your life is false."

Tears stop and my anger comes back, takes away the edge of my buzz. We talk raw and uncensored, pretty much forget that TJ is here. But he is. I look up and see him pretending that all is fine in the Land of Oz, shifting and channel surfing to hide his discomfort.

I wipe my tears away; tell TJ, "Sorry for going on and on and rambling like an idiot. You did not come here to see no crap like this. Look, you two go out and get your groove on."

He shifts, says, "No, I . . . We can go some other time."

I make myself laugh. "So, Mister East Africa, you really wanna go to a swingers' joint?"

"Eritreans get kinky too." He laughs. "Where do you think little Eritreans come from?"

"Aisle six at Kmart."

He laughs so hard he almost chokes. TJ thinks I'm insane.

I say, "No, you two go tonight. I'll be cool. Need to be by myself for a few anyway."

I notice him, the man with the provocative accent, the lover who will be the next photo in Yvette's album. The next season waiting to change. In my mind, he feels like a picture that has been left out in the sun, another image that is already fading.

Yvette says, "You sure?"

I say, "Get going. I'll probably be sleeping in the next few."

I make my way through her single bedroom to the bathroom. That's the design of her apartment; have to go through the bedroom to get to the toilet. I sit on the toilet and pee.

Fucking your husband.

I don't turn on the lights. I don't want to see the face of the woman in the mirror.

When I get back in the living room, Yvette and TJ are in the kitchen, cleaning up. I walk in just as they finish a kiss. She looks so soft and sweet in his arms. Yvette grabs her coat. TJ heads for the door. I get my cellular phone, grab a pillow and some covers and get comfortable on the sofa. I close my eyes, pull the covers up to my forehead, and pretend to be sleeping.

They leave.

The room starts to spin.

I fall off the sofa, struggle to my feet, and make my way through the fading ganja clouds. Takes me a while, but I make it back to the bathroom in time. I'm there for a while, sicker than a dog, on my knees, praising that porcelain god. Whenever I think I'm done, it starts over again.

I pass out on the cold linoleum.

A tapping wakes me up in the middle of the night. A relentless tapping that starts in my nightmare. In my dreams, I'm choking the snot out of Vivica A. Fox, Halle Berry, Jada Pinkett, Michael Michelle, Lisa Nicole Carson—all the women that I imagine to be Jessica. That tapping is the sound of me banging their heads against a brick wall. That tapping wakes me up.

I'm not on the floor in the bathroom anymore. I'm back on the sofa, pajamas on, underneath covers that are making me sweat. It feels like a woodpecker is carving out an ornate dining room table inside my head. I kick the covers off. The tapping is coming from my left, from the door. Somebody is whispering for Yvette. Whispering her name and tapping on the door. I'm dried out, have no voice right now, can't tell them to go away, that Yvette left with TJ, that you'll have to take a number and come back another day. That tapping is strong and steady. I struggle to my feet and weeble-wobble my way toward the door. By the time I get to the kitchen counter, that tapping sound messes with my mind and moves around the room, goes from the door to being behind me on my right, coming from Yvette's bedroom, as if somebody was trying to break in her window.

I hear a man whisper Yvette's name again.

Her bedroom door is halfway open. I stand hidden in darkness and I see my friend.

She's on TJ, riding him back to Africa, moving like she knows a nice, scenic route. Her scarf falls from her head and her locks sway with her movements. They move slowly, the way people do when they relish pleasure and want to delay orgasm. She and her young lover travel with each other, his hands worshipping her body—her thighs, her hips, her ass, her breasts—her experience, and her wisdom. Candles are burning, lighting up her wonderful sensuous den.

Yvette and TJ morph like characters in a movie, become a reflection of Charles and a faceless Jessica.

I'm angry again.

I shuffle back to the sofa, yank the covers over me. Something hard is under my back. I pull it out. It's my cell phone. I guess where the button is and push the one for home. I need to curse Charles out. He answers on the first ring, and my drunken anger flows like a river.

The entire catalog of things I've said to Yvette this evening comes out of my mouth. My voice is low and dehydrated. I remind Charles how I've been committed to him and our marriage, that I cook almost every day because I know he hates leftovers, clean better than Molly Maid, go to church, do laundry, bring up that sex-whenever-he-needs-me thing, let him know he had no reason to seek pleasure anywhere else. Then I went into the swallowing, backrubs, foot rubs, manicures, pedicures—pretty much cover the whole nine in one breath.

I rant for a good minute. He says nothing.

I say, "You there?"

He says, "Who is this?"

"Wait, who is this?"

Over in the bedroom, the tapping stops for a moment, then changes, has a new rhythm, a very aggressive cadence, the way it does when a man gets on top and starts to thrust.

The voice on the phone says, "David Lawrence."

"David Lawrence? As in David Lawrence, David Lawrence?"

"Yeah."

"How do you always end up on my phone?"

"You called me. You okay?"

"I'm distraught and constipated, thanks to you. Asshole. I should come kick your ass."

"I take that as a no. Look, I'm not doing too well myself."

"Answer me, dammit. How do you always get on my phone? I don't even know who you are and you've messed up my life. Do you have any idea how happy I was before you called me? Who are you? Did you ever stop to think that I was happy not knowing? You're irritating me, you know that? Why do I always pick up my phone and you're on my phone? Who are you? I know who you are. Irrrrr-eeeeeee-tating. You are Mister Irrrrr-eeeeeee-tating. That's why your wife was fucking around on you, Mister Irrrrr-eeeeeee-tating."

He hangs up.

The tapping gets intense. They're talking to God, worshipping each other toward heaven.

I fumble with my phone, try to push redial.

He answers on the second ring. I pick up where I left off with my drunken diatribe.

When my headache slows me down, I stop ranting. He says nothing.

I say, "Hello?"

"Baby, where are you?"

"Who is this?"

"Charles."

"Charles? Aw, damn."

"I love you."

"Yeah, yeah, whatever."

He sounds terrified. "Come home. Let's talk this out."

I hang up. The phone drops from my hand. The battery pops out.

That tapping gets faster, faster, and then eases down to soft thumps. It gets quiet enough for me to hear them on the other side of that wall catching their breaths. Then they whisper and laugh. The joyous sounds people have after good sex sneak into my space. Somebody walks across the room with a stride of pride. Yvette opens her bedroom door all the way and does a peek-a-boo at me. Her bedroom candles and the glow on her skin make her look like an angel coming down from heaven, give enough light so I can make out her silhouette as she comes close. I close my eyes. She touches my forehead, wipes sweat away. Her hands are warm; skin still radiating with the heat of fresh love. She adjusts the covers on me, then goes to the kitchen. I open my eyes. Yvette gets her lover a glass of water before she tiptoes back into her bedroom.

Talking. Laughter. Silence. Moans.

The tapping starts again.

7

That woodpecker in my head is working on another dining room table when TJ tips out at the crack of dawn. I hear the door opening and Yvette kissing him good-bye. She yawns as she checks on me again. I mumble something about being okay, and then ask her to turn the television on so I can see Katie Couric. Have to keep up with the news. She turns the TV on, puts the remote in my hand, and heads back into her bedroom. Then I hear the shower going. Yvette cooks for me, but I can't eat. Even the smell of the salmon croquettes and rice makes me ill. I try to drink water to ease my headache and get my system back on track.

I get on the phone and call Charles's job. "Jessica Lawrence. Well, when will she be back? Well, maybe you can answer this: was she there Monday when the incident happened in the parking lot? The damn fight that one of your teachers and Jessica Lawrence's husband were involved in. Look, you can turn that record over and play the other side because I know about Jessica Lawrence and Charles . . . Yes, that damn fight. This is . . . never mind. I'll call back tomorrow. Better yet, maybe I'll have a news crew come down and see if anybody around there can answer a fucking question."

I hang up.

Yvette says, "So, sounds like we don't need to make that drive to the school."

"Sounds like the whore don't work there no more."

"Fired?"

I pull at my locks. "They won't say."

"What you wanna do now?"

My answer is a stiff shrug.

I snap the battery back into my cellular phone, turn it back on, put in the password; it starts to beep and sing like crazy. I have ten messages from my husband. Some long, some short. All are in a down and desperate tone. Apologies and worry and please call or come home or at least meet so we can talk. He doesn't want me to tell anyone about our problems, especially our families. He's worried about his image being tarnished. All that plus he owns the fear a man owns when he's afraid his woman will do the same wrongs he's done. The fear that makes him toss and turn from dusk to dawn. He knows whatever I do, he can't question.

Two messages are from David Lawrence. He's telling me we talked last night. He's apologizing. And he asks me to call him if there is anything he can do. He says nothing about his wife. At first I don't remember, then everything is there, moving through vagueness—the tapping, images of lovers, the phone calls—it's all there, muddled and hidden behind clouds.

I ask, "How did I get on the sofa?"

"TJ carried you."

"Oh, God. I'll never be able to face him again."

"Freckles, you just don't know. You scared us big time. We were in there talking to you, taking your pulse, splashing water on your face. Thought you had gone Billie Holiday on me."

"I make a mess?"

"Don't sweat it. We cleaned it up."

She tells me she undressed me, changed me like I was a baby.

I ask, "How was the swingers' thing last night?"

She tells me they stayed an hour. I ask what they saw this time. She tells me that a white French girl and her African-American boyfriend put on a show for about thirty voyeurs. And the same girl that she had told me about before, the one who made oral love to a room of men, then had sex with just as many, she was there too, doing the same thing she'd done before.

Yvette says, "Something about her was . . . sad."

"What?"

"Don't know. Just . . . sad."

I go to the bathroom, shower the best I can, and come back in a T-shirt and panties.

I nod. "I need pencil and paper."

"Whassup?"

"Gonna write a grocery list for Charles."

She gives it to me.

Yvette bounces out to Billy Blanks's gym to hit a Tae Bo class, and she gets back when the sun is at its highest peak. She's eating a burrito from Baja Grill, energized, and wants to take me out for some retail therapy—shoe shopping at the Glendale Galleria, and then maybe bicycling on Venice Beach so I can sweat, but I can barely walk across the room, so I'm not feeling any of that. I need to go home, whether I want to or not. I don't want to avoid the inevitable. I'm not guilty of anything so I have no reason to run, no reason to hide. Plus, I need transportation. In Los Angeles, transportation is the first step to freedom.

"You really need to talk to Jessica," Yvette tells me on the drive.

I take out that sheet of paper I had been writing my thoughts down on this morning and add that to the bottom of my list.

I say, "I'll find her. And we will talk."

We're on the Hollywood Freeway heading toward downtown, lunchtime traffic so congested we're barely doing ten miles an hour.

Yvette says, "We'll go old school, roll up and put the fear of God in her heart."

"Let the windows down. Need some air."

She does, then asks, "You leaving Charles?"

The thought carves a hole in my stomach. "Think I should?"

"Your call. He broke the contract. But think about it long and strong. This ain't like dating. Not an easy out. If you do, get ready for a major financial setback."

"This is fucked."

"At least I got the condo in Georgia from those two years of indentured servitude."

Her words are the truth, and that truth hurts.

She says, "I don't care if I stand before God, Buddha, or Oprah, you break your end of the bargain and all bets are off. I've learned to only be as faithful as the man I'm dealing with."

"You're not faithful at all."

"I rest my case. Sometimes you have to get a head start on them motherfuckers."

"You are really cheering me up right about now."

"Keeping it real, just keeping it real."

My Mustang is parked across the street from my home, right in front of a small park that separates the larger homes from the smaller ones. A white van with a kelly-green logo is blocking my driveway: O'CALLAGHAN'S GARAGE REPAIR. A Hispanic man in jeans and a green company shirt that has a huge shamrock on the back is over there fixing the damage. The garage door has been taken off; the damaged parts are off to the side. I tore that tin up in a major way.

Yvette parks her SUV behind my wounded car and I cringe a thousand ways as we walk circles around the damage, lips sucked in and both of us moving in the same direction and shaking our heads. The front end is jacked up. Hood dented from where the mountain bike fell. The awesome paint job scratched to hell. Back end damaged where I rammed the garage door. Parts of the trunk scratched just as bad.

Yvette asks if I need her to come in, but I don't need her acting like Samuel Jackson in *Pulp Fiction*. I tell her I'll catch up with her later. With the garage repair person being in our house, I'm not stuck here alone with Charles. He's big on appearances and won't act a fool in front of the neighbors, and not in front of strangers. But I let my girl know that I might end up at her crib again tonight, depending on how things go inside my house of lies.

She gives me her spare key. That warms my heart. Makes me love her that much more.

We hug. Kiss cheeks. She leaves.

Charles's car is on this side of the street too. Not a scratch.

Not a dent. Undamaged. I look at my car again before I go in. I've messed up my classic.

Charles steps outside as I'm crossing the street. I stop and stare at him like he's a stranger inside my home. He walks back into the living room and waits for me to come inside and close the door.

I ask, "When you going back to work?"

My question asks a lot of things, about his job, about his seeing Jessica, about a million things. His eyes are swollen, both of them. He needs a shower. His hair looks dry.

We stand and face each other. Any other day there would be hugs and kisses.

Yesterday I would've died for him. Would've killed for him. Would've been the Bonnie to his Clyde, no matter what wrong he had done.

Charles says my name and I walk right by him. I go upstairs and change my clothes, put on a long black skirt and long-sleeved jean shirt, and then I go to the fax/copy machine. I'm trying to move like I don't have a hangover, and I'm doing a pretty good job, despite that woodpecker. I make two copies of the paper I've been writing on all morning, then I go back downstairs. Charles is standing in the doorway, talking to the garage man. Charles laughs with that stranger as if nothing is wrong within these four walls. That irks me, the pretense. I step out into the middle of their ha-ha-ho-ho man-talk. The garage man looks at me like I'm a woman driver, incompetent and dangerous. I'm unsmiling. He backs down. Stops laughing. He's about to get cursed out. I ask Charles to come inside so we can have a few words.

I ask, "Talk to Jessie?"

"No. That's over."

"Sure about that?"

"It's over."

Charles follows me into the kitchen. I sit at a bar stool. He does the same.

I say, "Your message said you were ready to talk about it."

"You don't know how bad I feel." He rubs his hair, plays with the curls and waves, then adjusts his sweats. "Just want you to know that I'm sorry, and that it's over."

"Not so fast." I cut him off with a curt hand movement. "I've worked it out. You know what we have to do to move forward?"

He has so much love for me in his eyes. Love and fear. Underneath my anger and disappointment, I own the same. I'm not ready for this, but I have to make myself be. I know how this goes, have seen this happen to friends, have seen countless coworkers come in distraught over some relationship gone bad, just never thought it would happen to me.

I say, "I'm gonna be honest with you. I'm very disappointed."

"I know."

"And I'm scared."

I don't want this to get ugly. I look for the right way to approach this. First I start with the good, tell him what I admire and respect about him. He's a teacher. An educator. Part of the overworked and underpaid that make it possible for others to grow up and avoid being overworked and underpaid. I even chuckle and remind him how we used to joke about how teachers are responsible for all the successful people in the world and should be like agents. If a student gets rich, the teacher gets a percentage. I don't mean average rich; I'm talking Michael Jordan and Donald Trump rich. We always laughed and agreed on that. We do that now. In this moment, things are okay. This is behind us and things are okay.

He says, "Those of us who grow up dirt poor'll always believe in the trickle down theory."

"Until we get too rich. Then it's every man for himself."

That line is an old joke between us.

He says, "The first time we joked about that was down in Florida."

"Yeah. When we ran away to Clearwater."

Right now I wish we were back there, back *then* in Clearwater Beach, Florida, at the Holiday Inn Sunspree Resort on Gulfview, in the same room facing the white sands and warm waters in Tampa Bay. We had a room on the ninth floor and made love on the balcony after midnight, started ten minutes after we stepped into the room. Did that to the sound of ocean waves and seagulls. I remember us laughing and joking about what would have happened if we had gotten too enthusiastic and the rail had given out and we had plunged down through the palm trees, coming and screaming. A day later, we made love in the ocean, moonlight over our heads and waves hitting us from the back. That was when we were new to each other. He was on hiatus from his job for the summer, and I was on vacation.

He chuckles. "And you got that speeding ticket in Valdosta. You were livid."

"That city was a speed trap." I shake my head, pick at my cuticles. "And that big confederate flag that greeted us as soon as we crossed into Georgia—"

"That had you going off for the next two hours."

"Well, you went off too. Went into that lecture-slash-history-lesson about that being slave country, and how dare those rednecks in Dairy Queen country keep that up as a reminder."

"Dairy Queens, Super-8 motels, and mobile homes were all up and down I-75."

I say, "And the Waffle Houses."

We chuckle now, in sync, and I can hear our laughter from back then.

For three weeks, we had driven through Miami and Tampa, then headed north to Atlanta to see some friends for a few days, then went out I-85 into North Carolina to see my family. Left Cakalaki and headed into Louisiana to see his family after that. Charles remembers the same. I know because his hazel eyes sparkle and he looks like a little boy. We almost smile at that memory, almost laugh like we did back then, almost put this wretched moment behind us.

But we can't. It's not that easy.

I look at Charles's swollen eye; see what David Lawrence has done.

The memories and the laughter fade. I become focused.

I say, "This . . . this . . . Our conversation is out of place."

He rocks and gives me no help with our transition from then to now.

My voice cracks. "How could you fuck somebody else?"

"It . . . it just happened."

"Tell me why it happened."

"It wasn't about anything."

I take a deep breath, open and close my hands as a tension reliever, and remind him about my relationship with my father, of how I've expected my husband to be a better man to me, but in the end, all he has been is a man. I tell him how I've always tried to build a strong relationship, how I've done all I can to make sure he was comfortable, how I've compromised myself to make sure he was happy. I try not to sound bitter, but I do, and I stop trying to fight what I feel. I let the few tears I have left come and fall to the counter. Charles listens and fidgets when I talk about the economics of divorce; I have to bring that up. Divorce isn't cheap, not on the emotions or the pockets. Somebody would have to move; somebody would have to borrow at least fifty thousand to pay off their part of the property, and to pay the lawyers. Then there is the possibility of pension entitlement, other things that wreak havoc on a person's livelihood, and right now, I'm not prepared to deal with all of that. I know that on his teacher's salary Charles can't come up with fifty thousand to buy me out. And I'm not giving him that much to go away and play with his girlfriend.

I say, "See what you've done to us?"

"We don't have to go there."

"All the damage that was in that garage, that's how I feel inside."

"Are you leaving me? Is that what this is all about?"

I say, "Before it comes to that, we have to try to work this out between us."

"Counseling?"

"Nope. Not yet. If you want to move forward, I've written down a list of things I have to know. I need to know this before we seek counseling, or talk to a minister, or whatever people do when they deal with shit like this. This is my query list."

"A query list?" He looks at me like I've lost my mind. "You've done a list?"

I nod, and slide a sheet of paper to his side of the counter. My eyes are on his wedding ring as he picks the paper up without touching me. Then my eyes are on my wedding ring, my other hand touching that metal, turning that circle as he reads to himself.

He reads a few lines, and then looks up at me in disbelief. "You're being a journalist."

"Sure am. And that's better than being an asshole."

It's the list I began this morning when Yvette went to Tae Bo.

I say, "To ease my mind, I need a comprehensive answer to every question."

"To all of these questions?"

"And I need your answers in two forms. The first being non-negotiable, and that is in your handwriting. And I would like to have a backup copy, Microsoft Word preferred. On a disk. That's the second form."

"Are you serious?"

"That's right, teacher. If you are serious about this marriage, that's your homework. I need your words in your writing, so that way you can't twist your answers later. You can't say I didn't hear what you said, or that I misunderstood something. I need facts."

"We can talk. I can just tell you."

"No, in writing. So by the time we get to number twenty-one, I can have a copy with me to hand out to everyone at the meeting. I want the same from Jessica."

"Are you serious?"

"Then I need to talk to her, woman to woman. And I want to meet her husband."

"You're joking, right?"

"Since my handwriting sucks, let me read it to you so we'll be on the same page."

Despite him telling me that reading the list isn't necessary, I read it to him anyway. I need to say these things out loud. He needs to hear them. Needs to hear how it pains me to have to ask him these questions. He needs to hear. This is our reality and I'm facing it head-on.

1. Did she know that you were married?
2. Did you know that she was married?
3. Do I know her? Have I met her anywhere at any time, even in passing?
4. How long has this been going on? Give me a start date. The first time it happened (location) and when. Last time. You claim this wasn't that serious, but her husband seems to think differently, so I need to know whose fuck 'n' chuck count is off. Guess how many times you were with her.
5. Where did you meet to have sex? Give me geographical locations. Cities, hotels, homes, apartments, parks, vehicles, all of that should be included.
6. Did you use a condom EVERY time? (If so, did it ever break or slip off? If not, what were you thinking?)
7. Did you give her oral sex at ANY time?
8. Did she go down on you?
9. Did you ever tell her you loved her?
10. Did you ever tell her that you didn't or don't love me?
11. Did you discuss our sex life with her?
12. After sex did you hold her?
13. Who else knows? How many other people? Give me names. Friends and non-friends. Coworkers count as non-friends.
14. How often did you meet? Approximate dates.
15. Did you date? (The answer is obvious.) Where did you go? And a DATE (to avoid any double-talk or ambiguity) includes being in separate cars OR traveling in the same plane, train, or automobile, and it doesn't matter if you split the tab or one of you picked up the check. It doesn't have to be a high-class dinner at Euro-

Chow or a discreet meeting at TGIF, could just be walking on the beach, in a mall, on Crenshaw, talking.

16. Did you fuck her the same days you made love to me?

17. Did you make love to me the same days you went off and fucked her? I know this sounds like question 16, but trust me, in my mind it's different.

18. Were you ever planning to leave me for her?

19. Did you ever want her to want you in that way, to take you away from me?

20. What did I do wrong? Or what didn't I do?

21. Since trust is no longer a constant in our relationship (your fault, not mine), we have to come up with a way to verify your answers. And to verify all of your answers, this is what we do: Arrange a meeting between David and Jessica Lawrence, not over the phone, face-to-face, like mature adults, at a neutral place, a public place where we can check ID (driver's license or passport) and verify that everyone is who they say they are, so we can sit down and talk this out and see where we all stand. We'll split the tab 50/50.

22. Questions 22–25 are pending. Don't worry, when my headache dies down, I will think of something to ask Jessica when we're face-to-face.

He says, "This is insane."

"I'm giving you a chance to be straight with me."

"I already told you."

My words blaze. *"You haven't told me shit."*

He lowers his head, rubs his temples.

I say, "Jessica owes me that much. You owe Jessica's husband the same."

He grunts and rocks.

I say, "Understand this, Charles. Choosing one thing is ultimately not choosing something else. Don't focus on what you want; focus on what you don't want. From me. From this marriage. I have to do the same, but it's hard to do without all the information. I need to understand your relationship with her, what went wrong between us, so I can see if this is something that will happen again, maybe not with her, but with some other woman."

"I said that it was nothing, that it's over, dammit."

"And I'm supposed to accept that? This scares me. I'm not gonna walk around being insecure. My marriage is supposed to be my place of solace, not a place of fucking grief, and my husband is supposed to be my friend, not my fucking enemy. Choose which one you wanna be."

I snatch up my purse and head for the door.

He rushes behind me. "Where are you going?"

I turn and look at him. My expression jars him.

"Answer those questions, Charles, or you're a photograph left out in the sun."

8

The all-news station is playing when I leave my planned community. I pull over in the parking lot at Coco's and pull myself together so I can make a phone call. He knows things. He has to. And I have to know what he knows. He agrees to talk. He tells me where. I take to the 91 freeway at Central, zoom east for three miles until it ends and becomes Artesia Boulevard, then I turn and go north at Vermont Avenue, ride toward the city of Gardena.

That woodpecker follows me, now pecking out an elaborate bookcase inside my head.

I want to turn back, but my anger and jealousy and curiosity steer me ten minutes from my home. This is an old city lined with palm trees and older buildings, no skyscrapers. A city that could pass for California in the fifties on any movie set. Gardena Boulevard looks like it's the main strip of the area. Hispanics. Asians. Those are the people I see walking the avenue, driving beside me. There are blocks of pharmacies, nail shops, sidewalk eateries, and all sorts of mom-and-pop businesses, all on side streets, hidden from the rest of the world.

My cell phone rings. I answer out of reflex, and immediately wish I hadn't. It's Tyra the Tyrant, my royal pain in the ass. Hearing her voice makes my head hurt more; my blood pressure rises to the point where I have to pull over and let traffic pass me by.

I blow air. "Whassup, Tyra?"

In her taut tone and get-to-the-point cadence, she tells me that a producer has had a sudden death in the family—she curses him to hell for that inconvenience—and he had to fly back to some hick town outside of Gainesville, Florida. Another producer has called in sick on a beautiful day made for rollerblading along the beaches, and since no one else can be reached, they need me to come in as soon as possible.

"Fuck." I lower my head; bounce it against my steering wheel. "I'm having a crisis."

"We all are having a crisis. What's the crisis?"

"Me and my husband . . . It's personal."

"Is he dying?"

"Would it matter?"

"Only if he needs surgery and you're the only surgeon in town."

There's a school shooting down in Orange County. A high-speed chase is heading south from Bakersfield. A fatal shooting at a dental lab down at Ball Road and Gilbert. An armed robbery. Car smashes into a school bus in Compton. Burglar kills himself in a standoff in San Gabriel. Another Catholic priest serial child molester has been exposed.

"I've got a meeting—"

"Stop making up these fucking excuses and get your ass in here."

"Tyra, I can't . . . My husband—"

She snaps out her frustration, "Get your ass in here, or don't bother coming back."

She hangs up, hard and strong.

I pull my injured Baby Blue back into the flow of traffic.

Giuliano's Delicatessen and Bakery pops up on my left, right before Normandie Avenue, across the street from Progressive Woman Hair Nail Boutique Gift Shop. That's what the mauve sign on that stucco walls says, all those words, back to back, with no commas, no conjunctions.

It's a busy area, one lane of traffic in each direction and free parking, the pull-in, pull-out parking spaces that are next to extinct. Most of the parking spots are taken, so I drive around the block and come back just as somebody is backing out of a spot across the street, in front of Andrews Printing Copy Center. No possessive punctuation is on the word Andrews. Must be an ordinance against excessive punctuation in this city. I park, jog across the street, and pace in front of Giuliano's. The sidewalk is cut in perfect side-by-side squares, the kind of design that brings back memories and makes me want to get chalk and play hopscotch up and down the boulevard. Or maybe get down on my haunches with a rubber ball and bag of jacks and see if I can make it up to my eight-sies.

White-haired men are out eating thick sandwiches and testing out their Poli-Grip, and a crew of firemen is pigging out at the green bistro tables in front of the deli.

I don't see anybody who might be David Lawrence. I check my watch every minute for the next ten minutes. Waiting, I feel like a fool. But I need to know what he knows, need to know things that no one else can tell me. So no matter how the city is falling apart, I'll have to wait until I decide he's not coming to meet me here, at the place he suggested.

My cell phone rings again. It's the station. I don't answer.

Out-of-season Christmas bells on the glass door clang when I step inside the pharmacy—a place straight out of Mayberry—and get a quarter's worth of Chiclets out of the gum machine. My reflection in the window shows me I look like shit. I peep outside. No one who owns my image of David Lawrence is out there. I try to keep myself calm by browsing around the knickknacks and miniature teddy bears, things that make me smile and remember when life was so simple. I buy a pair of sunglasses to hide my puffy eyes before I go back outside.

My cell phone rings. Again, it's the station. I start cursing and head for my car.

I'm at the door of Baby Blue when a Mercedes comes down the street, a two-seater, hardtop off. The car is an outstanding taupe color, its chrome shining from bumper to bumper. The driver wears sunglasses with rectangular yellow lenses and sports a dark brown afro, short hair that looks wild, nappy, and hip; like it was in twists then taken down and fluffed out by hand. His music leads him this way. I expect to hear Lenny Kravitz or Maxwell coming from his sound system, but country music flows as he cruises Gardena. It's that Tim McGraw guy singing that song about the cowboy in him making him do the things he does. The driver looks over near the deli, then sees me on this side and he slows, comes to an easy stop behind my car.

We make eye contact.

He makes a subtle head gesture, which along with mine, tells us that we are the two fools, the deceived souls in search of the truth. A space is open next to my Mustang. He parks there.

David Lawrence takes his shades off, gets out, and stands next to his car. He wears brown leather sandals and a white T-shirt that is stained in oils and paints, the same as his jeans. He looks as if he's been lost in the badlands of insomnia. His eyelids are bags filled with apprehension.

He glances at my ride and says, "Sixty-four?"

"And a half."

"I used to drive a sixty-six when I was in college."

"What happened to it?"

"Sold it to buy books and pay tuition."

I motion at his car. "What year is your ride?"

"Sixty-four."

"Doesn't look that old."

"Mercedes never change much over the years."

"That's a 350SL?"

"Nah, it's a 250SL."

"You've got it in top condition."

"Spent eighteen thousand getting it restored."

"You must have a great mechanic."

"Did most of the work myself."

He asks me about my car's engine, the equipment, and I do the same regarding his. It's strange, but for five minutes, that's what we do, stand on Gardena Boulevard, in the sunshine, underneath palm trees, stand there avoiding looking at each other, but looking at each other's car in admiration. He walks by me and touches Baby Blue, notices the scratches to my hood, the dents in both ends, and says nothing about them, just assumes that's the way it's always been.

He asks, "Have you eaten?"

"No. Not a bite. Had a rough night. Stomach is acting funny."

"Eat something."

I shake my head. "And I need to get to the station."

"Then I'll make this quick."

He takes a distressed black leather jacket out of the back seat, puts it on, tries to cover up, then finger combs his mane in an effort to make himself more presentable.

He makes a head motion and I follow him across the street to the deli.

He says, "You sounded pretty bad last night."

"I still don't remember talking to you."

He smiles a little. He has high cheekbones. Average height with features and a build that make him destructively good-looking. I had imagined him being overweight and weak, or skinny and weak, any combination of features and weak. He has a certain beauty, one that's more handsome and rugged than pretty and pampered. David Lawrence possesses the kind of magnificence that can make a weak woman forget half of the Ten Commandments, the kind of handsome that castrates her from her sense and sensibility.

I want to ask him where he lives, where Jessica lives, but I don't. I look at him and imagine that her beauty complements his, like Tracy Edmonds and Babyface, or Halle Berry and Eric Benet, Chante Moore and Kenny Lattimore, that her beauty supersedes mine. Again I imagine his wife, what she looks like, her beauty and availability to my husband in my day-to-day absence.

He looks more lover than fighter, but this is the man who kicked my husband's ass, left him with a black eye and wounded ego. The scorned lover who had gone insane and was going to gun down my husband in a schoolyard. I should be afraid of him. In some ways, I am. His body language, the way he keeps his head down, the heavy exhales, the clearing of his throat, all of that tells me that he's overwhelmed and distraught, and he is more afraid of me than I am of him.

My first face-to-face impression is that I can't understand why his wife would stray.

His wardrobe is unassuming. Levi's with mechanic's stains, like these are the jeans he wears when working on cars, if that's what he does. And they also have a rainbow of paint stains, as if these are the same dungarees he wears when painting houses, if that's what he does.

My phone keeps blowing up. I don't answer.

David Lawrence orders himself a chicken focaccia sandwich. He toys with his wedding band the whole time. His band is made of titanium, a shiny white metal. Trendy. My wedding ring is platinum. Old school. I touch mine as well. I don't get too close to David Lawrence, but people still smile at us. Because of our matching complexions, they think we're a married couple sneaking away on a lunch date. While he waits for the order, I go back to the pharmacy to get my food: crackers and ginger ale as an appetizer, with Tums as the main course, and take along a bottle of Pepto-Bismol for dessert. We sit at a green bistro table. He sees me popping the Tums and insists that I take the chicken soup he has. He's right. I'm weak and dehydrated, and I need to try to eat if I'm going to make it through the rest of the day.

I eat his soup.

I ask, "Where are you from?"

"Delaware." He leaves it at that. "What sorority are you in?"

"How did you know—?"

"Your key ring."

"Oh."

"Thought it was Zeta Phi Beta at first."

"Oh." I sip my soup. "Tau Beta Sigma."

"Never heard of that one."

"Music sorority. Marching band."

"Oh. What instrument you play?"

"In the band? Sax."

"Which one?"

"All of 'em. Alto is my favorite."

"In a band now?'

"Nah. I wish."

"Where did you go?"

"Johnson C. Smith."

"Never heard of that college."

"It's a university."

He shrugs as if that makes no difference.

I say, "It's in Charlotte. Golden Bulls International Institution of Sound."

I say that I started music in the fourth grade. Did violin for four years. Tried piano in the tenth, but was never good. Fingers were too short; couldn't span eight keys. I tell him that the sax is my friend. Another friend that I neglect because of my job.

He asks, "How did you end up in news?"

"Minored in journalism." I say that, then make a face that says "shit happens."

He yawns. "What kinda journalism classes you take?"

"Television broadcast. Editing. Copywriting. Public relations. Lots of stuff."

"You like it?"

I yawn in return. "Tragedy keeps me from being unemployed."

"Bad news every day."

"Nothing but the negative."

"Maybe you should do a good news show."

"Good news sells as fast as bottled water on the *Titanic*."

"Television producer."

"Yup."

"Sounds exciting."

"Shoulda gone into radio. Could play some happy music."

"What kinda music would you play?"

"Jazz. Nothing but jazz." I don't like this stranger asking about my life, so I move the questions to him. "Where did you go?"

"Delaware State. In Dover. Art major."

"That explains the paint."

"Yeah. I've been working on a painting."

"What kind?"

"Oil on canvas. Bright colors." He motions at the colors on his clothing. "Lots of alizarin crimson, cadmium red deep, cadmium red medium, raw umber, and yellow ochre."

"Sounds . . . exotic. What is it a picture of?"

"The outline of a naked woman, lying down, her back to me."

"You named it?"

"I call it *Grief: the morning after.* "

Our eyes meet then. In his eyes I see the reflection of my own curiosity. Both of us push our lips up as if we are wondering how we ended up here. Our spouses' infidelities are all we have in common. That is the transition to what our meeting is about.

He says, "I took my wife's SUV to the car wash about two weeks ago."

I nod. "Uh-huh."

"It was her birthday and I wanted to clean it up for her." He chews his food, swallows, and then washes it down with his soda. "I started pulling things from under the seat, making sure that no money or important things were on the floor."

"Right."

"I found a condom wrapper. That's how it started."

"A condom wrapper."

He nods. "She blamed it on one of her cousins out in Palm Springs."

I sip my ginger ale. It doesn't go down easy.

He says, "Then I went over some statements, saw a charge for a hotel in Rowland Heights, restaurant charges. There were movie charges on days she should've been at work."

He stops there, waiting for me to ask him to tell me more. I don't.

I say, "I didn't have a clue. Not until you called."

He chuckles, but the sound carries no joy. "After I found the condom, I went online and bought this software that allowed me to get her password, check her e-mails, all kinda stuff."

"They have software that does that?"

"Yep. Records everything that's typed from the moment the computer starts."

"Wow. That's . . . I'm not big on violating anybody's privacy."

"But you didn't find a condom wrapper in your husband's car."

"True."

"Sometimes I'd go home from my studio, and she'd be online on her laptop, then I'd walk in the room and she'd either power off, make the screen go blank—you know the routine."

I say, "Started acting suspicious."

He nods. "Anyway, I installed the software on Sunday, before I went to Canada for an art show. Got back Thursday afternoon. She was at work. I went into her account. Found a lot of e-mails and instant messages between Jessica and Charles. Thursday night, we had a fire in the hole."

"How long have . . . had they . . . How long?"

"You really have no idea, do you?"

"No." I sigh. "None at all."

He evaluates me. "Sure you wanna know?"

"You have the e-mails with you?"

"At my studio. You can read them, but you have to be sure you want to read them."

"What's in the e-mails?"

"The truth."

I fall silent, lower my eyes, and hide myself in chicken soup.

My cell phone rings again. I ignore that electronic leash. In that moment, I hate my job. Hate what it has done to my life. Hate the way it has made this moment possible. I think of the women I know who cheat on their unsuspecting husbands—and I do know quite a few—because of *his* inattentiveness, *his* lack of availability. I know how those women need emotional support so badly, need conversation, need to be held, need better sex, or different sex, women who are so thirsty for satisfaction that they are willing to drink from the closest river.

I'm wondering what David Lawrence didn't give his wife. Then I assume. He's an artist. Just like being a musician, or a writer, or anyone who thrives on long periods of solitude. He's in a self-absorbed occupation, where he can vanish into his work for days, weeks.

I hate what I'm doing, looking for an excuse to justify being betrayed. Betrayal is never the betrayed's fault. Charles made it sound like he was suffering, drowning in loneliness. I haven't been out having fun. I've been working my ass off, a prisoner of my own achievements. I've been lonely for him, lonely to tears. In need of affection. But my strength and honor kept my panties on. I have nothing to apologize for.

He asks, "You okay?"

I shake my head. "I have to get to the station."

"Look, the reason I came . . . the reason I almost didn't come . . ."

"I almost didn't come too."

"I wanted to apologize for calling you."

"Why did you?"

"Guess I freaked out, thought you might have known where they were."

"But they weren't together."

"If I'd known that you didn't know, I never would've contacted you."

"How did you know where I worked?"

"It's in the e-mails."

"So, Charles talked about me. They talked about me."

"About us," he says. "Time to time, they said things about us."

"What kind of things?"

"Things. In the last one, they started calling us their 'situation.' Wanted to meet and talk about how they were going to handle leaving us. The whole nine."

Silence.

He asks, "Done with the soup?"

"That's all my tummy can stand right now."

He takes the soup from my side of the table, eats some using the same spoon. Then he looks at me and it seems as if he reads my mind.

He says, "We're already biologically linked."

"Biologically linked?"

"With your husband and my wife fucking, we've already shared body fluids."

He's emotional and bold. His words create an image in my mind, one that I can't stand.

I ask, "Why do you do that?"

"What?"

"Plant seeds of discontent."

"I'm not planting. I'm just showing you the garden."

Silence.

I ask, "If it were the other way, would you have wanted me to call you?"

"Yeah, I would."

"I was better not knowing."

I thank him for the soup and I stand. He stands.

I say, "What did Jessica do while this fight was going on?"

"She wasn't there."

"Where is she?"

"Haven't heard from her since Thursday night. You talked to . . . ?"

"Charles is at home."

I want to ask him to show me a picture of his wife, but I can't bring myself to do that. I want to show him the list of questions I have given my husband, but I can't do that either. We walk across the street. I'm a couple of steps ahead of David Lawrence.

Again, silence.

"About the e-mails," I say once we get near our cars. "I don't want to know any more than I do. Don't call me with any more . . . information."

He watches me, his never-ending apology etched in his face.

I look into his eyes, irises swimming in a man's pain.

He says, "Really like that Mustang."

"Thanks."

"Makes me miss my sixty-six."

He takes off his leather jacket, tosses it into his backseat, puts his shades back on, and gets in his car. I get in mine. We both leave without any kind of good-bye.

9

I call Yvette on all her numbers. She calls me back while I'm on La Brea and crossing into Hollywood, and I tell her I'm almost at the station. I sit in the lot and tell her about the meeting with David Lawrence. She's doing some serious shoe shopping at the outlet in Camarillo, and the reception is bad, the call keeps dropping, we keep calling each other back, and I have to repeat a lot of things, then we finally give up on the conversation.

She says, "I need to hear this face-to-face. Need to see how you be doing too."

That gets a laugh out of me. "You know me. I'm okay."

"After I drop off my new shoes and water my plants, I'll swoop by and check on you."

"Come to the station and Tyra the Tyrant will make you work."

"Not if that big-titty heifer doesn't know I'm there."

Her phone beeps. She clicks over and comes back. It's one of her men friends.

I say, "You know where to find me."

"Bet."

It's a hell day and I'm scrambling to get five stories done in time. Tyra the Tyrant sees me working hard, trying to get everything together, and she doesn't bother to thank me for coming in to the plantation on my day off. That's typical in this world, the one run by her. My mood is funky the moment I get in, and I let it be known that it won't take much to set me off.

It's pure chaos in the newsroom. Another station has breaking news on a Robert Blake–type story and we don't have coverage.

Tyra the Tyrant rants, "Why the fuck didn't we get the story?"

In front of everybody, the assignment editor is being chewed a new orifice for excrement exit and is almost in tears, breaking her neck to get information.

Three hours later, Tyra and I are having a serious beef about one of my stories.

After I've been working hard on somebody else's crap, Tyra snatches it out of my hands and changes my words. That pisses me off to no end. Today, I can't sit on my emotions. I step into her office and snap, "If you change my work to what you want it to be, then it's not my work."

"This is the fucking way the story needs to be."

She's a child who always has to have it her way. I say, "I worked on that for over—"

"I'm your boss. I tell you what to do."

Then I stop, mouth open. It hits me: I have no control over anything anymore.

I pull my lips in. I don't fold my arms the way a woman does when she's breaking down, don't allow my voice to crack, or dip, or make it sound like I'm pouting. I keep the strength and professionalism in my tone and say, "I'm here day after day. I'm here on my off day. You know what? You think I need this shit right now?"

I tell her that I'm doing her a favor by being here. Remind her how she calls me in to produce holiday shows, and I do a lot of extra work, and make no extra money. I vent about how I do double work when someone is out, did it for months when someone was out on maternity leave, and extra money was promised, but none, not a red penny, has come my way.

People can hear us. That only gives her an audience and makes it uglier.

We go back and forth, cussing each other out for a good fifteen minutes. I end up walking away, heading to the green room, locking the door, and sitting on the sofa.

My cellular phone rings. It's my girl calling.

Yvette says, "What the hell is wrong, Freckles?"

I tell her that it seems like I'm coming unglued.

Yvette is a true friend. She fights evening traffic when she could be at home chilling and comes down to check on me at the station. Yvette stops on Melrose and brings me a snack from the Hot Wing Café, gets to the station at sunset, sits with me on the steps facing Willoughby. I put off eating my hot wings right away. That woodpecker is cutting me some slack, but I'm still not sure if I can stomach too much.

I have too many thoughts at the same time, and since I can't get my hands on some Prozac, I get my sax out of Baby Blue and play for a few minutes to calm myself down and clear my head. I'm not playing well, not really feeling it, a reflection of my fading hangover and my rising mood. Yvette hums along, actually starts to sing a bit when I do my own version of "Careless Whisper." She sounds pretty good.

Then, when I'm ready, we talk.

First I tell her about my run-in with Tyra the Tyrant.

Yvette says, "That bitch doesn't know what she's doing. Always running around and screaming at people like she's J. Jonah Jameson or somebody."

It feels good to have my girl on my side. I need that right now.

She says, "Gimme the juice on your situation."

I tell her how Charles reacted to the list, how he acts like what I'm asking is unreasonable. How he wants the situation to be over because he says it's over.

Yvette says, "Then you need to see what that David Lawrence person has in the e-mails. That might tell you something."

"Charles says it's over. Maybe I should let it go."

"Oh, hell no. Tell Tarzan it ain't over until you say it's over."

She knows me, knows that I don't want to let it go, that I won't let it go that easily.

I say, "If this has been going on awhile . . . damn. Why didn't I notice shit?"

"Been there, done that."

"I know."

"Hard to set a trap these days. Between niggas having twenty e-mail addresses, fifty-five pagers, I-pagers, post office boxes, who knows how many cellular phones, then the work phones, it just ain't that easy for a hunter to catch a rabbit."

"I know, I know."

"Freckles, I've told you over and over, you have to stay one step ahead of these niggas. Last nigga I was seeing, that motherfucker was still calling his ex, this bitch he was supposed to marry but she kicked his ass to the curb and treated him like shit, was breaking his neck to see her when she came to town, meeting her for dinner at Magic's TGIF, then tipping and meeting her when he went on vacation down in Miami, doing all kinds of shit."

That memory upsets her, makes her frown and curse every other word.

I ask, "You bust him out?"

"I told you. Didn't I?"

"Pretend you didn't and refresh my mind."

"Girl, your memory is shorter than a midget's dick."

"You oughta know."

"You know how I am. I gets to the point. I asked him if he was seeing his ex, gave him a chance to come clean, and he sat there and lied, told me to my face, said he ain't seeing nobody, wanted to know why I'd think something like that. Nigga asked me if I could prove it."

I ask, "Why couldn't he just answer?"

"His rule was no evidence, no crime. You ain't a criminal until you get caught."

"Typical."

"Honesty is a dying sport."

"Sure is."

"That asshole started calling me insecure, all kinds of shit, tried to make me feel paranoid when I knew what was up. Tried to flip it around and say that I was mentally abusing him."

"Typical."

She laughs and shakes her head.

She says, "They're getting married. He had the nerve to call me up and tell me that."

I pat her hand, sit close to her, and we both stare at the remains of the day.

She says, "Get the e-mails."

"What if I find out something I don't wanna know?"

"You already have. Freckles, you need to know the rest. Charles ain't gonna tell you."

I pull my lips in, hold my sax across my lap.

She says, "Get the evidence. Prove the crime."

Two hours go by. Tyra the Tyrant takes a red pen and mutilates two more of my stories. I know she's doing that to fuck with me. I've had enough and I confront her.

I say, "You always pull that shit. I do four hours of writing, use all of my damn energy, and the first thing you do is look at my work and change—"

"Read the name on the door." She raises her voice loud enough for everyone to hear. "Whose name is that? Mine. I'm the executive producer. You are not the executive producer. What does it say on your door? Oh. Wait. You don't have a fucking door."

"I'm talking about my creativity. I do a news story, you bitch about it being too much like entertainment. I do entertainment, it's too newsy."

She keeps going off at a hundred miles an hour, ignoring me, "If you have any doubt who makes the big decisions, check your paycheck. Hold yours up next to mine and you'll see who gets paid to make the big decisions. I have final say. That's my job, dammit. If you did yours the right fucking way, I wouldn't have to waste my time trying to change shit into sugar."

I stare at her. She has no husband. She has no man. Outside of this, like most of us, she has no life. I look at her and wonder what man in his right mind would want to be with a bitch like that. And I ask myself, Will I become a bitch like that if I stay here another year?

I push my lips up into a fed-up smile. "I'm leaving."

"You better not walk out that door."

"Fuck you. I've been here for the last twenty days."

She yells at me, and I keep going, turn off my computer, grab my purse, head for the door, and I don't look back. People are watching, telling me to let it go, because that's the way it is. They are followers, sheep kissing the ass of an aristocratic shepherd. I ignore them all.

I go to my car and sit inside, head down, fingers massaging my temples.

Tyra comes out, calling my name. Now, with no one watching her little executive producer show, her tone is different.

She says, "Okay, you're right."

"No, you're right. I'm incompetent. My work sucks."

"That's not what I . . . Look, I need you."

"Do it yourself." I start my car. "Fucking control freak."

I screech out of the lot and struggle down pothole-filled La Brea until I get to the 10, then cruise west, the opposite direction of my home, ride the madness with the wind blowing over the top of my head, drive as fast as I can until the freeway ends at Pacific Coast Highway.

My cell phone is blowing up. Caller ID shows me it's my job. I don't answer.

About an hour later, after I've driven up PCH into Malibu, I make a U-turn up near Pepperdine, head back and pull my wounded Baby Blue into the lot at Gladstone's, a restaurant on the edges of the water, down where Sunset Boulevard ends, then take my boots off and walk barefoot down to the sand and sit on the rocks, the cool breeze riding up my skirt. I pull my skirt up a little more; let the air flow through me.

I face the ocean, listen to the rolling tide, watch the seagulls flying under the moonlight searching for food, and I cry. I hate myself for doing that, for feeling weak right now.

I remind myself that tears are not a sign of weakness.

I cry until I feel ten pounds lighter. Then I go to my car and get the hot wings and fries Yvette brought me, go back to the sand, sit on a rock, and eat a capella. I leave the beach when it closes at ten p.m., drive through the beach cities with no destination in mind.

My cell phone rings nonstop. When my home number shows up, I answer.

It's almost eleven-thirty. My devoted husband wants to know where I am.

I clear my throat and ask Charles if he's done with the questions.

He gets frustrated, says that it was something that just happened, that it was nothing serious on his part, won't let me get a word in, and says a few things about how unreasonable answering all those questions is, and in the end stiffens his voice and says, "I'm not doing them."

I say, "No problem."

I hang up on him.

I call David Lawrence. I need to see his evidence.

10

It's between twelve-thirty and one a.m. I'm restless.

I stand in front of a red door. Red doors are supposed to be good in Feng Shui, supposed to create balance and harmony in your space. Trepidation wants me to turn around. Needing to know the truth makes me want to stay. I bounce my keys against my skirt. On my key ring is a small black container of mace. I bought it tonight, on the way here, just in case.

I ring the doorbell twice, then hear the sound of feet coming across a wooden floor.

The peephole goes dark.

The deadbolt is undone.

Chains are removed.

The door opens.

David Lawrence is barefoot, wearing stained, baggy jeans that hang low and show the edges of his black boxers, and a gray flannel shirt that clings to him. His mane is uncombed, nappy and chic all at once. Paint is on his face, in streaks, yellows and reds, like he has scratched his face with the side of his hand. I take him in for a moment, evaluate this stranger, then take a step into his studio and glance around, do that to keep from staring at him. The angst in his eyes tells me that this is serious, that he's not one to bullshit and this will not be easy.

We say nothing. We know what this is about, so there is no need to pretend.

An overwhelming fear slows my stride. His floors are made of hardwood and I'm wearing boots, so the sound of my heels, the way my pace changes with my growing anxiety, betrays me.

He stops and stares at me until I look at him. He asks, "You okay?"

"I'm fine."

I follow him. My walk is heavy-footed; a labored stroll that reminds me of when my grandfather died and I went back to North Carolina, that moment when I had to go into the Graham Funeral Home to view the body, that moment when I had to admit what I had been denying. I feel that way because what I read may funeralize what I feel for my husband.

Lots of tools are lying around. To make conversation, I ask what things are. He tells me they are printmaking tools. Etching needles, burnishers, and wood-carving tools. I nod. In my mind, those are things that can be used as weapons if David Lawrence is a psycho. He has several easels, a drafting table, paint-stained toolboxes full of paints and mineral spirits. Cabinets. Saws. Lots of odors are in this space. The turpentine has the strongest scent; its fumes are loud, even with the windows open.

I say, "You have a miter saw and a jigsaw."

"Use those for stretcher bars and wood sculptures."

The walls are bright, sage greens and melons and sunflower gold, and all have funky faux finishes that make each wall a work of art. From what I can see, all the interior doors have been faux painted to look like marble. And there are two skylights.

On his easel is the picture of a nude woman, painted in bright colors, red being the most dominant. She's touching herself. I make no comment, but I do wonder if that is Jessica.

I tell him, "I used to sand floors."

"You did?"

"Back in college. Summer job in Greenville."

I follow him across the room, glancing at erotic sculptures and sensual paintings along the way. A laptop is on a table. That technology stands out from the rest of the artsy decor, doesn't match the bohemian feel of the room. The laptop is a Sony, the kind that has a built-in digital camera and has the ability to make short videos. A guy at the station has one of those.

I stall when I see a gun on the table.

It's big, made of a dark metal, sitting there in the middle of paintbrushes and other things. It's not a cute little gun, but a man's weapon. I catch a chill and imagine him going after Charles with that thing, imagine him holding me hostage with that thing.

I say, "It's kinda cold in here."

"I keep the windows open most of the time. Need the ventilation. Some of the things I use are toxic. Can burn the lining in your nose and throat."

"Oh. Didn't know that picture painting was such a hazardous occupation."

"Almost as hazardous as being in love."

His emotions are raw, unhidden. I don't respond to that. I don't think he expects me to.

"Yep, my job is a hazardous occupation," he says. "I'm supposed to wear a mask."

I clear my throat. "Really?"

Chill bumps rise on my arms. This room is cold. I glance down at my nipples, then hurry and fold my arms across my breasts.

I ask, "Should I have one on?"

"One what?"

"A mask."

"You'll be okay. Just don't get any of this on your skin. It'll seep into your blood."

He moves to the other side of the room, to the windows. He closes the one nearest me, leaves the other two open. His work is intriguing. So detailed. I like the paintings the best. Some are in oils. One catches my eye because of its colors: reds and oranges and yellows. I don't know the specific names of the colors, not the way an artist does.

He moves some paints and pulls out a canvas. All around me, I see his vision. His talent speaks for itself. Discipline, I see that as well. I see his drive. I see all the things that kept me from being a great musician.

I ask, "Am I keeping you from your work?"

"Outside of finishing a painting that I'm behind on and not being in the right frame of mind to do it, I was looking at an evening of reading about the deconstructionist movement in abstract art of the eighties and nineties."

He laughs. I don't, but I smile. Not a big smile, just a fake one to go with his laughter.

I ask, "Is Jessica . . . ?"

"She never comes here. Can't stand the smell."

I hesitate. "Have you talked to her?"

"Not since she left me for your husband."

"So you think."

"Read what I have and tell me what you think."

I swallow some of my trepidation.

He asks, "Has your husband talked to her?"

"I wouldn't know."

We fall into awkwardness.

I ask, "How do we do this?"

He shrugs. "You read some or all of what I have. We talk about it if you want."

"Can I take it with me?"

"No. You read it here."

"Why?"

"Because that's the way it is."

I agree with a nod.

He walks to a black, three-drawer file cabinet. David grabs a stack of papers from the middle drawer, and then turns a small black fan off before he heads to close another window. He gets a big red-and-white cardigan, one that has DELA-WARE STATE HORNETS with some words about his alma mater embroidered on some sort of crest, and hands it to me.

I put it on. It's heavy and swallows me.

He apologizes for the room being cold. He says, "Sometimes, I'm so caught up that I can't feel the cold. When I've got a good painting jones, I don't have to think or feel at all."

"Sounds like me, when I'm into my music."

"Then you feel me on that."

"Well, the way I used to be. Used to get so caught up in a song."

"When I'm in the zone, it's almost like . . . like . . ."

"An out-of-body experience."

"Yep. When I'm there, in my zone, I'm not conscious of

colors or anything. That's how it was with *Grief*. The painting took over."

He hands me the stack of papers and motions to a queen-size futon.

I say, "This is a lot of . . . data."

"There's more. And things that we'll never know. Phone calls, or face-to-face conversations, things like that, so just imagine those in between their online chats."

"Look." My voice changes, becomes firm. I'm irritated. I toy with my hair, try to soften my tone. "Let me deal with this first and come to my own conclusions."

The frame is made of cherry wood, has a worn green futon covered with wrinkled white sheets. It's opened up as a bed. The room is about a thousand square feet with no divider walls, but there is a long mirror across one wall, a few more around the room, so the colorful room looks bigger than it is. The marbleized doors blend in with the kaleidoscope of hues that resemble autumn leaves.

Outside of drafting tables, bookcases, and other work equipment, the only other sitting furniture is two bar stools, unmatching, with hard metal frames, neither looking too comfortable. A small TV and a VCR are anchored to a wall facing the futon. The TV isn't on and the screen has a layer of dust. The small stereo isn't on. Pillows and covers are rumpled, as if he sleeps awhile, works awhile, then sleeps awhile.

I sit down on the edge of the futon, knees together, ankles crossed. I check my watch, lick across my teeth, take a breath, and start to read.

Charles [4:10 PM] I was supposed to go to a play with the wife.
Jessica [4:10 PM] What happened?

Charles [4:10 PM] She got called in to work an hour ago.

Jessica [4:11 PM] Seems like that happens a lot. Bummer.

Charles [4:12 PM] Was going to surprise her, get some quality time, take her to dinner and a play . . . even had made reservations at the W.

Jessica [4:12 PM] You didn't tell her?

Charles [4:13 PM] It was a surprise. Was going to take her to her favorite restaurant, this place EuroChow up in Westwood. They have great martinis and she loves the glazed prawns with walnuts.

Jessica [4:13 PM] You should've told her anyway.

Charles [4:14 PM] It's typical, us not being able to go.

Jessica [4:14 PM] What play?

Charles [4:15 PM] Female version of A Soldier's Play. That actress Tammy Barrett is starring in that.

Jessica [4:15 PM] You kidding? Tammy Barrett is hot. I have two of her CDs in front of me.

Charles [4:16 PM] We had a barbeque and she was over at the house awhile back.

Jessica [4:16 PM] You know her?

Charles [4:16 PM] Her husband's a writer and one of his friends lives right across the street from us. They all came over together.

Jessica [4:17 PM] She's mega large. And you have tickets to her play.

Charles [4:18 PM] My neighbors are out of town. He has a book thing in New Orleans, so they're doing a second honeymoon thing. I don't want to miss out, but I'm running out of options.

Jessica [4:18 PM] When?

Charles [4:18 PM] Tonight at eight. You want the tickets?

Jessica [4:19 PM] Don't tease me like that. I haven't been to a play in years.

Charles [4:19 PM] Then it'll be my treat. You and the hubby can have big fun on me.

Jessica [4:20 PM] The hubby is at his studio, caught up into his work, he'll never leave.

Charles [4:20 PM] Hate to throw a hundred dollars away. Guess I'll go by myself. Might be able to scalp the extra one at the door.

Jessica [4:21 PM] Wait a second. Okay, the play will be over around what time?

Charles [4:21 PM] Should last a couple of hours. Over by ten.

Jessica [4:22 PM] Where is it?

Charles [4:23 PM] Whitmore Lindley Theatre Center in North Hollywood.

Jessica [4:24 PM] Here's an idea. Tell me what you think, if you're not feeling it, no problem.

Charles [4:24 PM] What's the idea?

Jessica [4:25 PM] Since you don't want to waste a ticket, and I would love to see the play, we could always meet up there. No joke on this end. I really do want to see that play.

Charles [4:26 PM] We could do that. One condition?

Jessica [4:26 PM] What?

Charles [4:27 PM] Meet me at EuroChow. I'd already made reservations.

Jessica [4:27 PM] You're driving a hard bargain.

A date is on the printout. That was eight months ago. That's how it began for my husband and Jessica. Eight months ago. Damn near three seasons of ignorance in my world.

I look at David Lawrence; he stops working, steps into silence with me.

I ask, "You've known about this for eight months?"

"I wouldn't put up with this shit for eight months." He shakes his head. "Like I told you at the deli, just found out when I got back from Canada."

My leg is bouncing. "Uh-huh."

"Loaded the software, then took off for an art show up near Whistler. Looked at it when I got back on Thursday. Confused?"

"Some. Guess I'm fact checking before I start."

"Go right ahead. Fact check."

"These look like instant messages, not e-mails. How did you get all of these?"

"She saved them all, did a cut and paste. Doubt if your husband even knew she was doing that. She used to do the same when we were dating. Kept our e-mails in a special folder."

"And you went into her account?"

"The condom, charge receipts . . . did what I had to do."

I say, "A date is at the top. Is it correct or . . . ?"

"That's the date she saved the file."

I look at the thickness of what he gave me. "All of this . . . ?"

"There's more. Copied it to my zip drive. It would be as thick as a phone book if I printed everything she had in that folder."

A visible chill runs over me.

He asks, "Need a blanket, or a bigger jacket?"

"No. Not cold anymore. Not on the outside."

He goes back to painting.

I read Charles's and Jessica's instant messages from the next day.

Charles [8:03 PM] ☺ It's easy being with you. You were good company last night. Nice to see that you're not always in work mode. Always see you screaming at kids. You're pretty cool, Jessie.

Jessica [8:03 PM] That was sweet, coming from a boring social studie teacher.

Charles [8:03 PM] ouch

Jessica [8:03 PM] Joking. U are far from being boring. I like the way you call me Jessie.

Charles [8:03 PM] Just wanted to thank you for not letting those tickets go to waste.

Jessica [8:04 PM] NO, thank you. The play was off the chains. It was nice to get out for a change. I started teaching aerobics in the evening to fill up some time.

Charles [8:04 PM] Yeah, I feel ya. I don't get to do much outside of work. I want to get out, see a few movies, but it never works out.

Jessica [8:04PM] I love movies. Haven't been to one in months.

Charles [8:04 PM] Me either.

Jessica [8:05 PM] But I do have to put this out there . . . it was kinda strange

Charles [8:05 PM] what was?

Jessica [8:05PM] the way we acted at work, how we didn't mention it and just walked by each other like we barely knew each other, at least that was the way it seemed. I couldn't look you in the eyes today. Then I couldn't wait to get home and see if you were online.

Charles [8:06 PM] you felt that too? I was thinking the same thing ☺ Was so glad when you popped up in my screen

Jessica [8:06PM] What we did, it was innocent, right?

Charles [8:08 PM] yeah

Jessica [8:08 PM] Then how did we end up kissing for over
an hour?

That image stops me. I have to regroup, try to keep it
together.

I want to know the answer to that question myself. There
is a three-minute time gap between her question and the next
IM. Three long minutes. Charles has to be sitting at the computer, touching his wedding band, wondering what to say to
another man's wife.

I wonder what he was feeling right then, when he was at
the crossroads.

He never answers her question.

I look at the next time stamp and this time Jessica hesitates
before she asks the next question. Hesitates as if it were hard to
type that simple sentence. Since I don't know, I can only sup-
pose, so I imagine them being excited and scared all at once.

Jessica [8:11 PM] you tell your wife that you took me to
the play?
Charles [8:13 PM] we haven't really seen each other . . .
she didn't notice I had gone out
Jessica [8:17 PM] well, I didn't tell my hubby where I went

There's another time gap, another long pause. I imagine
them sitting there, thinking, fingers on keyboards, wondering
what to type next, maybe even typing things and erasing them
before they can be sent. Waiting for the other to make the
next move.

Jessica [8:23 PM] Well, I have to reciprocate for the play.
Charles [8:23 PM] You don't have to.

Jessica [8:23 PM] I do. I want to. So let me. How about hitting a matinee one day after work?

Y Tu Mama Tambien is playing over at the cheap theater. (next to Galleria)

Charles [8:23 PM] That could work.

Jessica [8:23 PM] Or you could come to one of my classes and we could go right after. You'd be back home in time to grade a few papers. ☺

Charles [8:23 PM] Sure. That sounds cool.

Jessica [8:23 PM] It'll be my treat. Popcorn, chocolate covered raisins, the whole nine are on me

Charles [8:24 PM] Any day but Wednesday is good for me.

Jessica [8:24PM] Nice to be able to have somebody to talk to.

They were typing fast, excited at being together again. They knew where this was going.

I look at another page filled with instant messages. One that's six months old. I see that on the date, then pull out my Palm Pilot. That day is a Saturday. The time stamp tells me that it's early in the morning. While I'm still sleeping in our bed a capella, Charles is in the other room at sunrise, on the computer with Jessica. They are sharing the sunrise, starting their day together. Things evolve between Charles and Jessica. They're less formal, more forward, not as worried about spelling. They start off talking about work, harmless conversations about other teachers, students, meetings; things that are pretty ordinary and boring. Then it changes.

Jessica [6:12 AM]: enough about work. i'm thinking bout sucking u again

I stop and take a breath after I read that. It hits me hard.

Jessica [6:13 AM] want to feel u in my mouth
Jessica [6:13 AM] feel your hands caressing me
Jessica [6:14 AM] love the way you kiss my stomach, shoulders, back
Charles [6:14 AM] tell me more
Jessica [6:14 AM] i neeeeeed to feel u again
Jessica [6:14 AM] want u hard between my legs
Jessica [6:15 AM] want you to get lost in me
Jessica [6:15 AM] stroke me hard and deep
Charles [6:15 AM] how deep how hard
Jessica [6:16 AM] as deep as u can go
Jessica [6:16 AM] want u to grab my ass
Jessica [6:17 AM] tease my mouth with your tongue
Charles [6:17 AM] i can do that

Again I look at David Lawrence.

I ask, "You read all of this?"

He says, "You sound . . . stressed."

My body language and my voice betray me. The smell of my rage rises from my flesh.

I say, "Just need something to drink, please."

"Water, wine, cranberry juice, or cognac."

"Wine. And a glass of water."

He moves across the room and goes to a mini-refrigerator.

I read on about my husband's secret life, about him and Jessica. The dates show months of interaction between them, so I can't pretend it's meaningless, that it was a thing that happened and went away. It's not a zipless fuck. Not a fuck 'n' chuck. They go on dates. Movies. Plays. To a comedy show at Lucy Florence in Leimert Park. He goes to her aerobics class and they go to Jamba Juice and Baja Grill, sometimes eat dinner afterward at the Cheesecake Factory. Santa Barbara for lunch. Getty Museum. Rollerblading on the beach. Riding mountain bikes from Playa Del Rey to Santa Monica. They go to see Maya Angelou.

This is not an affair. They are having a relationship.

I look at David Lawrence. He's opening a bottle of wine.

Without looking my way he asks, "Had all you can stand to read?"

"No. I'm not done."

But I take another breath, bounce the papers on my legs awhile before I go back to the words, to the lust and deceit. I feel like a fool for not knowing, for allowing it to be this deep.

As David Lawrence said, there are hundreds of phone calls between them that I know nothing about. This is only a corner of their relationship. I imagine them passing each other at work, their heads full of obscene thoughts, having two-minute conversations, flirting behind closed doors, touching each other the way teenagers do in between classes.

Charles [11:17 PM] She comes home so angry, vents for hours. I just want her to come in, hug me, kiss, and yeah tell me how your day was, but not like that.
Jessica [11:17 PM] Uh-huh Sounds emotionally draining
Charles [11:18 PM] It is. At midnight, I want a wife. I want a lover.
Jessica [11:18 PM] I feel you on that one. We could all use a little more attention
Charles [11:19 PM] I try to give her attention. I listen, but I've started having headaches the moment she walks in the door, anticipating the drama from dealing with her executive

producer, ranting about the freeway like she's the only one who gets stuck in traffic, the this, the that . . . LOL . . . here I am, venting to you, doing the same thing she does. Sorry about that

Jessica [11:21 PM] No it's okay. We all need somebody to talk to

Charles [11:21 PM] I need some positive vibes . . . that's what I like about you you're always so cheery and positive

Jessica [11:22 PM] How much do you guys talk?

Charles [11:23 PM] Our schedules are way off. We're passing each other in the hallway, when I'm awake, she's asleep. When she's awake, I'm asleep. She sleeps late. I'm up early because I like to get things done and still have a lot of day left.

Jessica [11:23 PM] At least you guys get to sleep in on the weekend.

Charles [11:24 PM] NOT. You know her off day is on Wednesday, and she works every weekend. She's there Christmas Eve, Christmas, Valentine's Day, my birthday, hers . . .

Jessica [11:24PM] I never would have known

Charles [11:26 PM] How do you call that a relationship, or a marriage? I'm used to her not being here too, not being available Sometimes I look forward to her leaving because then the house is peaceful.

Their emotional connection is growing. She is his shoulder, his therapist via AOL. He goes on for two pages, telling her things that he's never told me, the roots of his unhappiness.

Jessica [11:57 PM] How long has it been like that?

Charles [11:57 PM] For a while.

Jessica [11:59 PM] Forget work and traffic, she should come

in the door telling you that you're fantastic. I would. After midnight I'd walk in TAKING OFF my Vickie's Secret.
Charles [12:00 AM] ☺ Maybe you should call her and give her a few pointers
Jessica [12:00 AM] if I was your woman, sexy man, all you'd hear is that you're the sexiest sweetest man I've ever met, how you make me want to cook for you
Charles [12:01 AM] thanks Jessie. ☺ sexy?
Jessica [12:01 AM] ☺ Don't act like you don't know it.
Charles [12:02 AM] You're the one with the bad-ass bod
Jessica [12:02 AM] You're making me blush

David Lawrence pulls me out of that world when he says my name. He's standing next to me and I didn't notice him. All of my senses have fallen away, drawn me into the world of Charles and Jessica. I shift, put the papers down at my side, and he hands me my drinks. I thank him. He nods, then goes back to his canvas. The water is in an Evian bottle, the white zinfandel in a wineglass. I gulp a lot of the water, sip just as much of the wine, take a few breaths, tug my locks, pull my lips in, and think. I want to run away. But I pick the papers up again, and I read. Move on to a month later, move through more explicit conversations until I get to this.

Jessica [8:34 PM] want my orgasm to work its way up my thighs into my stomach and out my vagina i want your length and girth for as long as we can until we collapse into one big orgasm

I close my eyes and rock for a moment. Her words are too strong, too direct. Once again I check the date with my Palm Pilot. It's a Tuesday night. I'm at work.

Charles [8:36 PM] was looking at you at work today

Jessica [8:36 PM] really

Charles [8:37 PM] yup ☺ saw you running laps with the kids on my free period, then saw you on the playground playing volleyball with your class when I was taking my 5th period to the library. Your breasts bounce when you jump.

Jessica [8:37 PM] didn't think u ever noticed me

Charles [8:37 PM] hell yeah . . . been hard not gawking at you lately . . . real hard

Charles [8:40 PM] i get dreamy looking at you, start imagining and thinking "what if" I had met you before I . . . before.

Jessica [8:41 PM] r u just telling me words??

Charles [8:42 PM] nope

Charles [8:42 PM] for real

Charles [8:43 PM] imagined u being close to me

Charles [8:43 PM] that's why when you come in the cafeteria I start feeling all nervous

Jessica [8:43 PM] why come??

Charles [8:44 PM] dunno . . . I keep saying we should keep away from each other, then I see you every day, and that doesn't make it any easier, then I have to talk to you, then we end up somewhere trying to talk, then we end up either having sex in a hotel or up against a wall And I drive away wishing I could stay with you, spend the night with you, wake up with you

Jessica [8:44 PM] why do we do that to ourselves? is it because grass always b looking greener on the other side?

Jessica [8:44 PM] why why why? LOL

Charles [8:45 PM] I was wondering what it would be like if we were married to each other

Jessica [8:45 PM] Me too I wonder that all the time That

night we went to the play, I kept asking myself why it wasn't like that with David. You think we can stop cold turkey?

Charles [8:46 PM] no. i think we have an attraction to each other, a strong one, one that is beyond understanding, control. i can't make it not be there, you know.

Jessica [8:46 PM] i feel ya ☺ damn do i feel ya

Jessica [8:49 PM] isn't LUST grand?

Charles [8:49 PM] hell yeah. i want to be with u too much

Jessica [8:50 PM] you're dangerous Charles

Charles [8:50 PM] so are you

Jessica [8:50 PM] and you are so intense

Charles [8:51 PM] you're the intense one. if i was half as dangerous as you . . . damn . . . just imagined i could taste you . . . LOL

I swallow and lower the pages. Clear my throat, and have a hard time breathing. That suffocating sensation comes and goes. My hand is shaking when I down half of my wine in one swallow. Palms are soggy. I drink the rest of my wine in a gulp and want more.

Jessica [8:54 PM] seriously. with you i've got to b careful cuz my emotions start f'n with me. guess i'm not the sexually liberated woman i THOUGHT i was. i'll b eatin my words BIG time

A chill runs through me. I know her language. She's moving away from her husband, falling in love with mine, and trying to play down their emotional connection until she knows where they stand. Something tells me that David Lawrence is watching me walk through this valley of pain. My leg is shaking. I sniffle, touch my face. I expect tears, but my eyes are dry. I think I feel David Lawrence's eyes covering me. I glance his way and he's deep into his work.

> Charles [8:59 PM] being with you is soooo damn good ☺ hard to describe the warmth
> Jessica [8:59 PM] try
> Charles [8:59 PM] it's like i never wanna come just hold on to that feeling and watch you come over and over until you can't come any more
> Jessica [8:59 PM] what u wanna do? I really need to see you.
> Charles [8:59 PM] meet me at the spot on Thursday. After three, I can be there.
> Jessica [8:59 PM] i want to feel u inside me water pouring down on us from the shower hands sliding along slippery flesh smelling sweet bodies wet and firm and soft at the same time licking water off each other
> Charles [9:00 PM] i'll try to get the same room too
> Jessica [9:00 PM] you're the love of my life, Charles. I can't imagine myself living without you

Pages slide from my hand like concrete. Their words fall and crash on the floor. I stand. I have to move around. My boots click-clop a disturbed cadence over the hardwood floor as I try to shake this ugly feeling, but it clings to me. Charles doesn't mention me. He gives me no name. Either I'm *She*, or *The wife*. *Wifey*. Outside of that, I don't exist when he's with her.

David Lawrence comes up behind me without making a sound. I'm so into pacing and thinking about the e-mails that I don't notice him. He touches my waist. That scares me.

He says, "Your husband fucked my wife."

We look at each other and this time it's different. Now I know him.

"My husband didn't fuck your wife." My voice is soft. Not amorous, but the tone of a bewildered child. "They had a relationship, then came home and fucked us."

He pulls me closer, runs his hand up my back, puts his fingers in my hair, palms the back of my head. I don't pull away.

I say, "You wanna hurt me, don't you?"

"Maybe I do. Maybe I will."

I say, "I don't love you, so you can't hurt me. Charles is the only man who can hurt me."

"And he hurt you."

"Like a motherfucker."

David Lawrence takes his sweater away from me, does that slow and easy, the first step to undressing me, to undressing his enemy's wife, and then rubs me before he puts his mouth on my shoulder. I think he's scared, and filled with pain and confusion. And I think he's angry. Maybe those are just the reflections of my own feelings. One moment I want him to stop. And then I think about what he said at lunch, about us already being biologically bonded. We've never touched, but we're already partners, have been partners for the better part of the year.

That angers me more.

Still, I want to push him away, and I don't want him to stop. I look back at him. He's become my mirror, or I've become his. David Lawrence sees what I feel, closes his eyes, grits his teeth, the warmth of his angst a soft breeze on my neck.

Contradictory emotions flood the room; steal all sounds; smother the smell of turpentine.

His voice is serious, intent. "Stop me."

I whisper, "Don't stop."

His voice relaxes a bit, but he owns fear. "Stop me."

"I'm hurting and I want to feel good even though I feel so bad."

His hand moves from my waist, goes under my blouse, touches my breasts.

He shares my pain, this fucked-up-ness that's been dumped on us, and he's the only person who knows what I'm feeling. Silence rests between us. He turns me around, pulls me to him. His need for revenge grows against my ass. I back into him, letting him know that I'm in control, that I am fully aware of what's happening, and he can't do anything I don't want to do.

I whisper, "What does she look like?"

My eyes are open and I'm staring at the window. Darkness turns the glass into a mirror, and I see myself. This new version of who I am. David Lawrence puts his arm around me.

He says, "She's short, very dark, slanted eyes, high cheekbones. Shoulder-length hair in a layered style. She looks like a black Japanese girl from the neck up."

My nostrils flare and I snort. "Charles hated my perm. Always made jokes about me being behind the times, looking too plain, not ethnic enough for his tastes. Said he loved locks."

David Lawrence rubs against me, massages my breasts with kindness.

I say, "Don't be nice. Don't pretend. I know what this is about."

He takes my hand and sits me on the futon. We remain eye to eye as I lie down on his wrinkled covers, my skirt rising high on my thighs. He pulls his pants off, then his black boxers and stands before me. He raises my skirt until it bunches at my waist. Pulls my thong underwear down over my boots, tosses it away. It spins and lands on top of those sheets of paper. My legs slide away from each other, spread wide for him. We stop. We stare. My gaze lets him know that I'm not that weak, that I'm aware of what's going on. He eases down on me. My hands pull him down. He puts his face next to mine, enters me, and begins giving me his anger. I pull his T-shirt up, hold his back, pull him into me as he tries to reach his revenge.

He injects me with all that tortures him. Madness. Guilt. I feel it with each thrust. He tries to hurt me. He tries to hurt Charles. He tries to hurt his wife. I want him to stab me until what I feel inside me dies.

Then he stops. He lies next to me, falls into a realm of breathless silence, staring at the ceiling, his revenge interrupted by some thought, some feeling.

His face is ravaged by guilt. So are my thoughts.

Neither of us says a word, not for a long while. I turn away from him, rest on my side and look out the window into the darkness. Then I have to pee. I get up and walk around his things, avoiding easels and drafting tables, opening and closing doors until I find the bathroom. I turn the light on. The woman in the mirror, I don't know her. I've never seen her before.

When I get back, David Lawrence is on his stomach, his taut ass and the muscles in his back on parade. A warrior at rest. His left foot is moving side to side at an edgy tempo. My hand touches his hand and he stops bouncing his foot. His fingers curl up and rub my palm.

I ask, "What's on your mind?"

"Thinking about my mom." His voice is rusty. "My old man."

"Okay."

He says, "My dad was a Teamster, had a business not too far from the Teamsters building down off Route 13 at Naylor Street. Lot of the time my old man was supposed to be at work, he was laid up with some young girl that worked at the Wawa Market."

He closes his eyes, reminiscing.

He says, "Daddy got busted with the Wawa girl down at the Lakeside Hotel in one of the rooms on the backside of that joint. Momma parked her F-150 right out back, blocked the girl's car in, because that was who she wanted to have it out with."

"An F-150. Your momma sounds . . . tough."

"Momma was good at having it out with my old man's women. She called 'em all Wawa girls, no matter who they was, no matter where they worked."

"There was more than one, then."

"Yep. Momma had it out with a girl over at the Yodder Overhead Door Company, then a girl at Dutch County Market, kicked her ass on a Sunday at the Sunrise Motel. Dukes Lumber Company, Warren Electric, a few other places up and down Route 13 saw Momma in action."

Silence.

I ask, "Where is your mother?"

"Jail." He opens his eyes. "She killed one of my old man's women."

"She killed a Wawa girl?"

He nods, barely.

I ask, "Where is your dad?"

"Still in Dover. Riding up and down Route 13."

His pain heats his skin. I look across the room at that gun.

I begin to massage his back, knead his neck and shoulders, do that in the nurturing way I've done to Charles so many times. David Lawrence's muscles are tight. I work my way down his back to his buttocks. Then to his legs. His legs are hard, solid. Like those of a soccer player. I stop touching him and move away. Again, we're silent. He stirs awhile before he gets up and goes to the bathroom. I watch him as he walks away. His penis is large, swaying between hard and soft. I lie down on my side again. I hear him peeing. I rise up on my elbows, look across the room, my eyes searching for the gun he has on that table. I walk over and pick it up. It's heavy. I imagine shooting Jessica. Shooting Charles. Shooting myself.

The toilet flushes. He comes out and sees me, his gun in my hand.

He says, "Momma said to never point a gun at something unless you intend to kill it."

Again, we stare.

I ask, "What kind of gun is this?"

"Colt Defender."

"Loaded?"

He almost smiles. A chill runs through me.

I put the gun back down, then go lie again on the futon. I close my eyes. His feet sound as if they are trying to stick to the floor as he goes across the room to a sink. I hear him washing his hands, then messing around, and he comes back. David Lawrence turns me on my stomach, takes the rest of my clothes off my body. Something cool and sticky drips on my skin.

I jump.

He says, "Relax. It's lotion."

I turn my head; my arms stretch out like a crucifix. I jerk when he drips more liquid cream on my body, a long trail from my shoulders to my calves. He massages me from my neck down to my butt, then to my feet, and back up. His hands are strong and gentle all at once.

I say, "A lot is said in those e-mails."

"A lot is said. But a lot isn't said too."

"True. We don't know what they talked about face-to-face."

"We don't."

He rubs over the roundness of my ass, separates my cheeks, cups my vagina, lets its heat warm his hand, then curves his finger inside me. He pushes deep, then comes out and massages my clitoris. I try to pretend that I feel nothing, but my jerks and moans won't let me lie.

It's a struggle to sound normal. "How . . . how many . . . times do you think they did it?"

"Dunno." He clears his throat. "Don't want to think about it."

"You know you think about it."

"Yeah, I do."

"Guess."

"Thirty. Forty."

"In eight months."

"What are you thinking?"

"A hundred?"

"Don't know. In my heart, once is the same as one hundred."

He lowers himself and I feel his skin against mine. The room is breezy. My skin is cool. He works his penis against me, searching for the opening to my vagina. He bumbles at my butt hole and I arch my back, shift him south. I don't touch his penis. I don't help him find his way into his revenge. He finds my opening and moves inside me. I'm wet. Very wet. That surprises me. He waits, then moves up and down in a slow, nonstop rhythm. He pulls me hard, makes me get up to my knees. He holds my hips, pushing me away, then pulling me back into him, moves in and out of me with a better tempo, with more depth. I grip the sheets and anticipate each thrust. I'm so slippery. I don't want to, but I start to moan again. I start to feel.

I ask him, "You. Plan. On. Taking. Me. A. Hundred. Times?"

"If I have to."

He moves in and out of me, first slow and shallow, then hard and deep, as if he's punching me, and that feels good. I'm high on a cliff, jumping, falling in slow motion.

I look at my hand, see my wedding ring.

I pull the sheets. "I. Want. You. To. Stop."

"Tell me."

He moves and he moves, raises my energy level. That feeling of falling steals my wind.

At last I say, "Stop."

He doesn't, but he slows to a civilized pace, one not so urgent.

I try to go back to looking out the window; try not to feel this damn good.

I moan. "Jessica teaches aerobics too."

"Yeah."

"Her body . . . is it very nice?"

"Depends on what you like."

I feel him. Light pleasurable touches. In and out, over and over. Have to close my eyes, swallow my moans.

"She taller than me?"

"You're taller."

He rubs my skin, kisses my back, goes back to moving in and out of my sin.

I ask, "And softer? Is she softer?"

"She's toned, but your legs look better."

"Muscular?"

"Just toned."

"How does she dress?"

"She wears sweats to work."

"Outside of work? When she goes to plays, and movies . . . ?"

"She's a dresser. Loves her clothes."

"Her voice . . . describe her voice."

"Soft most of the time."

"Mine is harsh. Not romantic. Not seductive."

I'm done asking him to paint me a picture of her. He grips my waist, brings me back up on my knees, and pushes deep, moves in and out of me. He's not hard all the way.

He says, "I'll stop."

"Don't stop."

I'm thinking about Charles. Seeing him fornicate with Jessica. I see them a hundred times, a hundred ways. David Lawrence gets harder. He grows and I make sounds that let him know I feel him, that he has my attention. His movements become more intense, more aggressive. His skin slaps mine and I imagine him hitting my husband each time. David Lawrence strikes a spot and I lose all thoughts. I don't want to, but my body moves with him, bumps back against him. He swells inside me and I melt. I'm stretching so much. So many sounds are coming from me.

Then he slows.

I pant, choke on my saliva, try to catch my breath, and when I do I ask, "You come?"

Sweat drips from his face, splatters on my damp flesh.

His voice is tense. "No."

I whisper, "Don't come inside me."

He eases out of me, puts his mouth on my back, my shoulders, his teeth sinking into me, hurting me, exciting me, and again scaring me. He puts his mouth all over me, and then turns me over, puts both hands under my butt, lifts my hips, and brings my sex up to his face, begins licking circles, nibbling my clitoris, Puts his tongue inside my raw flesh. I put my hands on his head, grab handfuls of his hair; try to push him away. He's relentless. I stop pushing him away, let him lick around my vagina, let him suck on my clitoris. He's good down there. My breathing gets ragged. He eats me the way Miles Davis played his horn, and I sing all the notes. I tense up and grab his head, pull his thick hair, get more excited. I run from my orgasm and it chases me until I can't run anymore. My arms fall to my sides and I reach for something to hold on to. I struggle and make the sounds of a woman who is fighting the inevitable. My buttocks tense and electricity crawls up my legs. Electricity turns into fire and a scream escapes from me. Not the scream a woman yields when she wants to come, but one she makes when she doesn't want to give in to the orgasm, the guttural moans she makes when that feeling is kicking down the door. My orgasm crawls to my back, makes me arch, makes me jerk. I'm underwater trying to breathe. I hold on for dear life.

I come hard.

I come mean.

I come loud.

I come like an angry woman.

And before the feeling dies, another orgasm rises again. My back arches more than the first time and my screams and moans scare me. David Lawrence has his arms around my thighs, won't let me wiggle away. I slap his head. He won't stop. I come twice more. All of my nerves are alive. I'm too sensitive. I'm overwhelmed, shuddering, twitching, gulping for air.

He falls away from me, rests with his face near my vagina. Then he crawls back up to me, watches me have my after-orgasm spasms. I feel his ragged breath when David Lawrence puts his lips close to mine. He wants to kiss me, wants me to give him my tongue, and I want to kiss him, want to tongue him to keep this from feeling cheaper than it already is. Our tongues reach for each other, but we pull back. Hold our faces close to each other. All he can do is tongue my moist cheek, suck my neck, move my locks from my humid face, and do the same to my ear. Kissing is too personal for me. Kissing implies caring.

I hold his penis, move it up and down, feel him swelling. I put my mouth close and breathe on him, blow on his fire. He's shivering, gyrating, wondering if I'm going to take him in my mouth. He wants me to. I'm not. I'm being nosy, studying his penis while I tease. His is beautiful, almost poetic, has different shades of brown, from chocolate to almost pink, and when I stretch it out I can see all the colors in between. He has many hues, a breathtaking sunset on his skin.

I hold him, stroke him, watch him. He seeps. Lines grow in his face. He strains toward orgasm. I stroke faster. He gets close to coming. I slow down. Keep him at that level for a long time. I give him agony. His face owns three shades of red, glows like hot coals. His sweat drips from his forehead down his face. Veins rise and fall in his arms. His breathing becomes so choppy. He looks at me without blinking, but I know he's so gone that he can't see me. His world is blurred. He's having an out-of-body experience. I watch him. He grunts, closes his eyes, struggles, and reaches for me, wants to get inside me again, but I won't let him up.

I stroke him a little faster. Feel his legs tense, his hips moving against my hand. He's hard and I want to get on top of him, want to return to orgasm again and again, want that feeling to take away all the bad feelings that are messing me up on the inside, the ones that are fucking up my head. But I don't mount him. I stroke him faster. He digs his nails into the bed, reaches and touches my breasts, massages my flesh, pulls me close enough so he can put his fingers inside me. I shift, move my hips away so he can't finger fuck me and make me lose my focus.

His penis becomes so rigid, gets so much bigger, the change fascinates me, and then his pleasure spurts out. He thrashes, grabs sheets, and grunts out so loud. I hold on to his hard rage, keep stroking until I'm sure he's done, until the thrashing slows, until his cries die, keep stroking until his senses return and he puts his hand on mine, pats me over and over, asking me to stop.

I sit next to him, listening to him wheeze, smelling his odors, smelling my own, smelling our combined scent, watching his chest rise and fall, watching him return to normal breathing.

The pleasure he left on my hand turns cold.

We don't see each other. He sees Charles's wife. I see Jessica's husband.

I go to the bathroom, find a towel, and wash between my legs.

I want to be disgusted with myself. I'm not. Not yet.

It's four in the morning. The wee hours of a new Thursday.

I come back and put my wrinkled clothes on, stuff my panties and bra in my purse.

For a while, I stare at the pages that are scattered on the floor.

Then I stare at that gun.

I pick the pages up. I drop most of them next to the gun.

David Lawrence is on the futon. On his stomach. Unmoving. Staring at the painting of the nude woman touching herself. I look at his labor of love, at the image of the naked woman. She owns a stunning dark complexion, slanted eyes, high cheekbones. Hair permed and layered.

I leave.

11

Charles raises his voice. "Where have you been all night?" He's upstairs in the master bedroom. His voice comes down the hallway and meets me.

I don't know how I feel. I'm a passenger on a train that has no destination.

On the drive home with the top down, as the cold breeze chilled my flesh, I felt like a woman who was going back to her castle to slay the dragon. For a few miles I was so certain about my purpose. Now I feel like a wife who has violated the seventh commandment. Or is that the sixth? I don't even know what part of the Decalogue I've desecrated. Either way, I feel like a church girl who has moved off grid and now I'm on the express train to hell.

Charles's footsteps are heavy. He's upstairs, coming down the hallway, moving fast.

I close the front door and stand there, unmoving, wondering if I should've gone to Yvette's, or maybe to a hotel to clear my head. But this is my home. The castle I helped buy by working all those long hours at a stressful job.

He stops at the top of the stairs, up in the loft area that we use as a library. I can't see him, but I feel his energy. It's on high, heating up the house. Almost in the red zone.

It's close to sunrise, an hour that I haven't seen in ages. Charles turns on the light in the upstairs hallway and then comes down to the landing. He's barefoot and has on deep blue Old Navy pajama bottoms and a rust-colored wife-beater.

Again he asks, "Where have you been?"

When I don't answer, he breathes fire, takes hard steps, comes halfway down the rest of the stairs, tells me that my job and Yvette have been calling here all evening.

I don't hide from Charles. I click the light on so he can get a better view of his wife. His expression changes. He sees a woman whose locks are tousled, wearing wrinkled clothing, dried sweat on her face, maybe smells the scent of a strange man rising from her flesh. I see a man with a swollen eye, a man who was almost gunned down in a school parking lot, a man who has been tossing and turning all night, maybe for the last few days. Lies and guilt and fear create pillows made of concrete; make the softest comforter feel like it's made of stone.

I stand at the bottom of the stairs, purse in hand, and return his glare.

I'm scared. Scared of who we are now. Scared of who I am now. I'm a third person, hovering over this room, staring at two people I don't know.

I ask, "Was it easy for you to fuck her and come home?"

"Don't walk in here talking like that."

"You know what's fucked up? I could've become a widow and never known why."

"Not now," he snaps. "Let's not do this now."

"We do it when I say we do it, Charles," I snap back.

Everything becomes volcanic when I see him. Those words, all the things he said and shared with his lover for all those months, all of that pisstivity bubbles under my skin. I say, "After you fucked her *the first time*, you should've come home and repented your sins, but you went on like nothing had happened."

Head to toe, over and over, he takes me in.

"And you would've gone on like nothing had happened. Forever."

My words rouse him.

I say, "For eight months, you kept fucking that bitch and coming home to me."

His eyes widen and his anger changes to fear. Again he takes in my wrinkled clothing, my messed-up mane, maybe gets a whiff of the wine that rides from my breath.

I ask, "Was it a couple of times, Charles? Was it only twice in eight months?"

That vein rises in his neck, moves up and down with his rapid heartbeat.

I want him to fight. I need him to be that dragon so I can slay him.

But Charles isn't a dragon. He's a man. The man I married.

I ask, "You did answer those questions, right?"

He hesitates, fingers opening and closing. "Those questions are unreasonable."

"And having sex with another man's wife was reasonable?"

His hands remain closed, in fists.

I own a don't-fuck-with-me tone. "You know I can find out what I really wanna know."

"Look, where—" His voice is harsh, but he stops, his nostrils flaring. He pulls himself together, softens his tone, but can't get out his words. He repeats, "Where have you been?"

This time, the way he asks that question changes. He wants to know what I know.

I give him a thin smile; I almost laugh. Questioning me is ludicrous.

When I start up the stairs, he grabs my left arm. His grip is tight, a combination of desperation and irritation. I look at him like he's insane, then struggle and yank away.

I snap, "Touch me again and till death do us part will come a lot sooner than either one of us has planned."

He raises his palms in apology and I hurry by him. He's never manhandled me like that, but we've never been like this. I'm so nervous that I drop my purse when I get to the top of the stairs. The sheets of paper that were on top of my things scatter across the carpet.

Charles rushes up and stands near me. My heart beats faster.

I gather those sheets of paper and throw them at his face, wish they all were stones.

He asks, "What's this?"

I head to the bedroom and slam the door. I catch my breath and drop my purse in the leather chair. I wait for the dragon to come after me. Wait for the door to fly off of its hinges.

It's silent in the hallway. A strong silence that can be heard for miles.

Those papers were pages of messages between him and his lover. I stole those. I'm not stupid. No way was I going to leave David Lawrence's studio without evidence of the crime.

Jessica [6:18 AM] Busy today?
Charles [6:18 AM] Going to church. ☹ then the wifey is running to work after that ☺

Jessica [6:18 AM] David has an art show in San Diego, so he's gone for the weekend.
Charles [6:19 AM] ☺
Jessica [6:19 AM] ☺
Charles [6:19 AM] I'll be free by two
Jessica [6:19 AM] ☺ want u to be grabbing my ass by three
Charles [6:20 AM] ☺ by two-thirty

I imagine that Charles is outside that door, stunned, reading with his mouth wide open, then taking long, deep breaths and closing his eyes before he lets it all back out.

Jessica [6:59 AM] thinking about you had me wiggling in my sleep. I dreamed about you, woke up feenin for some more
Charles [6:59 AM] same here, we must be needing each other bad
Jessica [7:00 AM] i wish i could please you again right now . . . never had sex that good before, you're making a woman weak, keep saying I'm gonna be right, then I get to work and see you, look in your eyes, and all I wanna do is be with you
Jessica [7:01 AM] i want to make every fantasy a reality for you . . . just give me time
Jessica [7:01 AM] i love you . . . i want us to be together
Charles [7:01 AM] you know that's too complicated right now
Jessica [7:01 AM] I just hate thinking that anybody is touching you besides me
Jessica [7:04 AM] you make me happy . . . you make me want to be better than i already am. i am so blessed to have you. I won't get to be with you until Thursday
Charles [7:04 AM] ☹ Thursday seems like a month away

He's out there, doing the same thing I did when I read the lust letters, hoping the words will change, that this reality will disappear.

Jessica [4:33 PM] call me wanna see you
Charles [4:33 PM] okay, will call u later. She got called in to work.
Jessica [4:34 PM] call me at home asap
Charles [4:34 PM] only on the cell. Don't get sloppy.
Jessica [4:35 PM] I don't care about that anymore.
Charles [4:38 PM] don't get careless
Jessica [4:38 PM] he doesn't get back from Canada until Thursday
Charles [4:38 PM] That's no excuse. Don't get careless Jessie
Jessica [4:38 PM] Call me right now.
Charles [4:38 PM] told you I'm not alone yet.
Jessica [4:39 PM] We need to talk about how we're going to handle our situation. We need to figure out how we're going to do this.
Jessica [4:41 PM] hello
Charles [4:42 PM] be patient
Jessica [4:42 PM] can't wait anymore. Not being with you is torture. We need to talk.
Jessica [4:55 PM] Hello? U there?
Jessica [4:56 PM] Hello?
Charles [4:59 PM] I'll call u when she leaves
Jessica [4:59 PM] you're the love of my life. can't imagine living another day without you

The bedroom is a mess. Bed unmade. Three empty cans of Stroh's are on the nightstand. Clothes everywhere. Like he's had a fit. Black boxing gloves are in the middle of the floor.

Sweaty clothes are hanging over the side of the bathtub. His heavy boxing bag was down in the garage, blocking my parking space, that's why I had to park in the driveway and come in through the front door. He's been working out his anger today, trying to recapture his youth, banging that heavy bag like he's getting ready for the rematch of his life.

When I look in the bathroom mirror, a rainbow of colors has dried on my face and neck, even on my breasts. The reds and yellows, traces of the paint that came from David Lawrence's flesh, have streaked and speckled my skin. Even with my heart racing, the drumbeat of David Lawrence echoes between my legs. I turn on the shower, then stare out at the sunrise.

Charles is still silent. He has to be reading the last page by now.

> Subj: **What I feel for you**
> Time: 11:34:02 PM Pacific Daylight Time
> From: Jessica
> To: Charles

> Every time you touch me, a part of me walks away from him. Every time we leave our haven, our heaven, I feel guilty. Not for what we did, but for leaving you. I sit with my husband, talk with my husband, eat dinner with my husband, and I feel alone. I'm broken, a woman who is living many lives in many pieces.

> I have to see movies twice. I go with him and pretend that it's all new to me. And I know you do the same. This treachery is making me weary.

> Do you know how hard it is to be in love with someone

and I can't tell anyone? I can't put a picture of you up. I can't even own one. Do you know how bad I want to call you right now? I can't call you. I can't wait for your calls, because I know you're not going to call. I can't look at you too long at work. I can't speak your name in the tone it deserves, the one that rises from my heart. I can't make love to you and wear our aroma. I have to wash away all traces of us before I leave the room. And when I watch you do the same, see how careful you are, the way you make sure you have all of your belongings, how you make sure you leave with the same scent you left home wearing, one that has no traces of me. I remember the day you left your watch at the hotel. How you freaked out, had to go back and get it. Then you explained that your watch was a present from your wife. I said nothing, but now I hate that watch. Hate when you look at it to see how much time we have, because in my mind you're looking at her. Now I see how you keep all of your things in a neat pile so nothing will be forgotten, it bothers me. We wash each other as if we're washing the lies off our bodies. We shouldn't be ashamed of what we have, of what we feel.

I'm even afraid to dream about you because I might wake up in a haze, moaning your name. We're going out less and less, spending most of our time in rented rooms, rooms that many others come to rest in, to make love in, then go. I wish we could have our own space. Our own heaven, our own sheets that are unsoiled by the sins of others. I want a place where I can put pictures of us up. Maybe I can get us a place during the summer, an apartment, so when the both of us are off work for those months, we can come and go as we please. A place where I can wait for you, or you can wait for me, and we can bathe and massage each other. We can leave each other love letters.

I love you and I've never spent the night with you. I've never seen you in the morning's light.

What we have has gravity. The kind that I can't ignore. I'll give up all I have and eat rice and beans if you tell me that we can grow old together.

Your touch is liberation.

What I feel for you is incurable.

As always, you are the love of my life. The one I can't live without.

Forever goes by before Charles opens the bedroom door. He walks in, bouncing those sheets of paper against his leg, and stares at my reflection in the mirror.

His voice booms, "When did she give you . . . this?"

That confuses me, but only for as long as it takes me to blink.

He's smoldering. "What did Jessica . . . What did she tell you?"

He's pissed because he thinks I've been chilling with Jessica, that I've had a clandestine tryst with his lover.

His ignorance is bliss. That almost makes me smile.

I chuckle and say, "I'll tell you this."

I tell him how his affair started, almost pinpoint the date, tell him about their wonderful night at the *Soldier's Play*. I tell him about that first kiss, the one that lasted for an hour.

I don't play all my cards; just enough to throw off his game and halt his lies.

He shakes his head, speaks in a definite tone. "Don't believe her."

Where we are now, it's sad. So very sad. We're children in adult clothes. All of the education we have, it gets stripped away, and this is what we become. He reacts to me, and I react to him. Charles has taken away my choices. If he had come to me with honesty, I could've decided what I could do to fix it. But I can't fix something if I don't know it's broken.

Now he wants to talk. I turn the shower off because I want to hear what he has to say.

He sits on the arm of the chair, takes a breath, and tries to explain the unexplainable. My husband tells me that it was an affair of convenience, not one from the heart.

"Let's not pretend," I tell him. "Right now, we're not friends. Deception has put a rift in whatever friendship I thought we had."

"Okay."

"By choosing to be with Jessica, by not coming to me and telling me what was wrong, by not giving me a chance to work on our problems, you took away my choice."

"I didn't."

"When you slept with Jessica, that's what you did."

"O-kay."

"So, I took away your choice."

"What did you do?"

"I hadn't slept with anybody else since we started going out. I don't mean since we got married. I mean since we began dating. That's over five years."

"What did you—?"

"I took away your choice."

He pauses. Closes his eyes. "What the hell does that mean?"

"Don't get stupid on me."

His face looks like it's in a million pieces, a puzzle ready to fall apart.

His salvia is thick, almost glues his mouth. He furrows his brows and asks, "Who?"

"A stranger."

"A stranger?"

"Somebody I just met yesterday."

His hurt is so deep he trembles. "How could you?"

"How could *I*?"

That question makes me explode just like Tyra the Tyrant. Charles tries to smother my anger by exploding as well, but trying to shut me down makes me angrier. Our shouting match rumbles our peaceful home. I yell, I cry, I tell him about the movies, the plays, all the things I know he's done with Jessica. I tell him the shit that he said about me. My words shut him down.

My emotions exhaust me. We hit a calm, sit in the eye of the hurricane. The echoes of the screams fade. Silence returns. Birds are singing outside our window. People in our planned community are driving to work. The sun continues to rise.

I ask, "When did things change for us?"

The easiness of my voice, its earnestness, catches him off guard. He clears his throat, rubs his face. He looks numb. My hurt has run deep, has wounded his hypocritical ego.

He says, "Hard to say when, to give a date."

"Try."

"I think . . . I think things started to change when we went to Jackson, Mississippi."

"In Mississippi?"

"Yeah. Last year at your grandfather's funeral."

"How did going to Pa-pa's funeral change anything?"

He tells me that at my paternal grandfather's funeral, I didn't cry. He tells me how I sat there so detached. Looking so . . . cold. All around me, my relatives and Pa-pa's friends were crying, expressing sorrow, but I sat there, no tears in sight. People watching. Says that I reminded him of the news reporters at the shop, the way they reported on death without expression.

"That's bullshit, Charles. And you know that."

"This is who you are. I called you day before yesterday"—he motions at his wounded eye—"and no matter how I got hurt—"

"You called me and lied."

"Look . . . let's forget about that. For the moment." He shakes his head and lets out a rueful laugh. "No matter how I was injured, I told you I had a busted eye—"

"I was scared to death."

"—and *two seconds* later you were yakking about me watching some stupid news report on a woman who got bit by a pit bull. What kind of shit is that?"

I snap, "I was at work, Charles."

He retorts, "That's where your priorities are."

"I was at work, at work, at work. That's what I do."

"Yeah. That's what you do. You become insensitive. You turn off your emotions. You refuse to feel. And you do it well. And you do it all the time."

"I deal with death, rape, negative shit every day. I can't turn it on and off."

"I understand that, if you're at work. But I'm talking about after work."

"Do you really understand?"

"You think I don't deal with negative shit at work every

day? Between kids and parents and . . . do I bring that shit home and dump it on you?"

"You do and you know you do."

"Not every day."

"You . . . you just don't understand what my job is like."

"I understand."

"I don't think you do."

"How can I not? Your stress becomes my stress every time you come in that door."

"All I'm doing is sharing my day with you. It's called communication." My words fade and I pull at my locks, then massage my temples. I recoup and say, "I'm successful. Success cannot be attained without hard work, commitment, and determination."

"Of course. *You're* successful. *You* make the lion's share of the income. *You're* the head nigga in charge in this house."

I pause. "Is that what this is about?"

"Well, you were so quick to point out that I would need fifty thousand to buy you out of the equity in this house. Our marriage hits a speed bump—"

"Are you insane?"

"—and the first thing you do is calculate your losses."

"Don't confuse a speed bump with a brick wall."

"It came down to money."

"I have to protect myself financially and emotionally."

"That's very Dr. Laura of you."

"That's being real. I've worked too hard to lose all I have because you met some bitch. You're sitting over there trying to make it sound like your affair was nothing."

He goes on. "If you're successful, the producer who rides off to Hollywood every day, and I'm a middle-school teacher out in the friggin' desert, what am I?"

"What? I'm not saying that I'm successful and you're not."

"Yes you are. You're successful at work. But not here, not between these four walls."

That hits me hard. My mouth opens, lips move, but my words crumble. I can't talk.

He says, "Can you honestly tell me that you thought everything was okay with us?"

"Yes."

"Bullshit."

"I'm not saying I thought we were perfect. No one is. I didn't think that it . . . that we . . . that our marriage . . . our friendship . . . Didn't think that it was like this."

We sit here in our truth. It's not pretty; it's not comfortable. It's the way truth is.

He rubs his hands together, still bouncing his leg. "You think your work is hard, is so draining, well so is mine. I'm a teacher, a coach, a referee, a counselor, a surrogate parent to every black kid that has no dad at home, and that's damn near all of them."

He stops and rocks.

"They look up to me. Do you know how hard it's going to be for me to go back to work, to be their hero, how hard it's going to be for me to face them with this . . . this . . . shit."

"Well, you caused this humiliation. *Own it.*"

He chuckles. "Yep, you can be one cold fish."

I pull my lips in. "I'm not going to let you turn this around; I'm not the dragon."

He takes a breath and goes on. "Last year, I told you that we found out a kid was pregnant. A thirteen-year-old. An African-American. One of ours. One of the teachers did it."

"What does that pedophile have to do with—"

"And the first thing you did was try to figure out how to make it a story."

"*What?* I didn't."

"*You did.*" He nods. "Did you forget that you were pregnant at fifteen? Guess you forgot how that felt. Did you forget how scared you were?"

His words almost extinguish the fire inside me.

His voice softens. "Jessica cried about it. Didn't detach herself, she didn't try to make it a special report for the damn ten o'clock news. She did what real people do, she cried."

He wipes his eyes with the backs of his fists.

He says, "We're supposed to protect kids, not exploit."

I'm stunned.

"And I cried too." His lip trembles. "I felt like I was that kid's parent, you know? A lot of responsibility comes with my job. I do my best. And it hurt me because . . . because it felt like I had failed her. I called you that day, needed you, and I was in pain and you . . . ."

He stops and shakes his head.

He says, "You wanted to know what made me go to Jessica, now you know. It's the subtle moments that make you fall in love with someone. Or out of love. Too many hurtful moments make you want to pull away. We've had a lot of those moments."

"You should've come to me, Charles."

"When have you been available?"

"Every damn day. *I'm here every damn day.* I sleep in that bed with you every night. Dammit, you could've come to me eight months ago. You should've come to me eight months ago. I had to get a mortifying phone call at my job. Her husband had to hunt you down like you were an animal, beat your ass at your job, then he came to my damn job with this shit. And I had to read"—I motion at the white pages of IMs that litter the beige carpet—"that, all of that, to find out the truth. I could be a widow right now. Imagine me getting that shit after somebody had killed you over some . . . over . . ."

Words stick in my throat.

He looks at those pages. He asks, "What did she tell you?"

"I've become a 'situation.' " I motion at those papers. "I know more than that. A lot more. She kept every word you ever sent her. I've seen most of it."

He groans, tries to say things, but all he gives me is "I'm sorry."

"Sorry? This wasn't an accident. You took her to restaurants. To plays. To museums. You *planned*." My voice remains deflated, distant. "You had your own little Wawa girl. Paraded her up and down the 405 freeway. Guess that was your own little Route 13."

"What?"

"You violated another man's wife in hotels, cars; anywhere she would spread her legs. You swam in her for eight months. Right now, I don't give a shit about Pa-pa's funeral, or the pregnant kid, or any excuse you throw in my face to make this seem like it's my goddamn fault."

"God's last name ain't Damn."

"And Mother's last name ain't Fucker, but you're acting like one right now."

"Don't talk like that. I hate it when you—"

"You chose to put your dick in that man's wife over and over and over, and came home and did the same to me, over and over, went on like everything was fine."

"Am I proud of it?" His voice fills with conviction. "No.

Was I going to leave you? Thought about it. Would I leave you? No. Despite all the things I've said, or done, you're my wife and I love you. You are the love of my life."

"When did you realize that? Before or after Jessica's husband hunted you down? Maybe I should take a crew from the station and go down to the school and find out—"

He barks, "You will not go to my job."

"Try me."

"Do you understand? This is not a damn news story. This is my life."

"This is my damn life too."

"Don't . . . Just don't."

His threatening tone, the way he looks—all of that frightens me.

He rubs his face, calms a bit, but can't stop rubbing hand over hand.

Charles says, "I can't imagine myself being with anybody but you. If I wanted anybody else, you could have this house, my pension, whatever you think this is all about, and I would be gone. Would I do it over? No. Would I have gone on and not let you find out about it? I don't know. Can't say yes, can't say no. Am I glad you know? In some ways, yeah. I feel relieved."

"Do you?"

"Yeah, I do."

"Good. At least one of us feels better."

Again, loud and unnerving silence lives in this room.

The sun is up. No more darkness.

He stares at my wrinkled clothing. I stare at his swollen eye.

"Did you . . ." His voice almost breaks. He swallows. Straightens his back. His eyes intent, set on mine. His voice comes back stronger. Gives me hard eye contact. Now he's The Man. "You slept with somebody?"

He wants me to change my answer. His voice demands me to. Needs me to. Wants me to erase my scarlet letter and salve his wounded ego.

I nod.

He groans.

He asks, "You went out and . . . A stranger?"

I nod.

Bit by bit, his face changes. Jealousy rises and gives him insane eyes, then he blinks, and looks mortally wounded. For a moment, he has the same face that David Lawrence owns. Charles tugs at his hair; frowns, struggles to talk, but the words won't come. Then he clenches his fists, hunches his shoulders, veins in his neck become thick ropes, looks like he wants to kill.

"Don't play with me. Who. Was. He?"

I swallow, but don't answer.

"*Who?*"

Spit flies from his lips, his tone blacker than death. I shiver, but I don't answer.

"Why are the rules different for you?" I ask with force, my rage trying to match his. "You tell me to let it go, to forget about you and Jessica, but I tell you I do the same, you—"

"*Who?*"

His jealousy rattles the house. He has a Tyson-right-before-the-first-bell look on his face.

I'm ready for him to call me names, grab me, hit me, slap me, squeeze my neck, and bang my head against the wall until I lose consciousness. Part of me wants him to do all those things, would allow him to stone me, then to suffer from the pain he's brought into this house. Another part of me is terrified, telling me to flee, not fight with that dragon. My body is tense, easing into sprinter's position, but he's closer to the door, so I'm trying to decide if I should fight and scream, or scream and flee, or just scream until I die.

My voice is unsteady. "I've never called you Francis. Never."

Then he blinks; exhales in short puffs. The glow of insanity fades from his eyes.

I go on. "Low blow, Charles. Bringing up my pregnancy . . . that was pretty fucking low. "

He won't stop frowning at me.

"What was it, Charles?" I'm yelling at him, giving him my anger. "Were you being greedy? Was it because she was new to you? Was it just new pussy? Is that what it was all about? Why is it a crime if I do it, and I'm supposed to let you walk over me if you do?"

He refuses to release me from his scowl and won't blink.

Then I say, "Or did Francis do what he had to do to feel like a man?"

He blinks.

I ride our emotional roller coaster deeper into our insecurities and fear; refuse to let the ride end. He gives me a heinous scowl and I give him a Lorena Bobbitt glare, daring him to do what he's thinking about and then ever try to go to sleep inside these four walls.

I ask, "Is that what it's all about, huh?"

He bites his lip, touches his swollen eye, stands up.

I stand too. If we are to fight, if I am to die, I'll be on my feet.

Charles yanks up his boxing gloves, slaps them under his armpits. He scowls down on those scattered pages, moves around that black lust inked on white paper, marches away from our truth. His heavy footsteps fade down the stairs.

Sweat covers my nose, runs down to my lips. My world is hazy, hot, humid. Air gets too thick to breathe. I swallow, feel as if I'm suffocating, about to choke on my own saliva. I stand staring at the colorful pictures on the dresser. Our wedding picture is the one in front.

Two happy people.

I'm in a daze, thrust into an ugly, surreal world; wondering how do I get back to the world in that picture.

BamBam BamBamBamBam BamBam BamBam

The house rumbles. The walls shake. It scares me out of my trance. I yell, bumble across the room, bump my knee on the edge of the entertainment center, then yelp and fall, crawl over the carpet, try to remember that stupid earthquake procedure and hurry and get to the doorway.

BamBamBamBam

I lean against the wall, holding my leg, cringing, the pain bringing tears to my eyes. The house continues to rumble and shake, feels and sounds like car after car is ramming into the walls.

BamBam

My home is about to cave in. But it's not an earthquake. It's Charles's raw rage.

BamBamBamBam BamBamBamBam BamBam BamBam

Charles is in the garage, in his pajamas, punishing that boxing bag.

I rub the pain in my leg until it eases up enough to let me stand. The house continues to quake as I lean against the wall, rub my temples, wipe my eyes, take easy steps, limp to the bathroom, and blow my nose.

BamBamBamBam

When I look at the tissue, it's stained with soft streaks of red and yellow paint. I gaze at my face and see the beautiful colors, see the fingerprints of another man on my skin.

BamBamBamBam BamBam BamBamBamBam BamBam

I limp to the shower. The drumbeat of David Lawrence throbs between my legs.

12

Something nudges my memory. Makes me remember how we started.

A little more than five years ago I met Charles on a crowded bus heading to Mammoth. We were on a KJLH and Four Seasons West ski trip. Saw my future husband when I was struggling to toss my luggage under the bus at six in the morning. I wasn't interested in him at that moment. He came over and helped me, took charge the moment I met him. I liked that about a man. I wasn't in the talking mood, but when I saw him up close, I did my best to sip my coffee and perk up, tried to be grateful for his help.

He asked, "You skiing blacks?"

"What's that?"

"Advanced."

"Oh, no. First time. Taking lessons."

"Me too. I'll have at least one person to run into a tree with."

We ended up sitting across from each other, but I tucked a pillow under my head and went to sleep as soon as I got on the bus. After being up until two in the morning, not even a quadruple cappuccino could wake me up. But my people were yakking and getting their party on by sunrise, had the music bumping like it was New Year's Eve, so I had to wake up, and Charles and I ended up talking off and on. We ended up in the same ski school, with all that bulky equipment weighing us down, learning how to turn and wedge, and falling off the ski lift, then tumbling down the bunny slopes together.

We were a disaster.

After we'd had enough embarrassment for one day, we turned in our rented gear and warmed up our frozen toes in the crowded lodge, sipping wine and beer, raising our voices so we could hear each other over the hip-hop remixes that were rocking the building, laughing about how we looked on the hill, then talking about our jobs, dancing a bit, eating greasy entrees.

He asked, "What made you get into news?"

"My probation officer."

He laughed at my joke.

I said, "Back then I wanted to help control some of the images about our people. Show that we're not all drug dealers or rappers. Thought I'd get in and change the system."

"Yeah. Feel you on that. I wanted to change things too."

He was looking good in his colorful gear, reds and blues and blacks. And I was without makeup, my perm needed to be curled and was jacked to the max, and that schoolteacher still kept his eyes and smile on me.

I asked, "When's your birthday?"

"October 2."

Libra. Balanced. Highly emotional. High sex drive.

He asked, "When's yours?"

"February 24."

"Almost a month away."

"Twenty-two days."

Hazel eyes. Soft black curly hair. The kind of man you look at and start thinking about pretty babies. Because, who wants ugly babies? Not even ugly people want ugly babies.

He said, "You said you came up here by yourself?"

"Yeah. Traveling a capella."

"Most women won't go to a movie alone, let alone on vacation."

"Well, was supposed to come up with this guy I'd been seeing—"

"Uh-huh."

"But I wasn't feeling CJ anymore, so I ditched him."

"Sounds like that's over."

"It's been over for months. Just didn't need to drag it out and mess up my vacation. Tried to get my friend Yvette to come up, but she had plans to hit Atlanta for the weekend."

He laughed. "Lucky me."

"Since you put us on that page, where's your woman? Don't wanna get stabbed in the back of my neck while I'm sipping on my wine."

"Dag. That's pretty violent."

"I work in news. The world is violent, trust me."

"I teach social studies. I've studied history. I know about violence. This country was built on violence. There has never been peace on this planet."

I nodded. "Well, all I'm worried about is your woman rolling up on me from the backside. Last thing I need is to become the lead story on the six o'clock news."

He laughed. "You don't have to worry about that."

"So, Mr. Schoolteacher, you're not seeing anybody?"

"Well, Miss News Producer, I'm not gonna lie. I date, but nothing serious."

"Uh-huh. Like I said, don't get me stabbed."

"Don't worry. I'll protect you from all enemies, domestic or foreign."

"Yep. You are mos def a teacher."

Later on we were looking for each other at the big party. It had a New York theme, so there were four hundred African Americans dressed in New York Blacks. Designer leathers and wools. Sunglasses and fedoras. I sported a simple black dress. Seems like I always wore black dresses when I went out. I had my face made up, hair curled, couldn't wait for Charles to see me looking more like a woman than a tomboy. As soon as I saw him, he took control, took my hand and led me to the dance floor, and we started dancing and drinking and laughing until it was time to shut the place down.

He told me, "I love the way you walk."

"I'm bowlegged and slew footed, just like my momma."

"She must have a sexy walk too."

We sat next to each other on the bus ride back to Los Angeles, shoulders touching, heads on shoulders when one of us nodded off, comfortable, like we were already a couple. It was hard for him to catch up with me after that mini-vacation, because by the time I made it back to sea level, it was sweeps week at my job. He was back to teaching. It was back to reality.

But he had my cellular number, and he kept calling. And I kept calling back. I wasn't exactly waiting for Charles. I did date other men. I was single. Not committed to any man.

It took me and Charles six dates to get into bed. Six dates spaced over close to two months. That was still too fast in my book, but slower than the average three-dates-before-sex.

That was when I was slave to the chemicals and the queen of the perm. Used to spend my off day at the beauty shop, getting my bob hooked up. That was me, a standing appointment down in Ladera every Wednesday, wasting three hours at the beauty shop.

I try to remember. It all gets mixed up after a while, especially right now.

We started out as late-night weekend lovers, pretty much had to with our schedules. He couldn't do the late-night thing on the weekdays. Then came summer, and he was off work. Available twenty-four-seven. The next thing I knew, we were jonesing for each other. The way he looked at me. Said my name. The way he laughed. From day one, I loved it all. Then he had more free time and would come by my job at sunset, brought me Jamba Juices and burritos from Baja Grill. Listened to me play my sax. Used to tell me that my freckles were like stars in the sky, and my face had beautiful constellations. Then he sent me exotic flowers two weeks in a row. My heart was softening. I smiled ear to ear when I showed him around the newsroom, took away some of the mystery of news production. Introduced my new lover to Yvette. She made freaky-deaky eyes behind his back and gave me two thumbs up. Charles was fascinated with all the behind-the-scenes work, wondered if I could come to his school, talk to kids on Career Day. No problem. Would love to, even if I had to go in there half-awake. For him, I'd change the rotation of the world. Fifteen minutes after he drove away he called. Missed me. Same here. *If you're still up, come over when I get off.* The language of the booty call. *I'll cook for you.* The language of romance. *Sure.* Or I'd have passes to get into some event, or have to go with a crew to cover some premiere, and ask if he wanted to meet me in Hollywood or Westwood. And I'd show up in a black cocktail dress, something silky that draped in the back, showed off some flesh, took away some of that wholesome appearance. And he would smile. And that smile made me giggle a thousand times a thousand.

We hooked up after I got off work pretty much every night, and I cooked a late dinner for him, easier to cook for two than for one was what I had said, and that had us eating after midnight, then with the kissing, and his hard-on would betray him, we moved toward the inevitable, his fingers would find their way to my vagina, the way he traced the edges, made circles, massaged that button while he sucked on my breasts . . . that combination was dangerous . . . made my voice change . . . eyes tightened . . . pre-orgasmic growls came from deep inside . . . famished moans . . . then my panties were at my ankles . . . my skirt pulled up high . . . his change jingling as his pants fell and bunched at his feet . . . right there . . . kitchen counter . . . up against the front door . . . on the carpet . . . got to the point that if I knew he was coming over I wore a skirt . . . high heels that pimped out my calves and made my butt curve more . . . no panties . . . always played the role and waited for him to make his move . . . to get past all the talking about our families . . . about Bible study and church and God . . . about jobs . . . beyond all the laughing at each other's stupid jokes . . . starting off polite . . . watching the clock . . . waiting for him to shut me up and get inside me . . . melting when his lips finally touched my neck . . . playing cool and aching for the next level . . . dizzy when his hand held my ass . . . then . . . his erection pressing up against me . . . fucking our hearts out . . . sometimes candles burning . . . sometimes music . . . sometimes no time for sensual ceremonies and going all the way in a room with all the lights on . . . Venetian blinds cracked for the voyeuristic . . . in my old creaky bed . . . my first bed from my college days . . . first with condoms . . . then lust disguised as trust numbed the sensibilities . . . I'm not seeing anybody . . . you're not seeing anybody . . . I'm HIV negative . . . you're negative . . . I'm on the pill . . . never miss one . . . helps me with my period . . . then . . . condoms abandoned for real contact . . . moved toward recklessness . . . no barrier . . . skin to skin . . . so intense . . . was like starting all over again . . . he'd sex me awhile . . . stop . . . lay me down and stroke my clit . . . stroke . . . give me agony . . . stroke . . . make me beg . . . then his tongue dancing inside my pussy . . . turned his body until . . . until . . . invited his penis to find shelter in the warmth of my mouth . . . taking him slow . . . methodical . . . playing his sex like it was my sax . . . while being licked slow in figure eights . . . then using my hand and mouth . . . punishing him . . . being punished . . . trying to make him go crazy before he made me go insane . . . me, the woman who looks like a freckle-faced church girl, giving deep throat on a Sunday afternoon . . . me and the innocent-looking history teacher who dined on my clit like it was a French cuisine . . . then lying next to each other . . . caressing and confessing . . . feeling high and heady . . . couldn't help saying things from the heart . . . he told me he never met anybody like me . . . beautiful . . . *got that from my momma* . . . professional . . . *afraid of failure* . . . cooked . . . *got that from my momma* . . . kept a clean apartment . . . *from my momma* . . . so eager to please . . . *no comment on that one* . . . not flaky . . . *too busy working, no time for games* . . . no phones ringing all times of the night . . . *no time for conventional dating, no secret lovers* . . . not like the typical L.A. girls . . . *try not to be* . . . a total package . . . *damn, really* . . . a renaissance woman . . . then he massaged me with hot oils . . . painted my toes . . . scratched my scalp . . . oiled my hair . . . cooked Cajun dishes for me . . .

made my heart sing . . . always there when I called . . . reliable . . . romantic . . . the start of our inseparable summer.

Then once we were loving, all heated and living inside never-ending moans, and I was exploring his body, squeezing his ass, spreading his cheeks, and I glided my finger toward his perineum, that fleshy part between his testicles and his butt hole, was going to massage that tender spot because Yvette had told me that takes the orgasm to a new level. I overshot my target, touched his back door, and Charles jerked, lost his groove, jumped away. Freaked out.

He looked scared, then he grinned like the little boy he once must have been.

That left me embarrassed in the moonlight.

My words became stutter after stutter, a struggle to ask him what was wrong. Had to pretend I didn't have any idea, or at least be sure. He thought I was going to put my finger up his ass. That made him widen his eyes, broke the mood. I told him no, not unless he wanted me to. He shook his head, no. Said he didn't go that route. He asked if that was what my other lovers had liked for me to do. I said no. Another white lie to him. We all tell small lies. Have to save face and not hurt someone's feelings. That perineum thing, I explained that to Charles, said I got carried away and didn't realize what I was doing, that my fingers had taken on a life of their own, laughed to soften the mood, and said that I read that a lot of men like that. A lot of heterosexual men at that. Read that in a man's magazine. *GQ,* I think. Women too. Read that in a woman's magazine. Either way, I heard it takes the orgasm to a new level. That was a hint to try something new, a suggestion that went unheard. Or maybe it was something he chose to ignore. He asked me if I liked that, if I was into anal loving, and because of the judgmental sound in his voice, again I lied, shook my head and made a disgusted face. Wouldn't admit that, because of the orientation of my G, I could orgasm that way too. I wasn't the next Madonna, but I didn't want to give up my Madonna image and be looked at as a freak whore. Just said that I was still a back-door virgin and repeated that I had read about that pleasure technique in a book, maybe a monthly like *Essence* or *Honey*, articles written by upwardly mobile black folks with no shame on their game, and maybe in *Cosmopolitan* or *Vogue* or *Tempo*, mainstream magazines read by pretty much everybody, and thought he might like it.

He chuckled; said real men didn't get into that.

He kissed me, entered me doggie, had me in a position where he could control me and I couldn't grab his ass, and he stroked me harder than he had before. Loved me like he was the ultimate *Maxim* man with the quintessential dick.

That awkward perineum moment came and went.

We went on with our summer.

Halfway through his work hiatus we were spending almost every night together. My place. His place. Didn't matter. I hated being alone. I was in need. Needed consistent companionship and security. Late night drives up the coast. Lots of talking at Lucy Florence. Or sipping lattes and listening to jazz at Magic's Starbucks. He was in need too. Restless. Lonely. Horny. We were human. Needed satisfaction on all levels. He was there. He was available. We moved from being part-timers to having a full-time relationship. A scary transition. He had a toothbrush at my apartment. I had keys to his crib. I put a picture of us up in my living room. He did the same at his home and at his job. I stopped investing in D batteries and my pink vibrator with the clitoris stimulator went on indefinite hiatus.

That summer we were cruising through Lust City into

Loveville. In another weak moment, after he had cooked dinner and I had sipped two glasses of merlot, I got heady, started rambling out my emotions because a slight case of PMS was on the rise, and confessed how I was feeling first. Wanted to kick myself. Then he said it too. Said the L word to me. I damn near cried. And we kissed a thousand times. Then we couldn't stop saying the L word.

Then time went by so fast.

We talked about kids. Told him I wanted a couple. A boy and a girl. Or two girls. Would hate to have two boys. Too much testosterone. I'd give them both to their daddy. Gotta have a girl to play dress-up and shoe shop with. He said he wanted five or six, have a big family, just like his folks did. An old-fashioned man at heart. We laughed about that. I said that I already had a late start and needed to have mine before I got too old. He was surprised that I didn't have any. That was when I was so at ease in his arms, confessed that I was pregnant in high school. Major drama at school, at home. Was knocked up by this basketball player who had bad knees and ended up selling crack. He was my first lover. The taker of my cherry. Of course he denied it. Disowned me. Of course I had to make a decision. Baby or scholarship. Become a single mom on welfare, or move onward and upward toward the light. A no-brainer. What goes around. My first lover was killed in a drug bust, tried to shoot a cop.

I asked Charles why he wanted to be a teacher, why he was so into his students, because none of the teachers that I had back in junior high or high school owned his kind of passion. He told me his history, that he was abused as a child. The next-door neighbor's son, a teenager, locked him in a bathroom and sodomized him when he was in elementary school. Said the guy was huge, and he was scared. Kept touching his face. Calling him Francis, the pretty Creole. Said he loved his smooth skin. His curly black hair. The hypnotic color of his eyes.

Charles never told his parents. Never told anybody until he told me. His voice trembled.

Charles's first name is Francis. Named after a saint. But he was always teased about having a girl's name. Charles was his middle name, again the name of a saint, but he used that one. A boy named Charles gets more respect than a boy named Fran.

I asked him if that was the only time, the only thing that evil boy did to him.

He never answered. His eyes were dark, like a television unplugged.

Then, the television behind his eyes came back on, and he talked and talked. Said that he went to the Y and took up boxing. Lived at the gym. Wrestling. Judo. Kung fu.

Got stronger. Learned to fight, practiced day and night. And the women. Conquered as many as he could. Did what he had to do in order to make himself feel like a man. Was going to get skills and beat down his abuser. Always dreamed of killing that man. But that never happened. His abuser moved away. Charles was going to track him down. Then Charles found out his abuser died from AIDS over fifteen years ago. He said he salved his soul with a bottle of hard liquor that night. Drank alone, in the dark. Stopped boxing, not all at once, but over time. Felt lost for a while. Never got his revenge. Always wanted to, but never did.

That was so sad. The abuse, then how he abused himself in response to the abuse. I cried when he told me that. He cried too. We both cried a long time, and I fell in love with him.

* * *

Today he wasn't fair. He disrespected me. Used my shame against me. That isn't my only shame. Just like everyone else in life, I have more regrets than I care to mention. But that one, when thrown back at me, hurt me down to the core.

I didn't do the same with his shame. Trust me, I sat there and thought about it, because for every reaction there is an equal and opposite reaction, but I didn't take it to the level that I needed to to feel . . . satisfied.

I felt sorry for Charles. Felt sorry for my husband. Felt sorry for both of us.

It's so sad . . . how two people can love each other, and with one decision, begin to lose everything you've worked so hard to create.

13

Yvette tells me, "You look like shit, Freckles."

"I know. No sleep."

"It's more than that. Looks like you've been traumatized."

We're in the parking lot at the station, both of us just getting out of traffic that was as thick as a brick. We both end up parking at the far end of the lot at the white stucco-and-brick wall closer to La Brea. Tyra the Tyrant's convertible Jaguar is already here, that silver chariot resting in her private space that is closest to the door, away from the rest of the common workers. Right now she's probably in a planning meeting, terrorizing other people whose offices have doors. I don't rush to get in and find out if I still have a job.

Yvette asks, "Why didn't you call somebody and let them know where you were?"

"Sorry, *Moms*."

Today Yvette has on faded jeans and a fitted multicolored T-shirt that reads CERTIFIED LOCKDOWN WORTHY. Her jeans stop right below her calves, are low cut and show off the edges of her lacy black thong. She has on some funky clog shoes today; the heels make that Amazon three inches taller. I have on black jeans, black boots with thin heels and a pointed toe—real sexy shoes—and a light brown peasant blouse.

"Kill the sarcasm." Yvette gets serious. "Had me freakin' out half the night."

I ask, "You hear about the fire?"

"Hell, yeah. Twenty thousand acres and at least nine cribs have been burned down."

"That's gonna be the lead story tonight."

"Tyra will be coming and screaming all evening."

We hug each other, then she hands me a small bag that has a zebra-print design.

I ask, "What's this?"

"Your goodies from the ATL. I keep forgetting to give them to ya."

I know Yvette. My body language is screaming that I've had a rough night and my girl is trying to cheer me up, keep me living in the positive before I step into that other world. In the bag is a T-shirt from Atlanta's Underground, and a colorful box of Dick Tacs.

I shake the candy and laugh a little. "What the hell are these?"

"Look at 'em."

I open the small box and shake a few of the itty-bitty candies out into my hand. They are Tic Tac–like things shaped like colorful penises.

I laugh a little harder. "Where did you get this mess?"

"This spot in Little Five Points called Junkman's Daughter."

I pop a brown one. She pops two of the same color. Sax man Mike Phillips's debut CD *You Have Reached Mike Phillips* is one of my gifts. I smile big time. A book is inside the bag too. I take it out and read the cover. *Threesome: How to Fulfill Your Favorite Fantasy*.

I say, "Dick Tac. Romantic music. A book on how to do a threesome."

"Oh, snap."

"Uh, is there some message behind this?"

"That's not for you. I was looking for that book."

She takes it back, laughs all the way to the trunk of her SUV, and tucks it underneath a basket of laundry. While she does that, I open my dented trunk and put the bag of goodies inside, then lean against my car. She stands next to me and does the same.

Yvette says, "Okay, where were you last night?"

"What's up with that threesome book?"

"Research."

I ask, "Were you researching last night?"

"I was home."

"Self-medicating?"

"Alone. Never medicate alone. Was on the phone with TJ—"

"He has to think I'm an idiot."

"Nah, thinks you're a crack-up. First I was out on the Web researching the Eritrean-Ethiopian thing, called him because some of his 'facts' were contradicting what I was reading about the land dispute. I surfed the Web and pulled up tons of maps from 1902 that said the Ethiopians were in the right, found another article said the Eritreans have only released one map, and that's a Mussolini map from around 1935."

"Mussolini?"

"I was surprised too. I've seen photos of Mussolini riding with Hitler, so that puts a *phat* spin on the issue. Flash Hitler's face, throw in some of his atrocities, and mainstream people will be interested in watching."

"Can't believe that CBS is doing a miniseries on Hitler."

"You and me both."

"And they're gonna kick ass during sweeps."

"That's what I'm saying. Anyway, what I pulled off the Internet says the Eritreans have other maps that would damage their case, but they're keeping those to themselves. And they bum rushed the Ethiopians when there was no war, then rejected peace plans."

"Sounds like you had a romantic night."

"Didn't mean to go on like dat, but you know how I can get."

"I know."

"Put me in contact with your neighbor. I'd like to get her perspective."

"Sure. I'll give Tseday your number."

"Then TJ got beside himself, we started having a debate, then somehow and for some reason the conversation changed and he tried reeducating me on the Hutu and Rwanda."

I say, "Rwanda. We covered that, what, seems like ten years ago."

"At least. Were you in news then?"

"I'd just started working as an intern. Was trying to be a reporter back then."

"Long time back. When I thought long, curved, red finger-nails were hip, that a Jheri-Curl was underrated, had to have a gold ring on almost every finger, sometimes had two gold rings on a finger, and bright colors were the shit. And was dying to get a gold tooth."

"Yuck. Had that Master P thang going on, huh?"

"Got that from my momma. You shoulda seen my cousins out in Bessemer."

"Your 'Bama butt done changed a lot."

"Yup. Back when I was hanging out at J.O. Parker, pigging

out on the pig, and still sleeping on Africa." She reminds me that the Hutu massacred a million Tutsis. She talks on, "People over here would rather see a story on 'Only eight percent of the French are obese. What's in their diet?' than . . . than . . . geesh."

"It's about the dollars, Yvette. You know that."

"And that's why we know all about the Irish Protestants and Catholics, right? And how many more stories can we possibly do about Palestine and Israel? Shit, that neck of the woods is well covered. But Africans, in the news, we still don't exist. It's disturbing, don't you think?"

"Yvette, don't get political right now. I'm tired, head hurts, and I've got my own probs."

She gets back to her original question, "Where were you kicking it at all night?"

"You sound like Charles."

We talk underneath Hollywood's two o'clock sun and layers of brown air, a combination that will have people with bronchitis popping pills and getting breathing treatments all day. The echo of traffic out on both La Brea and Willoughby punctuates our words, irritated and bad drivers screeching and wailing their way into our conversation.

Tyra the Tyrant opens the double glass doors that lead inside. She stands at the top of the stairs, a dictator on her throne, peering down at the peasants. That stops us from talking. Tyra wears a deep green pantsuit, a colorful scarf over her head. She opens a piece of Nicorette, eases it inside her mouth, then folds her arms and stares at me without saying a word, almost daring me to come up those steps and step inside that door.

Yvette yells, "Whassup, Tyra? You can't speak?"

She gazes at Yvette, then at her watch, then back at Yvette

and raises a brow. Yvette doesn't respond to any of that. Everyone is rushing, so no one comes near us, but a couple of them give me the thumbs-up, letting me know they're my friends and on my team; they do that before they realize Tyra is at the door, then their demeanor changes. But just as many regard me in a strange way, almost as if they know that there is going to be a fever in the funk house and some static in the attic when I cross the moat and get inside of Tyra the Tyrant's castle.

In the midst of Tyra's silent threat, someone comes up behind her, looking for her, and she goes back inside, cutting her eyes at me until she vanishes.

Her little psychological move fucks with my head.

"Whoo wee." Yvette chuckles. "Looks like Citizen Tyra is gonna be in rare form today."

"I shoulda hit that bitch in the eye."

I give Yvette the real deal about what happened between me and Tyra, about how I drove away and left her begging, then move on and tell her the short version of the rest of the night.

"Whoa. Rewind. You went to see that David Lawrence cat by yourself?"

I take a breath, try to purge Tyra's bad karma from my system, and tell Yvette about the mountain of evidence. That gets her attention in a major way. To get away from Tyra's eyes, we walk to the side of the building, stand near the corner, and I talk my angst away.

Tyra appears at a side door, looks at me, then goes back inside. We walk back around and stop by our cars, continue to talk while our rainbow coalition of black, white, Asian, and Latin reporters, segment producers, line producers, they all pull into the lot. I notice that a lot of people are here on their off day. Looks like everybody has been called in. That means the world is falling apart. Always falling apart. All I care about is my world. That's what I vent about.

"You're joking." That is all my girl can say. "Charles been creeping for eight months?"

I repeat, "Eight months of roogoodoo."

"And you didn't have a clue?"

"I feel . . . stupid."

I hand her a couple pages of IMs. I tell her about all of their dates.

Yvette says, "He took her out in public? Getdafuckoutta-here."

I nod. "Took her to EuroChow."

She says, "Both of them, sitting up at your fave romantic spot, wearing wedding rings, holding hands, laughing, flirting, looking happy—"

"Yeah, yeah, yeah."

"On a side note, Freckles, we need to get a copy of this cyber software."

"Knew you were gonna say that."

She reads the IMs and each time she gets to something strong she cringes. "Snap. This is deep. Can't tap dance your way around your own words. Straight up pornography."

Mouth open, she leans against my wounded car, reads, and frowns. Once again, I see all of the new dents and old imperfections on my car, find myself cursing at the damage that has been done. I live in anger; it's not my true nature, but it's my reality now.

Yvette lowers the paper, stunned. "No wonder homey did a number on his face."

"And his ego."

"Charles ain't no joke, but that David guy opened some

serious Kick Ass. Looks like that David guy whupped his ass the way Todd Bridges stomped Vanilla Ice."

Still, I feel for my husband. Despite the madness, despite what he's done, or what I've done, my love for him runs deep. Love and hate live so close to each other.

Yvette says, "I read all of those IMs and you know what I see?"

"Two people cheating. Two adulterers. Two con artists."

"It's deeper than that. You know I tend to go deeper than the surface."

"Okay, what?"

"Two people crying out for something. It's sad. She's crying out for something, he's crying out for something. Maybe, at face value, it's just two people getting their groove on on the down-low, but one of them, or both of them, could be crying out for help."

I don't say anything. Hope she can't read my thoughts.

She asks, "What was that David Lawrence like?"

"Arrogant. Little cocky. Scary."

"Uh-huh."

"But at the same time . . . the brother is super intense. Passionate. And exciting."

"What he look like?"

"He's like . . . like . . . like Lenny Kravitz and Eric Benet rolled into one."

"Uh-huh. Weird and handsome."

"And he likes classic cars."

She hands me back the IMs and I struggle to not lower my eyes, words getting unsure and shaky, and I tell her about the loft, the art, and obsession with painting Jessica. Describe Jessica the way she was described to me, only I add some nasty words of my own.

She keeps saying, "Uh-huh. Fine as hell and likes classic cars."

She knows me. She's waiting.

I tell Yvette about the gun, the death-maker that David Lawrence took to Charles's job, the Colt Defender that is still loaded and waiting.

Yvette's face fills with concern.

I think about what David Lawrence told me about his legacy, about Route 13 and the Wawa girl that his mother killed, but I keep that frightening and heartbreaking part of him to myself.

"I slept with David Lawrence."

"*What?*"

I confess that in a shaky voice, a bewildered tone, don't try to romanticize what went down between midnight and sunrise. I slept with a married man. I keep touching my wedding band, reminding myself that I'm married, wondering if I've made myself a Wawa girl as well.

I say, "We . . . we . . . we did it last night."

"Freckles, are you—"

"In his studio."

"—insane?"

"On a futon."

"You spent the night with him?"

"Left after we . . . Was there a few hours . . . got up and left. Went home."

Yvette pauses, a look of disbelief etched in her face, and shakes her head.

Just like Charles, she sees me as a black Hester Prynne, can't accept my transgression.

Then she takes a hard breath before she speaks, "Two wrongs don't make a right."

I shrug. "Do I look different?"

"No. Why?"

"People who commit adultery should look different."

"You feel different?"

"Like a person I've never met before."

I shift.

"Sleeping with . . ." Her words fade. "What the fuck were you thinking?"

My girl comes at me with that judgmental tone of a true Gemini. She's giving and caring, very opinionated, but I'm defensive, not feeling any of that judgmental shit right now.

My anger gets the best of me. "Charles refuses to own what he did, dammit. All that motherfucker had to do was own it and give me the remorse I needed to see. I needed him to be sorry, to cry, to let me be right for a goddamn change. His machismo . . . hate that shit. Not that damn arrogance and refusing to answer my questions or do anything I need to get toward some . . . some . . . some resolution. He tried to turn this around and make it be my fault."

She backs down, sighs, and asks me to calm down.

I can't calm down, not before I give up what I'm feeling. "No remorse means disrespect and disrespect means it's gonna happen again."

She backs down and just listens.

I calm a little. "I have a lot invested. Too much. I'm losing it all, just like that."

"You gonna cry?"

"Yeah." That expressive Pisces part of me is in an internal battle; the emotional part wants me to shed enough eye-water to drown this city. I shake my head, "No."

"You need to."

I wave at a reporter as she hurries into the building. "Not right now."

"The stress . . . it's in your face."

"The city's on fire and I'm in a house that's burning down."

"Freckles—"

"Go on and go in before Tyra sends a lynch mob after you."

"Not without you. Can't believe you got with her husband. Why?"

"I think . . . and this is crazy . . . part of me wanted Jessica to walk in. Wanted to hurt her. Wanted to drive that bitch crazy. Wanted to fight her. Wanted to . . ." I pause and remember how that gun felt in my hands. "Wanted to do all kinds of things."

"That's not the way you do it."

And I think of David Lawrence's mom, incarcerated while her cheating husband drives up and down Route 13.

I say, "I know."

Her eyes tell me that she hears me, understands me, but doesn't agree with me, not at all. Her deep sigh is a serious song saying that I'm putting myself in a dangerous situation.

She says, "Let's walk."

I follow her. We pass by the guard's gate, wave, and keep moving across Willoughby into the single-family homes that lead into the geeks-and-freaks section on Melrose.

I motion at a billboard that's high on La Brea. It's super-sized with two actors and an actress from the sitcom *Scrubs*. I read the sign and nudge my friend. "Got Milk?"

"Not another one." Yvette's eyes follow mine to that billboard. "Is it just me or do those 'Got Milk?' ads look like they just gave somebody a serious blow job?"

We stare at the way the milk sits on those two actors and

that smiling actress's top lips. We crack up. Yvette makes me laugh when I want to cry. Everyone needs a friend like her.

I say, "Yuck. That does look pornographic."

"Makes the men look gay and the women look . . . downright nasty."

We walk some more, stay on the side of the street with the most shade. Cars are zipping up and down the narrow side street, a tree-lined area with restricted parking for residents only. After she eases me with laughter, she gives me silence. I fall inside myself and think.

She checks her watch. I do the same. We know Tyra is waiting. Her game is to rush us, ours is to not be rushed, to maintain control.

I ask, "Think I was crying out for help last night?"

"Screaming like an old woman does when you step on her corns." She shakes her head. "You should've called me. When shit gets like that, we have to call each other."

We walk parts of the sidewalk that are uneven and rising as either the aftermath of earthquakes, or trees growing and the roots causing the cement to buckle. We're shoulder-to-shoulder and silent, like two inseparable elementary school girls.

I ask, "When you did the creep-creep on your lovers, what was that about?"

"I didn't trust them anymore, didn't feel secure, wasn't anchored to the relationship, or was anchored to somebody I didn't trust and wanted to be unanchored."

I bite my bottom lip. "Anybody ever find out?"

"Only one guy did. This guy I was mad in love with, I told him just to spite him."

"And?"

"He went insane. Broke into my apartment. That immature troglodyte was drunk as a skunk. I mean, he had lost his mind. Kicked my television over. Slapped me around. Was dragging me down the hall by my hair and screaming 'how can you let another nigga penetrate you, how could you let him put his dick in you and invade my property with his sperm?' "

"You gotta be joking."

"Thank God I had that Jheri-Curl and he couldn't get a good grip on my greasy hair."

"Guess that Curl was your first line of defense."

"Then he wanted to fuck me."

"You're joking."

"No joke. He kicked my ass and got a hard-on."

"He wanted to have sex with you?"

"It's about power, not sex."

I stop walking. "He raped you?"

"He was too drunk. He got it up, but I wouldn't let him get it in."

"Damn, Yvette."

"I was so scared."

Her pager goes off. She checks it, frowns, then looks at her watch again. Then my pager goes off. We both turn around and we head back, moving a little faster.

I say, "Pavlov rules."

"You know it. Damn electronic leashes."

"Finish your story."

"Anyway, I got away and locked myself in the bathroom. Called me all kinda whores, screaming at me like he didn't have nothing to do with it. One minute his drunk ass was crying and telling me how much he loved me, how he wanted to marry me, wanted me to have his babies, then the next he was screaming that I made him do it all. Made him break in, made him jump on me, just kept kicking the door and going off on me."

"Sounds like that psycho had a chemical imbalance."

"Couldn't say nothing to make his ass calm down and leave."

"How long did that go on?"

"Hours. He didn't leave until the next afternoon. When I came out, he had trashed my place. Punched holes in every wall. Broke every picture."

I say, "I understand."

"Do you?"

"You're schooling me on the down low."

She repeats, "Ain't no forgiveness for women. Men do that shit, and start all over, get reelected, pedophiles put back in the pulpit, while we get shackled to our reputations."

"Still amazes me how men expect us to get over it, then they fall apart."

"A lot of these educated fools still have that Nigerian Muslim attitude. They want to sentence you to death for creeping, but they ain't criminals, haven't committed a crime."

I say, "The wacko who attacked you, he was the only one you tipped out on?"

"Oh, please." She chuckles. "C'mon, now. You know it's all part of the game."

"I was out of the game."

"You're never out of the game. That's why the Golden Rule always applies."

I say, "You're only as faithful—"

"As the man I'm seeing."

I smile a little. "That should be on a T-shirt."

"Print 'em up and I'll stand on Crenshaw selling 'em for fifteen a pop."

"Buy three, get a free bean pie."

"Now you're thinking."

I ask, "What about your Eritrean lover?"

Yvette sighs. "He's cool, but he's young."

"Uh-huh. What he do?"

"Had the nerve to ask me how many partners I've had."

We laugh.

I ask, "And you said . . . ?"

"Luckily he asked me about the men here in Los Angeles."

The way she says that makes me laugh again, this time much harder.

She says, "I do a state-to-state rule; I'm a born-again virgin once I cross state lines."

"Cool rule."

"Made that rule up when I was in college. Trips to Atlanta, Tampa, New York, sex on an island, or on a weekend ski trip, hooking up with an ex on vacation—none of that ever counts."

We high-five that rule. She amazes me every time I see her, always makes me feel better.

Yvette catches her breath before she goes on. "I mean, if a lover ain't all that, I shouldn't have to take credit for a bad performance."

"Oh, hell no."

"Bad sex is a candidate for selective memory. It just didn't happen."

Another high-five.

She says, "And if I didn't come, that can't count."

"Oh, hell no. No way."

"If the need was not met, then the action did not take place."

Double high-five on that one.

I say, "You have some good points."

"If I didn't come, it wasn't sex." She says that and smiles at her own words.

"That should be on a T-shirt too."

"Hell, no. That should be on a blimp."

We pass by the guard shack again, this time cackling like teenagers, wave again, and head back over near our cars. Again I think I see Tyra at the door, but I don't look that way, refuse to give her the attention she's demanding. My girl looks at her watch, and I do the same, the laughter eases up, stress lines grow in her face, my expression mirroring hers.

"Freckles . . . ?"

She says my name with concern. Work isn't the alpha and omega of her world.

I ask, "What?"

"That David Lawrence guy . . . ?"

"What about him?"

"You use a condom?"

"Of course."

"Just want you to be safe. Charles already has you at risk."

"Trying not to think about that."

She's a true friend and it hurts me to lie to her, but I feel like I have to.

She asks, "Last night . . . you come?"

"Oh, God. He was a pussy-eating king."

"He ate you out, just like that?"

Again, flashbacks make electrical tingles run through me. I smell him. Feel his echo. The sex, it sings. The primal chants. The oblivion. That animalistic state we were in.

I say, "Yeah. I came. So it counts."

"It amazes me how some of these brothers will just stick

their faces in the coochie without knowing you from Summer's Eve, and do it without a second thought."

Charles is a Libra and owns a pretty strong sex drive. I know him. He had to be the same way with Jessica, as intense and as enthusiastic as he was the first time he was invited into my body. Eating her out like she was the buffet of the week, impressing her with his moves, then coming home and kissing me, giving me Jessica's essence with a smile, holding me while her fingerprints stained his body, her invisible paint all over his flesh.

I wonder how they fucked. If they were as primal as those IMs make them sound.

That porno plays before my eyes, Jessica's name in bright lights; her dark face with the slanted eyes, that image becomes the lead actress in an endless triple-X movie. I make it vulgar. Make her the queen of whores. I can't bring myself to romanticize and give any meaning to their trysts, can't think of what they did as making love, no matter how many times they did it. Have to keep it at a rude and rudimentary level.

Yvette and I make a loop around the building.

She asks, "Was he a decent lover?"

"He was a PEK."

"Okay, could he work it?"

"Oh, yeah. He has that tongue-vibrating thing down to a science."

But David Lawrence, despite my scrubbing myself with my own soap, moisturizing my flesh with my own lotion, covering myself with my own perfume, his scent remains on my skin. I feel his girth inside my body. His rhythm lives. That drumbeat refuses to die down. My mind makes me cling to him as if he's the only thing that keeps me from going insane.

And I know that Jessica's scent lives on Charles's skin,

seeps into his pores. She's part of him for eternity. In a flash I think of all the days and nights I've tried to please him, made my body available to him as an offering of more than sex, but as love, as my gift to him, as his friend, as his wife, and yet all I've done hasn't been enough. He blames it all on me.

"I told Charles that . . ." My words fade as I try to think of the right word to use. I remain honest with myself. "Told 'im I fucked somebody last night."

"*No you didn't*. You're joking, right?"

I tell her that I was so pissed that I told Charles I'd had an affair, but didn't tell him with whom, and that drove him insane. I tell her how he was tripping, then breaking down, then asking to work things out, then how I thought he was about to kick my ass, then he was down in the garage for over an hour, rocking the house and trying to destroy that boxing bag.

She snaps at me, asks me why I did such a stupid thing.

I confess, "And look . . . okay . . . I didn't use a condom."

"Shit. What were you thinking?"

"It just sorta went down, you know?"

"No, I don't know. How could you not protect yourself?"

I have no real answer. All I can tell her is that I don't want a lecture, don't want her to make me feel bad, or stupid. But Yvette is Yvette and she does lecture, she does make me feel bad. I have no answer. Sensibility flew out of the window and I got caught up. Again I feel like a criminal for lying to her. A new guilt shows on my face. I feel like I've committed another transgression and now I have to confess to feel better, need her to give me atonement.

"You're out of control." Her words are firm. "Stay with me until . . . until."

"I'm not abandoning my home because he fucked some bitch."

"Freckles—"

"No."

She reminds me that she speaks from experience, and those memories put some tremble in her voice, some fear in my heart. She holds my shoulders, looks me in the eyes, and sounds tense and firm, scared and concerned when she rants on and says other things.

We open the door and step inside. The temperature drops, becomes a new season just that quick. Tyra waits down at the end of the hallway. Her expression chills me even more, consumes the last of my warmth. She shakes her head, walks away, both hands in fists.

Yvette says, "Looks like she's gonna give you the silent treatment."

"Whatever."

Already I'm freezing. Televisions are on all over the place, monitoring news on other stations as well as ours. Some are on *The Steve Harvey Show* and other sitcoms; at least one is on MTV, another on BET. And with all the equipment in both the offices and the control room, the place has to stay cold as a morgue to keep all of that high-tech crap from malfunctioning.

My cell phone rings. It's Charles. My heart wants me to, but I don't answer.

I get to my doorless office, to my secondhand desk that sits in a field of open desks that yield no privacy, open my purse, take out two Tylenol, and pop them without water. They go down rough, but they go down. Yvette stops by her desk for a hot second, then takes her sweet and sensuous sashay toward her editing world, her saunter and charisma lighting up the warehouse. Black, white, Latin, or Asian, everyone stops and smiles at her. They all love her.

Tyra passes by, shrieking and screaming at a co–executive producer, a tall, bony, bearded, Pee-wee Herman–looking guy who dresses nice and has some switch in his stooped walk.

I check with the assignment people and they give me the rundown on all the breaking news, then check the wires to see what's up in the country and the rest of the world so I can step into the meeting with confidence and knowledge. Can't sit in a meeting as a producer and have no clue what they're talking about. Today it feels as if my job is on the line.

First chance I get, I stick my head into Yvette's editing world. She's working her ass off and bumping *Nellyville*, adding some funky tracks to a hip-hop segment on the dance called the Crip Walk being banned at Crenshaw, Manual Arts, and Washington Preparatory high schools.

She speaks with sarcasm. "Real important stuff. Skip Africa and go for the Crip Walk."

We talk about another package on the man who killed his coworker this morning, try to see how we can pump it up and make it more sensational than it already is.

She says, "He only killed one person. Same race. That's not news."

"That's your final answer?"

"That came straight from Tyra. It'll be a filler."

When we're done with the business, she says, "One more thing, Freckles."

" 'Sup?"

"You're vulnerable. Love and hate are so intense, make you lose sight of who you are."

"I understand."

"Keep away from that PEK."

Her words are strong, and like a mother, she sees right through me. I leave.

Again, Charles calls.

I wait until the last ring, then I answer. His mood is different, no longer arrogant.

He asks, "Can we meet for lunch?"

"No."

That slows his roll.

"You coming home tonight?"

"Don't know."

He sounds depressed, as if he's not sure what to say, or how to talk to me. Like a stranger.

He asks, "This guy . . . was it somebody you used to go out with?"

"Why?"

"Are you planning to see him again?"

"Is that your only concern? Is that what got your attention?"

"Are you?"

"You violated the covenant first, Charles."

I hang up. My lip trembles. He calls again. He's irritating me to the max.

I say, "Stop calling me."

"I need to talk to you."

"I'm working. Don't do this to me at work."

"Always your job, right?"

"What didn't I do for you?"

"Your job is more important right now, huh?"

Guilt hugs me, won't let me go. I think about his eye, those shades of blues and blackness, that redness from it becoming bloodshot.

I ask, "How's your eye?"

"It's okay."

"He got in a lucky blow, huh?"

That bothers him. He makes a sound that is a mixture of pisstivity and irritation.

I say, "Take Tylenol. Ice it. And beating up that bag ain't gonna help."

"How you doing?"

"How the hell do you think I'm doing, Charles?" I catch myself. "Trying not to have a fucking breakdown, that's how I'm doing. And you know what, if it wasn't for my job, the way I can maintain, if I didn't know how to be a coldhearted bitch—"

"I didn't say—"

"That was how you described me. That's why you betrayed me with Jessica, right? Because she's so damn sensitive. Because she doesn't complain and make your head hurt."

"Baby, you don't—"

"After all that, why would you want to be with a bitch like me? Why would you want me when everything you said in the e-mails tells me that Jessica is the better woman for you?"

"Those . . . those were just words."

"*Your* words."

"I'm sorry. I fucked up. Look . . . listen . . . I'm . . . What else can I say?"

My breathing shallows. I peep around to see if people see me losing it. A couple of people are at their desks, on computers, on the phone, all watching me. I turn my back to them.

"I gotta go, Charles."

"Wait—"

"What, *Francis*? What what what, *Francis*? What do you want, *Francis*?"

That shuts him down.

I say, "My car is jacked up. My neck hurts. Stomach is upset. My leg has a big bruise on it. My husband is cheating. And my heart is broken. That's how I'm doing, Charles."

He says nothing.

I ask, "And how are you?"

"Look, I'm sorry for the things I said."

"It was your truth. Don't deny it." My voice returns to calmness. Another part of me reminds me that he is still my husband, and I'm still his wife. I say, "Put some ice on your eye. Food is in the fridge. Make sure you eat. You know how your head hurts when you don't eat. And make sure there aren't any clothes in the dryer that need folding."

I hang up. The phone rings again. Emotions swell and I hurry away from that chime, keep my eyes down and pretend I'm busy reading notes on a clipboard and slip away to the green room, make it there before I have a huge emotional breakdown in front of everybody, struggle to lock the door, then fight to pull myself together, wipe away a million tears.

A while goes by before I regroup and tip out to the bathroom, wash my face, then, as I redo my lipstick, stare at the woman in the mirror. The image startles me. Her freckles beg her to smile. She does, but her red-rimmed eyes reveal the wounded soul within.

I step into the control room and someone says, "You look really tired."

"I'm okay."

"What's the matter?"

"Nothing. Stop sweating me."

"My bad. Somebody needs to pop a Midol."

"Throw her some raw meat."

Laughter at my expense as I flip them off.

I have to get back to working. No matter where I go, people keep asking me if I'm okay, and I blame my sniffles and rosy cheeks on my allergies, try to laugh it off, then keep moving. Have to keep moving, stay busy, go into overachiever mode and become superwoman.

Over and over I pass Tyra in the hallway. All evening she does her best to kill me with silence. I put a story on her desk; two minutes later it's back on mine, mutilated and redlined to death. I make changes and put the story back on her desk. Again it ends up on mine, redlined top to bottom. She fucks with me all evening. I can't do anything right by her today, not one thing. She has that quavering air of superiority, moves as if this place is Asgard and she is a female Odin. The last time we pass in the narrow hallway, she's munching on fries in a super-size McDonald's box. We slow and give each other contemptuous eyes, but no one says a word. Whenever we're near, the building closes in on us, becomes a square boxing ring.

I have a million things to keep me distracted. Including a ton of voice-mail messages that came in after I left yesterday. Most of them are from Charles. Each time I hear his voice I make grunts that sound like *fuck you* and *I'm disappointed* and *you're so pathetic*. I don't listen to his words, just push "save" as soon as I hear his voice. I want to delete his messages, but I'm not there, not ready to purge him. I want him to keep calling.

One is from David Lawrence. My sinner in bohemian clothing. His voice invades my senses; first a chill runs over me, then fire creeps up and down my spine.

I swallow and close my eyes. If we did it once, it's the same as doing it a hundred times.

David Lawrence says, "I was served with divorce papers this morning. The money in my accounts is looking funny. Check yours. And I think your husband filed assault charges. We were man-to-man in that fight. That's punk of him."

My headache deepens.

His voice softens. "Call me."

I hang up, hesitate for a moment, and then I return David Lawrence's call. He's not there. I'm relieved. Want to talk to him and don't want to talk to him. I leave a message, my words jittery, businesslike, and brief. I tell him thanks for the information, but don't ask him to return my call. I call Wells Fargo. Check the balance in all of our accounts. All of our money is still there. The balance is off by a few dollars, but not enough to worry about. I'm not the best at balancing the books.

Then my office phone rings and I answer, asking, "Who's calling?"

He says, "It's Mister Irrrrr-eeeeeee-tating."

It's David Lawrence. He actually laughs.

He asks, "Remember that?"

I groan. "I was really sort of drunk the other night."

"Sort of?"

"I'm feeling really embarrassed over here."

He asks, "How you feeling today?"

"Stressed."

"I got something you can do."

"Uh-huh."

"Close your eyes for a minute—"

"Uh-huh."

"Remember Popsicles, lemonade, and running through sprinklers."

I smile and fall into memories of being a little girl in North

Cakalaki. Being a kid with kid concerns, long before life plagued me with grown-up problems.

He tells me, "I read the . . . don't know what to call the papers you left here on the futon."

"Those were . . . are a copy of my questions, the ones I gave to my husband."

"You want to know a lot."

"You should want to know the same."

Then he gets quiet.

I say, "Hello?"

"I'm here."

" 'Sup?"

He says, "First, about last night. We should talk about that."

I pause. We're serious now. I say, "Go ahead."

"Don't really have any idea what to say."

"That wasn't the real me, you know."

"It's okay. Just say what you want to say."

"No, you first. I'm surrounded by people, so it's easier for me to listen right now."

"You got the message, so you know my situation."

I ask, "Divorce papers?"

"Process server came by at the crack of dawn."

I shrug. "Sorry to hear that."

"Our wedding anniversary is this weekend."

"That's . . . Damn. How many years?"

"Three."

"Wow."

"Some anniversary present, huh?"

"Seen her?"

"Nope. Think she's hiding out in Palm Springs. She has family out there."

"She hasn't been back home?"

"As far as I'm concerned, she has no home. Not with me. I went by the house and changed the locks and the code to the alarm. She can't get in."

"Wow. Three years. I'm on my fourth."

"Yep. She tried to drain the accounts, and made plans to run off with your husband."

That annoys me. I say, "Charles didn't quit, or move money. Never packed a bag."

"You sure?"

"My money is fine."

"What he say?"

"Charles admitted the affair, to a certain extent—"

"Before or after you showed him the IMs?"

"Little of both. But said he wasn't leaving, not in the way Jessica told you."

Yvette passes by, in a deep conversation with another segment producer about a package. She doesn't see me, but her presence makes me conscious of what I'm doing. I pick up a pen and a notepad, furrow my brow, pretend I'm scribbling down important information.

"There any way I can see you?" he asks.

"For what?"

"To talk, face-to-face."

"Not a good idea. We already need to yell ten Our Fathers and ten Hail Marys, murmur an absolution, and get dismissed with a reminder to love God and sin no more."

"You're right."

"Wait." I suck my top lip. "There's a place near here. The Hot Wings Café."

"Okay."

"I might be able to meet you for a few minutes at sunset."

"But you're not sure?"

I ask him to hold on when a writer comes to my desk to ask me about a story on the high suicide rate in prisons. Before I get done with that issue, someone else needs me to answer a few questions. It takes me a couple of minutes to get back to my call.

I apologize for leaving him on hold. "It's crazy around here."

"What time at the Hot Wings Café?"

"Let's scratch that idea. Too many people from here eat over there."

"That would be a problem?"

"I wouldn't feel . . . It'd be a problem. Wait, it wouldn't be a problem. We can meet over there. No, over on Melrose at Jamba Juice. No, up at the Beverly Center . . . Damn, let me think."

"Where's your sax?"

"Huh? What about sex?"

"Sax. S-a-x. Your horn."

"Oh. Uh. In my car."

"I wanna hear what kinda music a floor-sanding sorority gal from a marching band at Johnson College in North Carolina plays on her alto saxophone."

He remembers most everything about me. Forty-eight hours ago I didn't know he existed. Twenty-four hours ago I hated him. Now, I'm worn and he's making me smile.

I reply, "Can't be any worse than that country-western crap you listen to."

He laughs at my attempts at humor. His tone gets an unexpected smile out of me.

He says, "I listen to a few, but Tim McGraw is the only one I dig enough to buy."

"Sure, I'll drag you away from listening to the white man's blues and studying about the deconstructionist bowel movement and school you on some Kim Waters, give you some jazz."

"Deconstructionist bowel movement?" He laughs harder. "Come see me tonight."

"That will be . . . late. You know, close to midnight."

"About the same time you came by last night."

With an innocent tone, he puts his desire to continue his vengeance out there. His soft voice makes my vagina moan. I'm not breathing, holding the phone and remembering last night.

I say, "If I come by, well, I need to get a copy of that software you have on your computer. Want to put it on my computer at home."

"Think he might have other women?"

"Have no idea. No idea at all."

"Come get it."

I say, "If I come—let's get this out in the open—all I want is the software, so don't expect anything from me but music. I'll stay a minute, long enough to play a couple of songs."

"Long enough for herbal tea, a little music, and a short conversation?"

"What do we have to talk about?"

"We'll play it by ear."

I rub my temples, cross my feet at the ankles, and squeeze my thighs. I remind him, remind myself, "All we have in common is our spouses' infidelities."

"Pretty much."

"God. How did we end up here?"

"Infidelity spawns infidelity."

Silence.

I say, "You were hurt. I was hurt. We were in pain. We comforted each other."

"How you feeling right now?"

"At this moment?"

"Yeah."

"If I was to go to church right now, the building would probably crumble."

I stare at my wedding ring, remember a white dress and black tuxedo, honeymoon in Maui, vacations to Florida, ski trips to Canada, laughter and smiles and promises. A picture of Charles sits next to my computer. Cherubs and photos of my man and me are in my face.

I tell him, "One phone call, and you changed my life forever."

"Your husband changed mine."

"No, your wife changed yours. She made herself available."

"What's your husband's excuse?"

"I'm not making excuses for him."

"He touched my wife every chance he could get."

"Read those IMs again. Your wife opened her legs anywhere she could."

"Yeah, she did."

"You're the one who found a condom wrapper in her ride."

"I guess a man can only do what a woman lets him."

We hold the phone.

Bad news is blooming. Everybody's going off the deep end; screaming hollering yelling cussing, and right now the station is demanding my full attention.

David Lawrence breathes slow and easy. I have flashbacks, his breath and anger on my skin. I want him to say good-bye, because I don't know how to end our conversation.

He hangs up.

I sit, holding the phone, my mind muting out all of the screaming hollering yelling and cussing. I'm remembering North Carolina. Growing up on Rosedale Avenue. Walking through Forrest Hills. Seeing a house with large glass windows. That was my dream home.

I'm remembering Popsicles, lemonade, running through sprinklers.

14

I have extra clothes in my Mustang, so I choose to crash at Yvette's.

We get to her place and we're both wide awake and restless. Dealing with Tyra the Tyrant and Charles has left me stressed out to the max and I could use a nice glass of wine, but I don't want to have another claustrophobic pity party, so we hop in my Baby Blue and go for a ride. I cruise Ventura Boulevard, pass by Jinky's Café, Baja Grill, and a million side-walk eateries. When I cross the 405, she tells me to keep going toward Encino. She tells me to make a few quick turns and we end up cruising through a high-end residential neighborhood.

I ask, "Where we going?"

"Houghmagandy."

"What's that?"

She tells me that Houghmagandy is the unwritten name of the swingers' joint. Its name comes from an old Scottish word that means fornication. And they practice houghmagandy here with no boundaries. The house is on a side street that runs parallel to the 101 freeway. A nice-sized home in the middle of a residential neighborhood, stunning topography, hidden in plain sight. Everyone parks two blocks away, then walks down. There's a short, thin, clean-cut man at the gate. He's hardly big enough to be a bouncer at a kiddie party. He smiles, asks us who we're looking for. Yvette says the magic word and he opens the iron gate and lets us in.

Yvette looks at me and says, "Relax."

"What if we see somebody who knows us?"

"Well, they're up in here too."

We walk underneath palm trees, across a lot, and step into a house filled with thirsty souls searching for satisfaction, willing to drink from any pool.

People are wandering through the house like vampires in search of blood. One sister has on a long leather coat, wide open, and all she wears underneath is a leather thong and bra, knee boots, and Mickey Mouse ears that have "Disney World" stitched across the front.

She stops next to me and talks like she knows me. "I got a man who I'm not sure about."

"Huh?"

She repeats herself.

I play along. "What's the problem?"

"I know he likes to fuck, but I don't think he's as open as I am."

"Uh-huh."

She adjusts her Mickey Mouse ears. "I like to be talked to like a porn star, and he doesn't do that."

"Too bad."

"But that's what happens when you marry a minister."

"I guess."

She smiles. "You're cute."

"Thanks."

A guy passes by with a bowl of condoms, reminding me of

the peanut vendor at Dodger Stadium. His bowl is filled with all kinds and all flavors of protection.

"Relationships are hard," the woman with the Mickey Mouse ears says, just when I think she's done. "It's a full-time job, and we ought to treat it like one."

"What you mean?"

"If your lover wants to bounce, they should give you two weeks' notice. And severance pay. And before they go, they should have to find you a temp."

We laugh a little. But I'm laughing at her, not with her.

She smiles. "You wanna do something?"

"No thank you."

She makes a disappointed face—the kind a brother makes when he asks you to dance and you turn him down—then she smiles over at Yvette. "What about you?"

"Strictly dickly, Minnie Mouse. Catch me next lifetime."

She frowns and walks away, adjusting those ears.

I say, "Geesh. Talk about a few loose screws."

"She was a little Ya Ya in the Sisterhood department."

A brother walks in and worms himself into a conversation with Yvette. The men around here waste no time. I listen to him try to feel her out. He was born in Nigeria, then went back to Ghana, then to Botswana, has been in this country for thirteen years, and is leaving soon to work on his master's somewhere overseas. He's intelligent and has her ear. Around us, the big screen has on a hardcore XXX movie and Yvette and the guy are talking about how beautiful Botswana is, about Zimbabwe, about Namibia being off the hook, while moans and grunts fill the air.

She asks, "What do you know about the Eritrean-Ethiopian conflict?"

I leave them chatting and go to the kitchen. There's a

crowd there too. I go through the refrigerator like I'm at home, eat some chips, then pour myself a glass of Riesling.

A bowlegged, handsome golden guy walks in sporting jeans and a Kentucky sweatshirt. He's a six-footer, clean shaven, built like an oak tree. He makes his way over to me and starts a conversation, very polite and gentleman-like, but still coming at me hard. He tells me that he is originally from New Zealand and is an undercover drug enforcement agent.

I say, "I always thought you were supposed to be under-cover, not getting under the covers."

He laughs.

I ask him about his wedding ring. Without hesitation he admits that he's married, about six months into his vows. He asks me about mine. I tell him I've been married for four years.

He asks, "How's it going?"

"It's going."

He asks, "You wanna do something?"

"No thanks."

He shakes my hand and walks around checking out the rest of the swingers, then gets into a conversation with a Latin lady. She's wearing a blue and white schoolgirl uniform, suck-ing on a lollipop, and carrying a small whip.

I people watch for ten or fifteen minutes. Lots of new faces are coming in. Lots of people are walking by sipping on beers, eating chips. At least two girls look like they're barely out of high school. The men gravitate toward their apparent youth and assumed inexperience; follow their blond hair and blue eyes from room to room.

A lot of people partner up and vanish to all parts of the house, and I don't see Yvette. I get worried. Hoping she hasn't been kidnapped and turned into a sex slave. I quicken my stride and walk from room to room, from session to session, and finally find Yvette standing around the fireplace in the master bedroom, watching the show. My heart rate slows when I find her. I pretend all I see is no big deal. We stand in the thick of the crowd, hold our drinks, and watch the DEA have sex with six enthusiastic ladies, all of them looking high-rent and educated, like doctors and university professors. The DEA is putting on a show, sometimes working with two of them at a time.

"Uh-huh," Yvette says. "Now, dat's what I'm tawkn' 'bout."

I say, "For real tho."

The DEA smiles at me, a stimulating lover who gives them orgasm after orgasm. One by one, they gather their clothes and stagger away in post-coital bliss.

Me and my girl walk around after that. I'm tingling. Moist.

The environment is mixed, no low-rent people in sight, mainly upper-middle-class people of European pedigree, ages from twenty-one to about sixty.

Yvette says, "Let me know when you're ready to bounce."

"Let's look around and then we'll raise up out of here."

We float from room to room, then drift outside, hunting for the best action to watch. Fellatio and cunnilingus is in full swing at poolside, but it's boring to watch. At least that's what I tell Yvette, but she wants to stay. We blend in with the elite audience of intellectual and unemotional connoisseurs. One guy is attentive, his wife's mouth is open, breathing ragged, face tense like she's about to scream, moaning and orgasming in a tone that sends chills up my vagina. Her husband is so into pleasing her. For a moment, I'm her and he's my faithful lover.

Maybe Charles wasn't into me sexually anymore. Maybe he was pity-fucking me.

There were times I needed him so bad, he was sleeping, and I'd cry myself to sleep. Just wanted to be the best of everything to him. His lover. His wife. Wanted to have his children. As many as he wanted. I gave 400 percent of myself and still came in in second place.

Yvette taps my shoulder. "You okay?"

"Yeah."

We move by those writhing people and go to the guest house. All the rooms have doors. The shy people are out there. We can hear them moaning through the thin walls.

There are a lot of different rooms. Some with open doors. One candlelit area has a large bed that has a rainbow coalition of people on it. In another room with soft lighting, it looks like a butt-naked sorority meeting. Women are pleasing and touching women. It's not my flavor, but it's more sensuous. We watch them too. The minister's wife with the Mickey Mouse ears is the best carpet muncher in the bunch. She has the room hot enough to get third-degree burns.

For an hour I wander and watch people in search of carnal knowledge work it out, walk from room to room the way a person tours a museum.

It's a major turn-on. But it's sad too.

There is no love in this house. And without love, sex is violence.

We head back through the main house.

The DEA traces his lips with his tongue, then smiles at me as we keep going toward the door, stops me long enough to take my hand and say he hopes to see me again.

I take my hand away from him and ask, "Is it that easy?"

"What you mean?"

I point at his wedding ring.

He says, "Stay awhile."

"What for?"

He laughs the laugh of the world's greatest lover.

I wave my ring finger as my answer. I ask, "Your wife know where you are?"

He answers with another laugh. The DEA tells me bye-bye and heads back inside.

I wave good-bye to the crowd of sex athletes and hedonists and head away, sashay out into palm trees and darkness, Yvette right behind me sipping on bottled water.

I leave, tingling to the point of aching.

I tug at my locks as I drive us into the night, top down, crisp air cooling us down.

Yvette says, "You're quiet."

"Thinking."

"What?"

"Wild. All the men up in there with wedding rings on . . ."

Yvette says, "A man's need to come takes over. That's the bottom line."

I ask, "What's the women's excuse?"

"They get to dominate. They pick. They get to be love goddesses."

I hum out a curious sound. "And people have no idea these places exist."

"People know. They're in every city. I went to a private club in Charlotte."

"Whoa. You went to my old stomping ground and didn't tell me?"

"Thought I did."

"I would remember that."

"Actually it was outside of Charlotte in Fort Mill. Drove over there from Atlanta."

"When was that?"

"Back when Miss North Carolina gave up her title because of those naked pictures."

"I pulled that story off the wire. That wasn't that long ago."

"Me and a friend stayed in downtown Charlotte at the Adams Mark, hit the poetry at Club Aqua, partied at CJ's, then the next night we hit the private spot in Fort Mill."

"Fort Mill ain't even on a map."

"Hadn't ever heard of it."

"How'd you find out about it?"

"On the Internet."

"Are you serious?"

"They have a Web page."

"Damn."

I let my left hand dance in the wind as I drive in the crazy traffic on Ventura Boulevard. Bright lights and plenty of people are still out on the strip. Bottom feeders in search of pleasure.

"C'mon, 'fess up." Yvette laughs. "You was digging Houghmagandy."

"Yeah. But I was kinda disappointed."

"What up?"

"Most of the guys . . . they weren't that cute, and they were, you know, regular sized. And they didn't really do nothing impressive. No foreplay. No after play. Nothing sensual."

"No pretense, Freckles."

"No deep and slow kisses. No romance. I wanted to see romance."

I drive toward Studio City. All the shops are closed and the Jerry's Deli down this way has burned down. The closest JD is a nice drive from here. We're hungry, but we decide that we aren't in the mood for JD tonight. L.A. is a county that loves to sleep. My cell phone rings. My home number glows on the caller ID. It's Charles, wondering if I'm coming home. I don't answer, just cut the phone off. Our last conversation left me too spent.

Yvette asks, "How was it when you were watching me and TJ?"

"What?"

"I know you saw us."

"You saw me?"

"Yeah. Saw you stumbling and staggering around the kitchen."

"Was . . . uh . . . was that intentional?"

"Don't flatter yourself. No, but after I saw you . . ."

"TJ saw me?"

"He never said, but his rhythm changed for a sec. Couldn't help hearing you on the phone, trying to whisper and arguing. Drunk people always whisper louder than they talk."

"Damn. He has to think I'm a dingbat, an alcoholic, and a Peeping Tom."

"It charged us up. Took it to another level."

"Yeah?" Vague images come to mind. Me stumbling toward her door. Seeing them in the bedroom. The expression on Yvette's face. "From what I remember, he was working it."

"Truthfully, he ain't that big in that department, but I like the guy, so it's satisfying, the way he makes me feel. He's real gentle when he needs to be, rough when I want him to be. When it comes to that, he's a good listener. A damn good student. Straight As."

"Then why don't you just stick with him?"

"We've only hooked up twice."

"Then kick it with him and see what's up."

She shakes her head. "The Law of Diminishing Return."

"What that mean?"

"It's my take on an econ theory."

"And it means . . . ?"

"The more often we experience something, the less effect it has. If a man sleeps with you a lot, it loses its value, he gets tired of the same old bump and grind, wants new pussy."

"I don't think that law applies to sex."

She says, "It does."

"Doesn't."

"Why do men cheat, when they already have a willing partner at home?"

I answer, "Opportunistic."

"Why do some women get their freak on, on the down low, when they have a man?"

"Emotional void."

"You need to come off that idiotic crap. Be real. If you ask me—"

I cut her off, "And I didn't."

"The excitement of the unknown hypes it up. Doing wrong is a turn-on. Hell, the sister can be a beautiful Oscar winner, and she still has the same problems as a butt-ugly mud duck."

"The Law of Diminishing Return."

"Creates a very vicious cycle."

I ask, "Where do you come up with this mess?"

"I'm a thinking woman's thinking woman."

"You really need to come off that Oprah crap."

"No, serious. I understand men better than most women. The way they really are, as opposed to how we would like 'em to be. Read all the books you want. Go to all the seminars. Face it. We can't change 'em. They can't change us. Let them be them and keep it real."

"Do you?"

"Like Charles . . ."

She speaks his name and I cringe. "Don't go there."

She goes on, "You give him everything—"

"I show him my love."

"—and it wasn't enough."

"You can stop reminding me anytime you're ready."

"No, let's talk. You cook for Charles."

"Out of love, not servitude. And I love to cook."

"You clean."

"Out. Of. Love."

"He can hit it when he wants it."

"We're married. I get just as much out of it as he does. Hell, I get more."

"It's too available. Available has no value. Available gets boring."

"Yvette—"

"That's why even great sex gets predictable and it's easy for him to turn you down."

"That's some lonely, single-woman bull if ever I heard it."

"I'm just the messenger, don't hate on me. I mean, I know it's a dichotomy, because I've been married, I've been where you are, and you're in the right, that's what you're supposed to do, and you get burned for it. You were doing what you were supposed to do, loving him."

"And there was no pretense. That's just who I am. I'm not like you."

"You think I'm into pretense?"

"You know what I mean."

Pisces rises and anger rules my tone. That heats her Gemini blood and shuts her down. I drive in silence for a couple of lights. Yvette hums and plays with the wind. She knows I want her to say something, but she keeps quiet. She knows I can't stay mad at her. She says she's a realist, but I think she's a frustrated idealist, frustrated because she knows that idealism sucks. In her own heavy-handed, keep-it-real way, she's always trying to educate me. She has a huge heart, wants the world to be perfect, but she knows it isn't and has grown to accept it the way it is. She recognizes the passions and the sins, acknowledges the madness and dreams of the human heart, and she lets them be. Day after day my girl sees the same idiocy, hypocrisy, and brutality I see, and we don't try to change what can't be changed. I love her because she's pure.

"I know what I'm talking about, Freckles." Her voice is curt. She's emotional. I can tell because her 'Bama accent always flares up when she's pissed off. "That's why every relationship I've been in, the first kiss was just the beginning of a long good-bye."

"I don't like you saying that."

"The thing about dating in L.A. is that you're always breaking up with somebody. Always between relationships. Even when you're in a relationship, you're between relationships."

"You're so damn cynical."

"I don't like it either. But when you're single again and again, those are the facts."

"You happy?"

"I'm happy." She laughs a little. "I'm happy with my sex life."

"I mean with your whole life. More to life than sex."

"I have my freedom. I can go out to eat, if that's what I

want. Or go to a play. And for the most part, I enjoy my own company. I'm out of that codependent phase."

"Are you happy?"

"I answer to no man. I'm on hiatus and I can have fun on any playground I choose. I can explore the things that being in a committed relationship keeps a woman from doing."

"Is that what I have to look forward to over the next five years?"

"That and more frequent rectal exams. Pills that won't kill the monster cramps. Fibroids. Reflexology won't work and Midol will be a joke. Oh, yeah, it's gonna be a blast."

But I'm still miffed to the max. I don't want to think about divorce, not tonight. Just wanna have fun and pretend life is good. Thinking about thirty thousand dollars in legal fees alone makes my head hurt. And losing the house, that's major. L.A. is a dual-income city. You can make 40K a year and still not be able to afford a good house, and if you find one, it's a fixer-upper that looks like Fred Sanford's crib. And divorce. Can't deal with that concept right now. Divorce is second only to the death of a spouse on the psychic pain meter. Death, then divorce. People have panic attacks behind that shit, flip out and spiral down into major depression.

I tell her to kill the mad face and tell me what she's thinking. She says, "Eritrean."

That gets us both laughing.

Then she asks, "True or false?"

"Yvette, c'mon now. Let it go."

"The first time a man sleeps with you, it's powerful, has the full effect."

She can be so stubborn. I give in to her conversation and nod. "I'll go with that one."

"You never get that original effect again."

"It doesn't diminish. It can always be good. Sometimes it gets better."

She says, "Let's just agree to disagree and change the subject."

"I'm not agreeing with that crap."

"It's all about the excitement of the chase. The sperm chases the egg. The egg doesn't chase the sperm. The egg is stationary. It's settled. It's in their nature, the perpetual chase."

I'm cracking up.

She says, "So it's a man's destiny to hunt."

"What's a woman's destiny?"

"To buy shoes."

I'm laughing too hard to drive straight.

I ask, "How do you come up with this bull? This is some 'Bama talk, right?"

She laughs with me and shows me two middle fingers of love.

"You need to stop running like Flo Jo and find you a steady man," I tell her. "Why don't you meet one of those nice Southern men on those trips back down to the ATL?"

"Nothing but a bunch of gay men down there."

"In Atlanta?"

"Going into Lenox Square is like stepping into a Li'l Richard and RuPaul convention."

"That bad?"

"Brothers are switching up and down Peachtree acting more feminine than I'll ever be. And there are too many bisexual brothers down there."

"That's messed up."

"They are taking that brotherly love concept to a whole new level."

"Damn. Can you imagine catching your man with another man?"

"I'd mess around and have to kill a nigga."

15

It's almost one a.m. when we get back to Yvette's place. We warm up some leftover pasta, bump Jaguar Wright's CD, and the conversation changes a thousand times, eventually landing back on work, and how she wants to do more important work than she's allowed to do.

Yvette says, "I want to give people social significance."

"Oh, please. We're in Hollywood. People here aren't socially experienced."

"And I'm tired of working for the psychologically unsophisticated. I told Tyra that shit."

Then she gets a phone call from one of her lovers. She checks the caller ID, answers with a snap, "Why are you calling me this late?"

Then she laughs and blushes, and hangs up.

She asks, "You gonna be okay by yourself?"

"Handle your biz."

She rushes, packs a bag, grabs her toothbrush, tells me that she'll see me in the morning.

I need to be alone. The Pisces in me yearns for solitude.

Nothing is on but those damn low-budget erotic movies. And even sex with bad lighting, weak editing, and whacked choreography is a reminder of what the world should be doing at this hour. Since Yvette has a stash of booze, I break open a bottle of merlot, collapse on the sofa, covers around my shoulders, and watch fake breasts and beautiful bodies do some bad fucking.

A glass of wine goes down like Kool-Aid. My body craves something with more of an edge, but ever since I met that woodpecker, I'm avoiding hard liquor and hangovers for the next ten years, so I violate her space and search around for one of her medicinal cigarettes. In her jewelry box, I find two fat joints left over from my pity party.

I smoke half of one, holding the herb in my lungs and never giving up one cough, then down another glass of wine, and close my eyes.

The sandman comes to me in beautiful colors.

Angst and a full bladder team up to wake me at three a.m., long before darkness has given way to a new day. After I pee, I'm feeling antsy and dirty from all the negative energy. Need to scrub away all the bad karma that is clinging to me. I want to bathe so I can soak awhile, but I can't find the stopper to the tub. I say three tears in a bucket and go for the shower. I close the door and get the water hot enough to make Yvette's petite bathroom steam up like a sauna, and I strip down, look at my bruised knee. I ran into the corner of that metal entertainment center harder than I thought. It's a dark purple, like a swollen eye. Looks worse than it feels.

I shower by candlelight.

My body holds so much tension. I'm still buzzed. Water feels so good. I put my hair under the showerhead and baptize myself. Her showerhead is detachable. Cool. I take it off and clean my arms. Water down my breasts. Wash my stomach. When the water sprays between my legs, the sudden pressure gives me the tingles. I hold the showerhead right there, allow tingles to create warmth, and that heat becomes a fire. I work the detachable showerhead, find the pulsating setting, get the water at the right temperature, then find the right pressure.

Damn.

I prop my left foot up on the faucet, back against the wall, use my left hand to touch my vagina, pull back those fleshy folds and expose my spot, let that pulsing stream of water arouse me, and give in to the orgasm. The release is sudden, makes my right leg tremble nonstop. The acoustics amplify my moans and groans. I'm chanting a capella, in my own concert. My left foot slips off the faucet and I lose my balance, almost fall through the glass door, have to drop the showerhead and push back into the wall, slide down on my haunches while I catch my breath.

My release helps, but doesn't liberate me from enough stress. The tingles won't subside. My panic stole corners of my orgasm and that irritates me. I rest on the floor of the tub, chest rising and falling. Water up high. Showerhead going wild, my lover wiggling like a snake, having its own perpetual orgasm, water spraying all over my skin, saturating my locks.

Damn.

My hands take on a life of their own, start squeezing my nipples. I want to stop. Can't. My hand moves from my breast to my vagina. She's on fire and slippery. Fingers come to life. One-finger loving myself. Then two-finger loving myself. Three-finger loving. Chewing my lips. Swallowing the sound of my growing orgasm. Moans echoing like I'm in a hollow cave.

I give birth to Momma Orgasm, then lie there, winded, wounded, jerking, twitching.

The water turns cool. I need to turn the water off, but I

can't move. The showerhead continues to squirm and cleanse me. I sit up. My hair is heavy. I pull my soggy locks from my face; use both hands to wring them out.

I'm getting cold. I turn the water off. The showerhead goes limp.

My world becomes silent.

That felt good, but it also felt like a waste.

Water drips.

Loneliness rises.

I bring my knees up to my breasts, hug myself, sit in the candlelight, steam fading, the scent of ganja perfuming the air, merlot on my breath, thinking about how many nights I've had to please myself, touch myself, love myself, fucking a capella while Charles slept, and me never knowing that Jessica had fulfilled his carnal appetite long before I made it home.

An hour later.

I have on a pair of Yvette's tattered Old Navy sweats. Dark blue top and a gray bottom, both wrinkled to the max. The sweats swallow me, give me the appearance of a hip-hop'n tomboy. I have on no shoes, just a pair of my girlfriend's white socks.

David Lawrence has on worn jeans and a faded gray Los Angeles Marathon T-shirt. Paint speckles his skin; colors stain one side of his face. The smell of turpentine remains strong and his loft is just as cold as it was yesterday. I walk into his space and he hands me a sweater. Across the room on an easel is the stunning picture painted in bright colors, the one of Jessica touching herself. I gaze at all the erotic images of Jessica. Her sensuality surrounds me.

David Lawrence says, "Didn't think you were coming."

"I can leave."

Neither of us speaks a word for a moment. Again I look around at his printmaking tools: etching needles, burnishers, wood-carving tools. Get a whiff of the volatile odors in this loft.

He says, "Your hair is wet."

"And your Afro is whop-sided and nappy as hell."

"I was 'sleep."

"Thought you didn't sleep."

"Time to time."

"I can leave."

He says, "You're . . . You look buzzed."

"Not really. Coming down from my Jamaican high."

He motions at the case in my hand. "Your sax?"

"Yeah. Too late for your song?"

"Not really."

"Let's get this over with. Where's the software?"

He points at the table. There's a CD next to his gun.

I put my saxophone case down at the foot of the futon, put my blue and white neck strap on, and take my horn out. I blow a couple of notes before I look down. At my feet are pages of Charles's and Jessica's IMs, lust still scattered where I left them. I reach in my pocket, fumble around and pull out the other half of the joint I'd started at Yvette's.

I say, "You mind?"

"Go ahead."

"Gotta match?"

He goes to a small wooden table that has a lot of his work tools and he moves things around until he finds a book of matches. He tosses them to me. I read the cover. G. Garvin's. An upscale restaurant on Third Street. I fire up the joint, hit it once, then saunter to him, turn it around, and put the fire end in my mouth, blow him a shotgun.

He stares me down as he inhales.

He takes the joint, hits it twice before he does the same shotgun for me. His breath enters my lungs. I smell him. Feel the heat from his skin. Our lips are close enough to kiss.

I say, "Fuck me."

We're naked. Sweating. The PEK earns his title, then strokes me with a hard and steady drumbeat, the cadence of a true warrior. My body listens, hums, sings. I ride him the same way, giving him my own beat. We don't kiss. I need kissing. We come close, I bite his skin, suck his face, he licks my lips, tries to feed me my own scent, but I turn away, won't give him my tongue.

He goes to the bathroom. He pees, door wide open. Flushes. He turns on the faucet.

My feet are cold. I sit up, go through my pool of borrowed sweats so I can find my thick white socks and put them back on. I get my golden sax, dampen the reed on the red mouth-piece, and start to play my own quiet storm version of Aali-yah's "Rock the Boat." I'm no Kim Waters, but I'm decent, better than Jane Average. David Lawrence's passion, his work, surrounds me. If I had stuck with mine, had possessed the type of discipline I see before me, all over this room—

He says, "Sounds good."

I stop a second. "Better than 'Achy Breaky Heart.' "

The loft has nice acoustics. I keep playing. He comes to me with a wet hand towel. While I fool around with a few melodies, he cleans between my legs, uses the warm towel to clean his milk from my belly, then cleans himself, and drops the towel on the mountain of IMs.

He rubs my breasts, gets my nipples brick-hard, touches my damp locks.

I keep playing. Tingling and playing.

David Lawrence goes to his blank canvas, one that's already stretched and sanded. He's naked; his dick half-erect, thick veins making it look muscular, still swaying like a pendulum.

I ask, "You gonna work?"

"Li'l bit."

"I'll leave."

"Keep playing."

"I'm cold."

"Hungry?"

"Not really."

"I have fruit. Or I can make you a turkey sandwich."

I smile. "I'm cool."

He closes the windows. Lights a few candles. He looks at me as he walks across the hardwood floor, his feet sticking, and gathers yellow ochre paint and pencils. He settles down in front of his blank canvas, studies me, asks me to move a little this way, a little that way, and I become self-conscious of every freckle, of all my flaws. My sax hides me. I close my eyes and play song after song. I warm up with "That's the Way Love Goes." I feel so damn good. Play Candy Dulfer's "Lily Was Here." Then I blow the hell out of David Sanborn's "The Dream."

I move from commercial songs to the real deal, allow "Love Supreme" and "My Favorite Things" and "Peel Me a Grape" to Coltrane and Rodgers and Frishberg their way through me. All that's bad leaves my heart, and my soul rises. I play. Eyes close when it starts to get good. I'm no longer here. I freestyle myself into another world. Where it's spring-time and all I see and feel are the wind and trees.

Dawn appears outside the windows.

I play until sweat runs from my brow.

David Lawrence studies me in silence from across the room, dissecting every part of me, mixing colors that match my complexion, does the same for my hair, my breasts, my thighs, putting his vision of me—of me in this moment—on the canvas.

He stares at my eyes with a depth that I'm not used to, as if he sees something in me that others don't. His intense gaze flatters me, gets me warm in my heart, moist between my legs.

His voice is soft. "Too bad."

"What?"

"We had to meet like this. It's too bad."

"Yeah. Too bad."

He comes back over to me. Penis rigid and promising. Moves my alto to the side.

He says, "We've met in the middle of a war."

"Are we at war?"

"Yeah, we are."

"Yeah. I guess we are."

I lie back, spread my legs. He eases down on me, grunts when he penetrates me, holds my ass, pulls me into him over and over. I grip his back, moans and hips rising to meet his rhythm. His rage feels wonderful. I show him mine. He flows deep. I squirm and he chases me, yanks me back into him. The futon scoots, the sound of wood screeching against wood cries out. He pulls my hair. Bites my neck. Sucks my skin. I pull his 'fro, refuse to let his Herculean passion be greater than mine. He sucks my breast and I chant, shiver, and lose control.

I kiss him. Everything changes. We stop moving, and all we do is kiss.

His tongue teases mine, then he sucks on my tongue, my lips, my neck, then takes my tongue again. Then we move against each other. Rising. Falling. I call Jesus and his father. My broken heart and lonely vagina hug him tight. He gives me multiple orgasms.

When we're done, the futon rests at a new angle, scooted a good six feet from where we started. He relaxes on me awhile, chest rising and falling against my breasts while I play in his thick hair, then he moves next to me, sweating. I'm hot, out of breath too. The colorful paint from his skin melts into my flesh, reds and browns rain from me into his white sheets.

I say, "I'm thirsty."

He staggers across the room and comes back with a tall glass of water. We sip from the same glass. I'm sluggish. Dizzy. I look at the platinum wedding ring on my hand. Then at the titanium wedding band he wears. He asks if I'm okay. I'm feeling bowlegged, pigeon-toed, and cross-eyed. I create a smile, fluff my damp locks, and nod that I'm fine. Very fine right now. I struggle to sit up, yawn, and grumble that I need to get back to Yvette's apartment. He rubs my leg and says that he wants me to stay. I tell him I need to jet before traffic gets thick. And I want to zoom back to Sherman Oaks before Yvette gets home from her booty call. He touches my face, tells me I look groggy, asks me to chill out a little longer. His voice is soothing. My body is getting weighty. I lie back down on his white sheets. He crawls next to me.

A breeze from an open window rakes my skin while we pillow talk about classic muscle cars. The '72 Nova. '69

Dodge Superbee. '59 Rambler. '69 Ragtop Camaro SS. He likes the '57 Corvette. I'm a bigger fan of the '63 Corvette because that baby has the speed and the ride.

I embrace his penis the whole conversation, measure its girth, flop it side to side, make it smack his thighs. His penis owns shades of pink, brown hues, and a deep blackness. It's smooth and the most beautiful I've ever seen. I don't envy it; just think it's odd to have something that extends from your body like that. Something that grows and shrinks, has no bone, changes from flaccid to firm. I wonder what it's like and don't hide my fascination with that flesh.

I say, "But I love being in a ragtop Mustang, zooming down Pacific Coast Highway."

His hand rubs against my skin. "Wouldn't mind finding a '67 Nova Super Sport."

"Get one with twin four-barrel carbs. That's the bomb."

He rubs my hair as I make his penis flip-flop. I stretch his flesh out. I'm buzzed, feeling silly. He says nothing, as if he's used to women being in awe of what he has. Then my eyes settle on those images of Jessica, all as naked as I am now. My stare lasts forever. I stop playing with his penis, then turn over on my stomach, morning air crawling over my back and butt.

His hand rests on my butt, then moves back and forth, tickles the curve down my thighs.

I ask, "Can I look?"

"You've been doing that."

"Not at your thing. Your work. I wanna see what you did over there."

He taps my skin in a way that tells me to go see for myself.

I do. Take slow steps and stand naked in front of an image of myself.

It's unfinished but I can see what it's going to be, earthy

and erotic. Me sitting on the edge of the futon, eyes closed, deep into playing my sax, like I'm my own symphony. The red and orange undertones of my brown skin, my cinnamon freckles—it's all there. I'm nude and my nakedness doesn't look offensive, in shades of reds and browns, all of what he's done praising my body and spirit. I look sexy. I look smart. I look talented. I look like a woman.

I look happy.

The positive sensation that runs through my body gets summed up in one word, "Wow."

"Your beauty has been immortalized."

I look at him, questioning how he views me.

He smiles. "Look at the one to the left."

I move that way and I'm stunned. It's me again. It's unfinished, but it's me. Sitting on the futon, reading the IMs. My mood, my shock and pain, it's all there.

He says, "I'm going to call that one *Revelation*."

I look back and forth between the two images of me. Stand between two emotions.

I say, "Call the other one *Sunset*."

Then I hand-comb my locks, go back to the image that gives me the most joy.

For a moment I imagine this loft being filled with the sound of my sax and images of me. Imagine myself sneaking here for a noon rendezvous, then returning for a cup of late-night sin.

Those wrongdoing thoughts scare me, steal my smile, knot the insides of my stomach.

I should leave now, run back to Yvette's, flee to anywhere but here, but I feel sexy, wanted. I go back to him, stand over him, stare down at him, then choose to lie with him, his skin both warming and sticking against mine. I touch him. He doesn't push my hand away.

I ask, "You love your wife?"

"It's changing."

Pain rises in his voice. On a scale of one to ten, his sounds like a twelve, equal with mine. This isn't easy. He's handling it like an alpha man, internalizing and suffering in silence.

"Yeah," I say, my voice so low. "Everything is changing."

I wait for him to ask me the same question. He never does. I'm glad he doesn't.

He says, "Right now I'm not feeling too married."

"If I were single, I would've slept with you."

"I'm attracted to you too."

Our sweat cools and dries.

I smell our combined scents, our after-sex smells. That aroma is different with every lover, has its own fingerprints. His aroma seeps into my pores. I think of the men who came before today, who came before Charles. I've experienced a lot of lovers, and still not many who loved me, but more than enough for me to not want to get out there again.

I understand Yvette right now. And I respect her freedom. I admire and envy her sanity.

I manage to ask, "What's your zodiac sign?"

"Scorpio."

"Figures."

I understand him. Scorpios are physical beings, very sexual. Faithful. But they're controlling and vengeful. I've loved a couple, so I know them. And I know me. Pisces and Scorpios have so much sexual chemistry that it's frightening. But when it goes bad, it goes bad.

He asks, "You ever think about dying?"

"Where did that come from?"

"Do you?"

"Not really."

"Everyone does at some point."

"Not me."

"Good for you." He rubs against me. I tingle. He says, "Sometimes I can see my funeral. The one I made my mom promise not to have, she has it anyway."

"What kinda funeral did you tell her not to have?"

"Don't want one. Just a memorial service. No open casket and shit. I told her that."

"Why would you tell her that? What was going on at the time?"

"Just told her. Wanted her to know my thoughts on it."

"When did you have that conversation?"

"Last time I went to see her."

"How was she?"

He tells me he had to sit at a row of cages with Plexiglas fronts and use a telephone, just like the movies. He says, "It's horrible. Prison has robbed her of everything that matters to her."

"I can only imagine."

"Was hard looking at her like that. She was radiant and slim when she went in."

"And you talked about dying."

"She told me where to find her paperwork and stuff if she dies first. I used that as my opportunity to tell her."

I move closer to him. He pulls the covers up to our waists.

Honesty rises and I say, "I used to think about dying. Back when I was fifteen."

"What happened?"

"This guy dumped me."

We share the same pillow, but we're not snuggling. I'm

warm; so I kick one leg free, allow my body to stay cool. His strong hand drifts over my soft skin, rests on my belly. Morning shines through the windows.

Everything is peaceful.

My eyelids become heavy.

I pull the covers up over my face to block out the light.

I fall asleep.

I jerk awake and stare straight up at a painting of Jessica. This painting looks lifelike. Her dark face, with the permed hair and the slanted eyes, is crisp. The beauty, the features in her face are so much clearer. Her skin is poetic, as blue-black as the night sky after a hard rain. The tears in her brown eyes look real.

I blink.

The painting blinks too.

It frowns.

Then it screams.

16

Jessica screams.

My heart tumbles into my stomach. I clutch the white sheets and struggle to cover myself, and then I try to jump up.

Her voice fills the room. *"Who are you?"*

I'm squinting, groggy, ready for flight, but will fight if I have to. My heart beats so fast. I'm grabbing my borrowed, oversized sweats from the floor, yanking the pants on backward and not bothering to turn them around. I wrestle to get the sweatshirt over my head as fast as I can—don't want to leave myself defenseless—but my arms get stuck in the sleeves. I didn't wear panties or a bra. My socks are still on my feet. My sax is at the foot of the futon, propped against its black case, resting near that stack of IMs.

"Who the fuck are you?" Her voice becomes sharper each time she yells.

I scramble toward the drafting table, put space between us, try to catch my breath, get my focus. Jessica has on dark Lycra stretch pants and a pink see-through mesh top with the words DIME PIECE across her breasts in red letters. I stare at her and my rage rises in my gut. Jealousy turns me into another person. Into another monster.

She's here. The P.E. teacher. The aerobics instructor. The woman I've been biologically linked to for the last eight months. My enemy.

She demands, "Where is DL?"

She frowns at the rumpled covers on the futon, then at my tousled locks and dry skin.

She steps toward me, then toward the tables with all the tools that now look like weapons. She's intimidating, has firmness in her body, toned arms, abdominal cuts in her stomach. My adrenal glands work overtime. Fear races throughout every capillary in my body.

I rush to step between her and the tables. Then I move to David Lawrence's gun.

Jessica swallows and stops moving.

Mentally, I'm picking up the gun, aiming at her, pulling the trigger, the explosion deafening me, then sitting down, waiting for the sirens, for the police to come have a tête-à-tête.

I touch the gun. Feel that rush again. Then glare at her. Wonder if she's afraid of Death. She can't be. She knew that dying was an option when she fucked my husband. Just like it's an option because I fucked hers. But I'm closer to the gun.

I know what David Lawrence's mother felt when she killed that Wawa girl. *Righteous.*

My fingers move across the gun.

She's scared, about to scream something, then her face changes.

Her head cocks to one side like a bewildered dog. She says, "I know you."

"You should." I move my damp locks from my face. "My picture is on his desk."

Her eyes ricochet toward David Lawrence's desk.

I shake my head and say, "At the school. On Charles's desk."

"Charles . . . ?" That bewilderment magnifies as her eyes go to the floor at the foot of the futon, to my saxophone. This is my overnight face, not as pretty now as I am in the pictures. She studies me—my height, my features, my locks. There's a pause. She does some Sherlock Holmesian deduction, it all adds up, and realization paints her face. *"Oh, my God."*

"Yeah, *Jessie*." My tongue glides over my teeth. A bitter taste has cemented itself to their surface. "That's what Charles calls you, *Jessie,* right?"

"How . . . What are you doing . . . ?"

She blinks a million times. Lips move but no words come out. Then she stops blinking and stands wide-eyed and mouth open, none of this making sense. Not right away. She's processing what she sees. Her expression morphs—she's angry, afraid, confused all at once.

We glare.

I pull the sleeves of my sweatshirt up and get ready for whatever.

I don't want to fight her. She's ushered an unwelcome change into my world and I need much more than that. I want to make that bitch disappear. Want her to not exist.

Hatred encourages me to put my hand on the handle of the gun.

Lines bloom around her mouth, shadows around her deep-brown eyes. She doesn't have the ethereal glow of eroticism that is in the army of pictures surrounding me. Hers is the face of a wounded whore who hasn't had any sleep for days. Angst has been her jagged pillow. Just like mine. She's heartbroken, the weight of that stress heavy in her eyes.

Insanity and sanity wrestle inside me.

Charles swam in her, ate her pussy for days on end, then came home and kissed me. Stuck his dick in her a hundred times, gave her raw sex, then came home and let me suck him.

I pick the gun up.

She's seconds from no longer existing. I'm minutes from being on CNN in handcuffs.

She doesn't flinch. That pisses me off.

I start raising the gun.

Keys jingle.

We both jump and look at the door.

That abrupt sound startles me back toward sanity. I see myself in the mirrors along the wall. See the woman in the mirror. My image frightens me. I hold the gun at my side, sanity and insanity kung fu fighting each other. I can't put the gun down.

The door opens, bumps against the wall.

David Lawrence comes in.

He sees Jessica and is startled, almost drops the Starbucks container he has in his hands. He pauses. She smiles. He smiles. He loves her. Her hands flutter to her face as if she wonders how she looks. Or maybe she's just nervous. Or wiping away her guilt. David Lawrence opens his mouth. Then he frowns. He remembers he hates her. His frown changes into the sneering, livid face of a man scorned. Then he looks toward me. He's wearing the same jeans he wore the day we met, an L.A. Lakers jersey that sports Kobe's number, and worn sandals. He takes a harsh breath and forces a smile, maybe telling me that it's cool, the situation is under control.

Even after seeing me standing there, gun at my side, my face so tense, he remains under control.

He tells me, "I brought you a cup of hot apple cider."

Jessica asks, "What's going on here, DL?"

I blink, swallow. "Thanks."

Jessica asks, "What the hell are you doing here?"

David Lawrence says, "Hope you take it with caramel and whipped cream."

I say, "I do. Thank you."

"What the hell is going on here? *Answer me.*"

She has a lot of silver fillings in her bottom teeth and a slight gap in the front of her mouth, flaws that aren't seen on canvas. I want him to kick her ass, to at least scream at her, but he doesn't. He reacts to her by not reacting to her. He makes her invisible, makes her not exist.

She glares me down, shakes her head, hand-combs her hair, shifts from foot to foot.

I bounce the gun against my leg. It's heavy. "I'd better raise up."

His voice is firm. "You were invited. Stay."

Jessica looks at the futon, at us, then does something I don't expect her to do.

She laughs.

And her laugh isn't joy; it's a criticism. Her lover's wife being naked in her estranged husband's loft, holding a stainless steel Colt Defender at her side, then her husband coming in with cups of Starbucks, our conversation, what she sees and hears, to her, I guess it's ridiculous.

She screams, "Answer me, dammit. What is going on here?"

He brings the cup of apple cider to me. It's hot, steam rising, bringing that pleasant smell to my nostrils. He looks at me, then at the gun, sees something in my face that tells him I'm still walking that line, and takes the gun from my hand, holds it by its handle, pointing at the ground, goes across the room, opens the black file cabinet, and puts the death maker in the top drawer.

Jessica says, "Fine. Well, let me ask you then."

She's talking to me again. I don't say anything.

She says, "Fine. Then let's just call Charles."

A new fear rises in me, one that is born out of love and foolishness, and that sudden jolt makes me move toward her. I snap, "Put the goddamn phone down."

"Oh, now you hear me."

David Lawrence says, "Let her call."

"Put the goddamn—"

"Get her away from me, DL. I'm going to call—"

He snaps, "He already knows."

There is silence.

He repeats, "That motherfucker already knows."

My eyes are on David Lawrence. He's not looking at me anymore.

He says, "We're at war."

I absorb the implications behind his words, but I'm too scared now. He wants payback more than anything. I've wanted to face Jessica, wanted to corner her and question her, wanted to ruin her, but now I have to get the fuck out of here. She's across the room by the easel when I hurry out the door. Then I have to turn back around to get my horn. I can't leave my horn.

The door isn't closed. They're arguing. I stand there and peep inside. Become a voyeur.

"You painted her," she says with so much envy. "You painted her."

"You slept with another man."

"You painted her."

Jessica looks broken for a second, wipes her eyes, moans like her world is falling apart and she's messed up everything. She loses it, has an emotional turn and goes at David Lawrence full throttle, about how he's always been more passionate about his work, never has time for her, and never nurtures her, not like Charles. My husband made her feel special. Like a woman. She vents that David Lawrence never took her out, was always in his studio.

He loses it. "This is what I do, dammit. This is what I was doing when we met."

She tells him how she felt when he wouldn't come home for days. How she was more of a sex buddy than a wife. How she cried and cried and would plead with him to give her some attention, to take her out, to come home and have a romantic dinner, but he was so determined.

She puts her hand over her mouth and when she takes it away a string of saliva sticks to her palm. She coughs, then talks as if her tongue is heavy and swollen.

She says, "And you're still not a superstar."

"And you're a whore."

He's in her face now. Tells her she can't cook worth a shit. And fucks without passion. Says that her problem is that she's busy pointing fingers, not taking any responsibility.

She tells him that he is doing the same. Tells him that he was a lousy lover.

He says, "You had me served divorce papers."

"Is that what I have to do to get your attention?"

He tells her that she never wanted to compromise, always had to have things her way, asks if that's what Charles promised her, a world perfect in her eyes.

She snaps, "I don't like being number two."

"You were not number two."

"Your work was your main marriage. I was the other woman."

"What? How can you even say that? You know I have deadlines."

"You find time to do what you want to do."

"You're selfish. Want the world to revolve around you all the damn time."

"And you're a wacko from a wacko family, a long line of whacked-out wackos."

Again David Lawrence's voice booms, points out how fucked up things have been, how this was who he was when she met him, how she wanted to be pampered, how he still accepted her As Is, but all the things that intrigued her about him were the same things that eventually turned her off.

He says, "You told me he makes you happy. To know that he really makes you happy . . . that really hurts my heart. That I couldn't do that for you."

Jessica cries, "DL, I don't wanna fight with you. I don't. I came . . . I came to apologize for hurting you. And . . . uh . . . want you to know I love you very much. Always will. You were good to me. In my heart I want to beg you to, you know, take me back, give me a second chance, so we can find peace together, be happy like we used to, and be silly and laugh like we used to all the time. But because I love you so much I want you to be happy. I really, really do."

"Jessica, don't do this to me."

"I know you go through so much other stuff in your life, dealing with your mom, your family, and I want you to be happy. Like I said, I wish we could find that peace together."

"Jessica, don't."

"And I want you to know that I will always love you . . .

uh . . . more than . . . uh . . . I really hate that I did so much to cause drama in your life. I'm sad, really vulnerable. My friends have never seen me this way before and I don't really know how to . . . how to handle it. Say something. Please? I'm opening up to you. DL, I'm really struggling here because I miss you a lot."

They say nothing and look at their feet. Part of me wants him to grab her by her hair and drag her out of this space. But the bigger part of me wants him to hug her until she stops crying.

He barks, "That motherfucker betrays you and you come back to me all broken down. He dogs you out and you come crawling back home all humble and shit. Is that what this is?"

Just like that she's a teardrop away from drowning.

He remains caustic. "Tell me what happened."

"Nothing."

"*What happened?*"

"It's not important."

"You know what, *get the fuck out.*"

She wipes her eyes over and over.

He booms, "*Get out. Whore. Go before I throw you out.*"

She gets up to leave. He grabs her arm. Without a struggle, she sits on the futon, elbows on knees, hands in hair, head down, so uncomfortable on the rumpled sheets that smell of sex.

He softens his tone. "Where you been staying?"

"Palm Springs."

"With . . . ?"

"With . . . with . . . with," she stutters that word, "my cousin."

"Which one?"

"Toyomi. We talked. I see . . . see things clearer . . . clearer than I have in a long time. Over the last few months . . . told a lot of lies. We gotta come clean. Have to do that . . . come clean."

"How have you been holding up?"

"Not good. Not good at all. Been taking Xanax to sleep. Took Prozac too."

"Prozac?"

"Just a couple . . . couple . . . couple . . . couple." She stutters again, then tries to hold back a nervous chuckle. "Had a panic attack. Took a couple of Toyomi's happy pills."

"Got you taking Xanax and Prozac?"

"It's not that bad."

"That crap work?"

"Happy pills can't make me happy right now."

"He really hurt you." He's gnashing his teeth. "That motherfucker really hurt you."

Their emotions humidify the loft, make it hard to breathe. They look so human right now. Stripped down to the bare essence of them. They're just people. Just like me.

He rocks and grunts out, "That motherfucker made you happy."

"DL, you can't not have any communication, not so much as a grunt for a damn week and expect me to be with you like that. I need that communication. I need to know that you think naughty about me. I need to know that, hell, you can talk to me about current events and not only talk when you want some either. Communication is the key to my heart."

"And he . . . that's what that motherfucker gave you."

"I need you to touch me before we get to the bedroom, need you to hold me just because, need you to ask about my damn day, need you to make me feel safe, need unconditional love."

"Answer my question."

"Hell, I watch ESPN to spend time with you. I pretend I like the Lakers and the Raiders and keep up on the latest sports info so we can have a conversation about something."

"Answer me."

"We should be able to have conversations about anything and everything."

"Answer me."

I bump against the door on purpose. I don't wanna hear her damn answer.

David Lawrence jerks toward me. Lots of surprise in his eyes. Jessica does the same. Hers is a disturbed reaction. She wipes her eyes some more, tries to not look so broken down.

I'm halfway inside the door, all the way into their truth. White socks. Locks in disarray. Skin dry. Breath kicking. His scent and the smell of ganja rising through my borrowed sweats.

I motion and say, "My sax."

I take quick steps over and grab my horn with my right hand, get the case with my left. There is no jingle when I walk. There should be a jingle. I look down at my pockets and there is no bulge. I slow and shake my right leg. Still no jingle. Then I remember my sweats are on backward. I shake my left leg. No jingle. Shit. Now I have to look back at them. They're watching me with two different expressions, one concern, and the other straight-up abhorrence.

I say, "My car keys."

The silver objects shine at me. With my head, I motion at the floor, near Jessica's feet. My car keys are on my blue and white Tau Beta Sigma key chain, resting near that stack of IMs.

She kicks them and they spin across the dusty part of the hardwood floor, stop twirling at my feet. We stare at each other. My eyes let her know I didn't appreciate that. I put my case down long enough to grab my keys, and struggle to stuff them in my backward pocket.

David Lawrence tugs at his Afro, then releases a strong sigh, and tries to say something to me, but the words won't come. The expression on his face, it's strange, like an apology.

I ask David Lawrence, "How does Charles know?"

He licks his lips, looks up at the wall, and shakes his head. "I'm sorry."

That's all he gives me.

I nod, let him know that I accept my blame, my irrationality and irresponsibility. Just like him, just like them, I got caught up in my pain. Tried to trade nightmare for fantasy.

Jessica says, "Close the door on your way out."

I walk out and leave the door wide open.

Someone moves across the wood floor, steps echoing.

I keep going, my locks dancing, keys jingling, horn and case bouncing on my hips.

Part of me wants David Lawrence to come after me. Then I'll feel better about the wrong I did, about the illusion he gave me. About my sin. Part of me wants Jessica to give chase. At first I don't know why I want her to, but then I do. I want her ass to apologize. I was with her husband, but she wore my shoes long before I tried on hers.

The door to the loft closes hard.

The smell of turpentine fades from my nostrils.

The sun is unrelenting. Smog, merciless. Traffic, unforgiving.

That motherfucker already knows.

I pull my cellular phone out, turn it back on. It goes crazy. I have forty-three messages. Forty-three calls in the last two hours. Each time they hesitate like they're thinking about what to say, or what not to say, a really eerie silence, then they fumble with the phone, hang up, and call right back.

Each hang-up makes me more nervous.

That woodpecker is coming back to carve out more furniture inside my head.

That motherfucker already knows.

I grip the steering wheel and wonder exactly what Charles knows.

17

Someone gets shot at the ticket counter at LAX. My pager starts blowing up, and as soon as I get to Yvette's, I have to shower, rush to the station, and get out to the airport with the crew. We're reporting live all day. No time for me to think about my own life. People get trampled. The SWAT team has guns on everyone, even the people trying to get their luggage. Every news station in town is here. The 405 is shut down and that brings the traffic in the South Bay to a halt. It's so insane that nobody can get a glass of water.

For twelve hours I live in terror, see things that will never be shown on the news. And I can use twelve more hours. Anything to keep me from thinking about this morning.

Charles doesn't call. Not once. In the back of my mind, that bothers me.

Tyra the Tyrant calls me, asking a thousand questions about another story dealing with a serial rapist in Torrance. She's curt with me, snapping at me, and I almost lose it.

Then I have to call down to the station and talk to Yvette for a few seconds. All business. I don't ask her where she was or who she was with last night. She's busting her butt putting together packages about a guy who shot his girlfriend in the abdomen, arm, and leg, then kept her locked in his garage for six days.

I welcome all drama, feed on it, ride it, and let it overshadow all of my problems.

At the end of the night, after the show is over, I have to go home and face Charles.

The new garage door glides up and I'm mortified. Fist-sized holes have been knocked in all of the walls. I leave my dented Baby Blue in the driveway and look at the destruction.

I'm scared to see what the rest of the house looks like.

The door sensor beeps three times when I open the garage door and hurry inside.

Again, I'm in shock.

The house is spotless. Looks like Molly Maid has come through and cleaned from ceiling to carpet. Music is on. Jazz. And I smell food. I take slow steps into the kitchen and there is a four-course meal on the stove. A Cajun meal. Gumbo. Catfish. Sweet cornbread. And a three-layer chocolate cake on the counter. The plantation shutters are open, so I can see out onto the patio. The deck is clean. The colorful lights that surround our small yard are on. And the fountain we have in the back is on, giving that peaceful sound of running water.

"Hope you're hungry."

I jump when I hear Charles come up behind me. He's barefoot, has on black jeans and a white shirt. His curly hair is brushed back in a wavy pattern. His bruised eye puffs out at me.

He says, "You look tired."

"I am."

"Me too."

We stand there and play the stare game.

He says, "I wanna show you something."

He holds the railing and walks up the stairs.

I follow, moving like a condemned woman being led to the gallows.

He passes by the bedroom. The bed is made up. Carpet has fresh vacuum tracks.

We slow at the laundry room. The door is open and a pile of dirty clothes overflows from the hamper, colors mixed with whites.

I say, "Never mix whites with colors."

He closes the door to the laundry room. "I'm no good at the laundry thing."

"I know."

"Didn't want to mess our clothes up, so I left it alone."

I whisper, "It's okay."

He goes into the office. The computer is on.

He pulls the chair out for me.

I sit, back stiff, hands in my lap.

He moves the mouse and the screen comes to life. Windows Media Player is up.

He says, "When I leave the room, start the little movie your friend sent me."

He walks out.

I sit there. Unable to blink. Too nervous to raise my hand.

The music stops playing downstairs. Then I hear three beeps. Charles has left the house.

Bam. Bam. Bam.

He's in the garage. The blows are strong, but they're flat. He's hitting the bag.

Then he stops rocking the house. Silence follows the sound of violence.

I stare at the computer screen. Stare at the mouse awhile before I touch it, move it until the arrow lines up with the symbol for play, then I click on the icon.

First I see the early morning sun outside a window. So many beautiful colors at sunrise. Then the camera pans the room. Shows artistic walls done in autumn colors and faux finishes.

Then the paintings of Jessica come into view. That collection of pictures that are in David Lawrence's studio. The sensuous art of Charles's lover drawn in all of her eroticism. Jessica beautifully drawn in hues of reds and browns and yellows. The image of her pleasing herself, the camera stays on that one the longest, as if it were meant to taunt.

At first I think it's a video camera, then I remember the high-tech laptop he owns.

The camera moves around the room, passes over cabinets, the other faux painted walls, and comes to rest on a pile of sweats at the foot of the futon.

I swallow.

Then the camera pans and shows a golden saxophone resting near its black case.

I moan, long and hollow.

The camera moves up over rumpled white sheets, up to oversized white socks dangling from small feet, up bare legs, calves, hips, over bare buttocks, stalling on the beautiful breasts, on the black nipples of a woman sleeping on her side.

Her chest rises and falls with each breath. Mine does the same now, only faster. Then the camera pulls back and shows her angelic, freckled face. Tousled locks. When the woman in the movie reaches up to scratch her nose, the cameraman focuses on her wedding ring.

Her ring looks like mine.

I shake my head over and over, want her to not be me, but the picture is so clear I can count my freckles. I'm sleeping. Peaceful. The camera pulls back and shows my body at rest. Thirty seconds of my nakedness fills up the huge computer screen.

Two powerful pictures of me come up. One sad. One happy.

Then my nakedness returns to the screen.

The lens turns, going up, breezing by the artistic walls, the ceiling and the skylights, then stops and does a close-up on a makeshift ashtray holding the roach from the joint we smoked.

The lens rotates, comes to rest on David Lawrence's facetious smile. His mane is matted on one side. He stares into the camera for ten seconds. Pain and vengeance darken his eyes.

The video ends.

I sit in silence, shaking my head. Asking what kind of man would do something like that, then go out and get me a cup of Starbucks.

Bam. Bam. Bam. Bam. Bam.

Over and over, I ask myself why he would do something like this to me. But I already know. It's not about me. Never was about me. He wants Charles to feel what he feels.

Bam. Bam. Bam. Bam. Bam.

The banging stops again.

Winds rattle the palm trees outside the windows.

I hear three beeps. Then Charles's footsteps in the hallway.

I remain unmoving.

Othello, he killed Desdemona for her alleged infidelity.

Charles puts his strong hand on my shoulder, then touches my neck.

Othello suffocated his wife.

My husband's fingers are damp.

I look up at his face. Sweat runs down over his nose.

He asks, "Hungry?"

We sit at the dining room table. Food in front of us. Wedding pictures on two of the walls remind us of the day we signed the contract and promised to stay faithful to one another. Family pictures inside the entertainment center remind us of our witnesses.

Our elbows aren't on the table. Two adulterers. We aren't looking at each other.

I sip water and let Charles eat a few spoonfuls of the gumbo first before I take a small spoonful of mine.

We try to talk about this. We try to remain civil. It's hard.

I say, "I met Jessica."

"I know."

"You talked to Jessica since . . . ?"

I leave it at that. He knows I mean since his fight with David Lawrence.

He shakes his head.

I ask, "No phone calls?"

He shifts, agitated. "She left messages, but I never called her back."

"When?"

"Every day."

"Oh, so she's still calling you. Why haven't you called her back?"

"It's over. I just want my life back." He chews. Swallows. Sips. "You met her."

"Interesting choice you made. She's immature. Dramatic."

He doesn't respond.

I ask, "What made her so special?"

"Don't know."

"Were you bored with me? Is she better in bed?"

"Don't ask me that."

"Tell me something, dammit. Is she a better cook?"

"She can't cook."

"Then what is it all about?"

Silence bores into us.

I say, "Her husband is pretty intense."

"He's a sociopath. Somehow he got the e-mail addresses from . . . her . . . and he sent copies of our . . . correspondence to everyone in the school system. Teachers and administrators. Some went to parents. And somehow the kids ended up with them. They're being passed around."

I'm stunned.

I say, "The fight. The e-mails. You've been home every day because you lost your job."

"Parents down at the school are in an uproar."

"Was she fired too?"

He shrugs. "Don't know."

"Charles, what if this hits the news? What if—"

"What if this gets out and makes you look bad, right? That's what you care about."

I shake my head and stare at nothing.

He says, "I saw that video and I wanted to end it."

"End what?"

"My life. I thought about driving to the beach and ending it."

"Imagine how I felt when I read your love letters. I did die. I died, Charles."

Again, we stare at each other.

I say, "You love her?"

"No."

"Don't bullshit me, Charles."

"I answered the question."

"Bullshit. You're not intimate with someone for eight months and feel nothing—unless you're the sociopath."

"It's not love."

"Will you come off it? It was more than shits and giggles, more than a fuck 'n' chuck."

"I don't love her."

"I'm a big girl, Charles. I can take it."

"She's immature, self-centered, like the kind of woman who wants to run around, have fun all the time, party as much as she can."

"Then explain it to me, because I don't get it."

"Can't."

"Is it a dick thing? Was she exciting? Did she make you feel alive? What?"

"We shared troubles. I was lonely. Can't explain it."

He puts his hand on mine. I let it rest there a moment, feel his skin against mine. I want him to touch me. Want to feel him like that. I remember Jessica. Then I pull my hand away.

I ask, "Then how are we supposed to move forward if you have some soul-poisoning desire for Jessica that you can't explain?"

"You want one answer, some solid motivation, and there is never one reason."

"Then name as many as you can. I'll wait."

"There is no reason or answer. We were friends. We shared troubles. Something jumped off and one thing led to another. It got out of control. All I can say is that it's over."

He bites his cornbread. Chews forever. I wait for him to

swallow. When it's safe, I nibble mine. He makes the best cornbread in the country, but right now it tastes like nothing.

He asks, "Did you use a condom?"

"Yes."

He stares down at his food. "You answered that real quick."

I keep chewing, my eyes those of a thief. He speaks as if his sin is written on a blackboard in white chalk, and his voice is the wet sponge that erases all of his wrongs. And in return, I've become a reflection of the mirror before me. I answer his loyalty with loyalty, his trust with trust, and his lies with lies.

He asks, "How many times were you with that guy?"

"Twice." But sometimes the truth is more powerful than a lie. "The last two nights."

His skin reddens as if he has a fever. He makes fists.

I say, "See how easy that is, Charles? All you have to do is speak what you feel, and not what you think I want to hear. That's all you have to do. It's called the truth."

"That was evil, what he did."

"And what you did wasn't?"

"I didn't intentionally hurt you."

"And he wasn't evil for the hell of it. Don't you think he had motivation?"

He snaps, "I'm hurting, dammit. Angry. Humiliated. Embarrassed. Destroyed."

"Then you feel what I feel."

"You feel something for him?"

"We're being honest and living in truth, or are we still bullshitting each other?"

"No bullshitting."

I answer, "I do."

He marinates. "You love him?"

"No. Of course not."

"Lust."

"The emotion doesn't have a real name, or make sense, but it's there."

"I mean, damn. Why him?"

"Don't know. Needed a painkiller."

Charles says, "He violated me. Did it through you. I'll stomp his ass."

I say, "Of course you will."

That makes Charles mad as hell. Mandingo mad. He glares at me with a crazy love in his eyes that says he wants to shove the table to the side and grab me, fuck the shit out of me in that "I'm your man and you're my woman no matter what the fuck I do" kinda way.

"*The man is a coward*. He came up behind me and hit me. And there were parents and kids out. I couldn't just beat him down in front of kids. I could've kicked his ass, but I couldn't do that in front of the children. He didn't face me like a man. Everything he's doing is punk."

"You can hit that bag all you want, you can have your tantrums and knock holes in all the walls, but that bag and walls have the same thing in common—they don't hit back."

"What, you think I can't beat his ass?"

"Ask your eye."

"Ask your friend after I beat his ass into the ground."

There is another change in his hazel eyes. The way his hair is brushed back makes him look like an angry child. He's Francis again. He's back in that bathroom. That wild gaze only lasts as long as it takes him to blink it away. Then he has the eyes of a warrior king.

He repeats, "Why did you have to go to him?"

"Like you said, no real answer. No definitive reason for why people do things, right?"

He asks, "You played your sax for him?"

I nod without shame.

He says, "That means you like him."

"I ain't gonna lie, I felt empathy for him. We had a connection. You and Jessica created that. I was infatuated by his talent. Flattered by his attention."

"Until he flipped the script and betrayed you."

"My heart was shackled to you. You betrayed me. What he did was a reality check."

We eat. He chews. I chew. He swallows. I swallow.

The colorful lights on the patio are so romantic. The sound of running water coming from the fountain is as peaceful as a mandolin rain. The breeze makes the flags in front of the model homes flap, brings some coolness into the house through the cracked sliding glass door.

I say, "Jessica was special to you. You loved her."

"I love you."

"Maybe you loved us both. I'm disappointed, but I'm not as angry as you think I am. I was, but not anymore. Maybe because I understand how and why you could love her."

"Because you were with him."

"His name is David Lawrence."

Charles's eyes go black. He breathes through his mouth in short spurts.

"All you say are positive things about him," he says. "You really felt something."

"But I could've walked away from it. Would've under any other circumstance."

He runs his hands over his black hair, messes up the wavy pattern.

My voice deepens with my thoughts, and I whisper, "It's amazing how quickly feelings toward someone can be shaped because they give us the attention we crave."

He straightens his back. Becomes the Man trying to solve our problem.

Charles asks, "You want a divorce?"

"What do you want?" Love weakens my tone. "You started this downward spiral."

"I just want this to end. Look, I want this to be over. I regret meeting her."

"She has a name. Not saying it won't make Jessica not exist."

"I regret meeting Jessica," he snaps, then pulls back. "I regret it all. I accept it all. I was weak. It was a mistake. Can we move on, or am I going to lose everything because of her?"

"No, *we* are going to lose everything because *you* had the Restless Dick Syndrome."

"Why are you such a smart ass all the damn time? How am I supposed to talk to you when this is what I get when I open up to you? Can't you understand I'm doing the best I can?"

"You swam in David Lawrence's wife for damn near a year, Charles. He loves Jessica. Jessica left him for you. She said that you were the love of her life. That messed him up. Don't you get it?"

"It's over. That is over."

"Your saying it's over doesn't mean it's over."

"It's over for me."

"You don't get it, do you? You just don't get it."

"What am I not getting?"

"A woman has to have the last word; a man has to win the war."

We're not eating anymore.

His demeanor softens. His leg bounces. He sighs and has a hard time looking at me. Feeling guilty is so hard for him. It's killing me too. Eating us alive. He gazes at me and I want to forget everything about Jessica, want to take back every sin I've done over the last forty-eight hours. Because all I can see is the man I fell in love with and married. He's still here. The man I used to laugh and play with. The really down-to-earth, charming, sweet, affectionate man from Slidell I had so many late-night conversations with. The man who couldn't wait for me to get home from work so he could kiss me for fifteen minutes, maybe rub my feet and bathe me.

My vulnerability rises. I lower my shield. My sarcasm withers.

Whatever energy he gives me, I give it back to him. That's the way I am.

I say, "I don't want a divorce. I don't want this to be a starter marriage. I don't want to fail. I don't want to have to call my momma, tell my sisters, then call your momma and your daddy, don't want to have to explain this to all of your relatives . . . I don't want a divorce."

"Then we can get past this."

I run both hands through my locks, tug them, and take a hard breath. "I can't move forward while things are unresolved. You know how I am. I like everything clear."

He leans forward, elbows on the table, his face in his hands.

"Before we do anything, baby, I really need to know that it's over between you and her."

He asks, "How do I prove that to you?"

"Don't know."

"Well, I need to know the same about you and your friend."

I say, "David Lawrence."

Charles swallows and rubs his temples.

I should let it go, but I need to know so much. That part of me won't go away.

I whisper, "Were you gonna leave me?"

He struggles with that question, shifts, and pulls his lips in, runs his fingers through his hair, and rubs his hands. Then his eyes become moist and he nods. "But it wasn't that simple."

I close my eyes. "That hurts. That really hurts."

"It got too complicated."

"Did you move money?"

"I believe in family."

"Please, just answer the question. Did you move money?"

"I did. I moved it back."

My face turns red. Tears come.

My voice cracks. "You should've gone to the beach."

I leave the table.

18

Subj: **Closure**
Time: 3:31:56 AM Pacific Daylight Time
From: Jessica
To: Charles

Charles—

I'm forwarding a copy of this to your wife's e-mail address.

My husband and I have talked and we both want to reconcile. We're going into counseling. This is hard for him, and it is hard for me. I've lost my job. He can't focus. Our world is so messed up right now. But I want to make it right. He gave me a list of questions to answer. Questions he said he got from your wife. I'm answering them. Each answer is the truth. And each answer makes him cry. Each answer rips out part of my soul. Each answer devastates me. I have to take responsibility for my actions so we can move forward. We're trying to save our marriage. He wants answers and I want to give him that clarity.

But it goes deeper than what we did.

Charles, seeing my husband with your wife, walking in

on her naked, knowing both of them had just been in bed, I can't begin to describe how that made me feel. That cut deeper than I can describe. It made me realize how much I love DL. Charles, I want you to know that this is over. I want your wife to know that this is over. But I need closure. And I need to see her to make sure that her affair with my husband is over. Charles, at this point, I think that you'll agree that you need to know the same. I don't want any drama, so you don't have to worry about that. I just need closure, and this is the only way I know how to start that process. All I have done goes against who I am and it hurts me. If your wife is willing, I would like to meet you and her, face-to-face, as soon as possible, today if possible, to apologize.

My life feels like that woman in Bridges of Madison County. I saw that with DL on our first date. Did you see it? The woman in that movie was bored and unfulfilled. The part I always remember is when they were in the rain. She was riding in their truck with her husband. The photographer was in front of them at the red light. She was trapped. The sky was crying. Everyone in the theater was crying because they wanted her to leave her husband and go to the photographer. I was crying for her too. I wanted her to get out of her husband's truck and get in the other one. I wanted her to get out of that truck and be happy for a change.

I got out of that truck. So did you. We never should have.

It's time for us to get back in our trucks and go our separate ways.

We have to meet. I need this. You need this.

To keep this civil, I suggest we meet at a public place.

Let's end this where we started this. EuroChow.

I'll be in Westwood tonight at six. I'll wait until six-thirty.

That e-mail is on the kitchen counter when I get out of bed. It's almost eleven. I go back upstairs and look in the guest room. Charles is gone. I call him and he's down in Hawthorne, eating breakfast at Chips.

I'm pissed. "How did she get my e-mail add—You know what? At this point, it doesn't matter. Who does she think she is?"

We talk about closure.

He says, "If that's what we need to do to move on, let's do it and move on."

"Look . . . I'll let you know."

He tells me that he's going to see about teaching in the L.A. Unified school district.

I say, "On a Saturday?"

He tells me that a frat brother from UCLA is hooking him up with a special meeting, pulling a favor and getting Charles a weekend interview. That way he doesn't have to go into the main office with his eye swollen. And with it being a different school district, and with the shortage of qualified teachers, he thinks that he can have a new job by the time his eye heals.

I wish him luck.

Yvette reads the e-mail, then asks, "What you gonna do?"

We're outside in the station parking lot, sitting under a smog-filled sky. Both of us are just getting to the plantation. We're here thirty minutes early so we can talk this out.

I tell her that I want to see Jessica face-to-face. And I need to see how she reacts to Charles. How he reacts to her. How they are together. How he reacts to me in her presence.

She says, "So you going?"

"What would you do?"

"You know me. But it's all about what you need."

Yvette says, "E-mail her back."

"And say what?"

She knows almost everything. After I had left Charles at the dinner table, I'd gone upstairs to the master bedroom, closed the door, and called my girl, tissue in hand. She had told me that it was okay to call her when things were rough, and she meant it. We were on the phone for two hours. I told her everything. About sleeping with David Lawrence again, about Jessica showing up while I was naked on that futon, about the words I shared with Charles at dinner.

I'd told her that he was going to leave me.

"But he didn't. Remember that."

A sister always has to call her girl.

"Make this little picnic be under your terms," Yvette says. "If you have her wait or meet you somewhere later, like at Jerry's Deli, I can get up there after work, maybe have one of my friends tag along, and we can lay in the cut in case she tries to get stupid."

"I can't sleep. I can't think right. I want to do it now."

"You have to give it to her. Sister has a little class."

"Whatever." I mock Jessica, *"I want to end it where we started it."*

"Oh, please."

"It'll be my last time going to EuroChow, you can believe that."

"Heads up. We have company."

I look up the stairs. Tyra the Tyrant is in the doorway. She's been watching us awhile. Then she opens the door and comes down the stairs, the coat to her pinstripe business suit open, her right hand bouncing sheets of paper against her thigh as she walks the walk of a true HNIC.

We're leaning against Yvette's SUV. When Tyra gets too close, we stand up straight.

She says, "I need to have meetings with both of you."

I ask, "Now?"

"Not at this second. I have another meeting. While I'm working on keeping our ratings up and the rest of my staff employed, continue your little gregarious and loquacious outing."

She tells us that she wants to see me in her office in the next hour, before things get rolling, then she wants a one-on-one with Yvette later in the evening, before the newscast.

I ask, "Am I getting fired?"

"One hour. My office."

She hurries away, her coat flapping against her long torso, auburn weave swaying, breasts bouncing like two midgets on a trampoline, leaves us wondering what the hell is going on.

She's going up the stairs, her pumps click-clacking, when I mumble, "Bitch."

Tyra stops walking. Her stiff body language tells me that she heard me and she's about to turn around. I think she's looking straight ahead, but her eyes are on our reflection in the glass doors. Her eyes are on me. Seconds go by before she resumes her pace and goes inside.

I say, "Gregarious and loquacious?"

"I hate dem damn SAT words."

"She's going to fire me. I can feel it."

"She wants a come-to-Jesus meeting with both of us, Freckles, not just you."

"Think she would fire you?"

"That grinch would fire her momma on Christmas Eve."

"Hmmmm."

Yvette says, "Bet she found out about us chilling at Houghmagandy."

"Oh, God. You think?"

"Hell if I know."

"We need to take her up there and introduce her to the DEA."

"Or Minnie Mouse."

That cracks us up.

We sit there. I read the e-mail again. Laughter ends. Yvette reads the e-mail again.

She asks me, "What do you need to get back to peace? Think about that."

I say, "I need to see them together. Then I need to have a conversation with her one-on-one. There are some things I need to say to her. Lot of shit I need to get off my chest."

We head toward the plantation.

She asks, "Planning on leaving him?"

"Adultery isn't grounds for divorce."

She says, "Used to be."

"But it ain't no mo'."

"Wonder why they changed that."

I shrug. "Guess because then nobody would stay married."

"At least nobody in California."

"Think adultery is still on the books down south."

She holds the door open for me and we step into the cold building.

Yvette says, "I want you and Charles to work it out."

"Why?"

"I want to believe in happy endings. I need to see one."

"Never knew you felt like that."

"You're my hope, Freckles. You've always been my hope."

* * *

Tyra has me come into her office. I close the door and sit in a chair facing her desk. Pictures of two little girls are on her walls. A cup of Starbucks and a bottle of Coke are on her desk. An old photo from her modeling days and so many awards are on her walls.

She says, "This was pulled off the wire yesterday."

She slides me a printout. One of the Associated Press stories is circled in red ink.

She sips the last of her Coke, then pops a piece of Nicorette and says, "If it weren't for the shooting at LAX shutting down all of the local news, local affiliates would've picked this up and it would've been run last night."

My eyes won't leave the printout. It's about two teachers having an affair. Same school where there was a pedophile incident. A fight between a teacher and his lover's husband.

Tyra says, "Not as hot as the child abductions, but it's local news, and that story could be hot. It has sex. Internet. Parents. Kids. Morals. Hypocrisy. That's news."

I hold the printout. Reading the words over and over, wanting them to change.

Tyra says, "I'm not one to get into anyone's personal business, but I have to ask. One of the names is the same as your husband's."

I finally look at her.

I ask, "When is this running?"

She says, "All I need is a nod, no explanation."

I look away from her.

She says, "Is this your husband?"

"If it isn't?"

"If it isn't, it's a story."

I say, "It's me. It's my husband."

She has the upper hand. I look at her again, expect her to smile, or laugh. She doesn't.

"Then it's not a story." Her face remains serious. "Not at this station. Not on my watch."

It takes me a moment before I can find any words. I say, "Thank you."

I sit there holding the printout, waiting for Tyra to say something that lets me know I'm forever in her debt. She says nothing. I don't understand her. I don't understand any of this.

She says, "Are we done?"

I say, "Can I ask you something, Tyra?"

"Make it quick."

"Is my work that bad? Am I just that incompetent at what I do?"

"No. You're one of the best. You have room for growth, but you're good."

"Then what's the problem? I do something to offend you?"

She leans back in her executive chair, rocking and thinking of how to answer that.

She says, "My husband left me for a dancer who looks just like you; I have to look at you every day."

Uneasiness grows inside of me. I have no idea how to respond to that. For a brief moment, she looks vulnerable as well, awkward, as if she wishes she hadn't told me.

"So, now I'm a single mom. I have problems, just like you. I put a lot of energy into what I do. I have two kids I hardly see. By the time I leave here, they're asleep. I can't read my own children bedtime stories because I'm here. The most contact I have is when I take them to Westchester Lutheran early in the morning. No husband in my life. Not since he left me. I have a nanny to give me a hand. She picks them up from school, cooks for them, does the laundry, helps with the homework, and puts them to bed. The nanny gets all the quality time."

"I didn't know."

"Now you do. So, I'm busting my ass here, trying to maintain for my children. You understand? Don't think I don't sacrifice every day. My kid gets sick, I can't leave. I have a breakdown in a relationship, I still have to come in here and be professional. We all do."

"You're right."

Before it gets too uncomfortable between us, she stands and raises her shield.

She says, "You called me a bitch."

"I apologize."

"If I were a white man and ran a ship the way I do, I'd be called a CEO. But since I'm a black woman, I have to work twice as hard and get called a bitch more times than I can count."

"I feel you."

"No you don't. And I hope you never have to."

We stand there facing each other, neither of us moving. She says, "Are we done?"

I say, "One more thing."

"Make it quick."

"I just found out about my husband's affair on Tuesday night. When you called me in on Wednesday, my off day, I was a wreck, was trying to handle it then."

She sighs as if to say she's sorry. Or maybe to say we all go through that, get used to it.

I say, "I really need to leave early. I need to take care of this."

She nods. "Just make sure everything is handled or delegated before you go."

"Thanks."

"Just remember who you're calling a bitch around here."

We both walk out the door. Tyra becomes queen of the Leos and falls into her type-A rhythm, goes right back to roaring at people and demanding the best from everyone in sight.

I watch her and I feel strange. I'm looking at myself ten years from now.

19

My world becomes a haze. A dangerous haze. I don't remember leaving the station. Don't remember driving out of the lot and getting on La Brea. Traffic is bad twenty-four-seven in this part of the world, and on a Saturday afternoon it's straight-up hell. I have to become a road warrior to get from point A to point B, and right now I don't remember making a turn, or getting caught at a light, or taking Sunset Boulevard from Hollywood toward Westwood.

But that's where I am when my mind comes back to me, on Sunset Boulevard at La Cienega, on the outskirts of Beverly Hills, miles of red brake lights in my face.

This is not the route to take when you're in a hurry.

I want to do this, but I don't want to.

I'm trapped at the same light for three cycles, carbon monoxide blowing in my face, and cursing that Jessica bitch for having me out in traffic.

My cell phone rings. It's Charles.

He asks, "Where are you?"

I tell him, then ask him the same.

He says, "On the 405 and the 90."

"You should get there first."

"Where should I meet you?"

"At the martini bar."

We hang up. That woodpecker is messing with me again. All I can do is pop two Tylenol, swallow them dry, blow air, pull at my locks, and shake my head.

I've had so much drama in such a short space of time.

This all started because David Lawrence was being a loving husband and washing his wife's SUV on her birthday. Ended up finding a friggin' condom wrapper on the floor. That was sloppy. I can't think of any woman that careless. He finds out she's been creeping with my husband for almost a year. Confronts her. He's an in-your-face kinda man and she's very emotional, so it had to have gotten ugly. Very loud and very ugly. She had to be scared to death. Jessica breaks down, bounces to God knows where. Skips work on Friday, ends up MIA the whole weekend and her husband's going crazy thinking that she's run off to be with Charles.

They're going through drama and I'm working and going to church, just knowing that my world is unshatterable.

I've been thinking about all of that so much that I forgot where I was going, forgot to look at myself and see how I'm dressed. I have on jeans and a peasant blouse. Good enough for Melrose Boulevard, but not high-rent enough for a spot like EuroChow.

But this is about business, not aesthetics.

Forty minutes later, I trade the insanity on Wilshire for the madness on Westwood Boulevard, make a quick U-turn, then line Baby Blue up behind three cars at valet parking. Everyone is being let out like they're movie stars. A couple of them are.

EuroChow is in a landmark Mediterranean building in Westwood. The station did a story on the restaurant when it opened back in the late nineties. It's always been my favorite spot. My territory. It's so international and the food is orgasmic to the nth degree.

The weekend air is blowing in from the Pacific, getting crisp, asking me to come away and flow with the breeze. I look up. It's close to sunset. It's my time of day. The skies fill with so many colors, become so beautiful I want to climb inside. The end of daylight. I want to leave, find a beach, and stick my toes in the sand, or go to Kenneth Hahn Park, sit in the grass and look for four-leaf clovers, go somewhere and have my moment, but I can't.

An eerie feeling creeps over me. I know where I am, and I feel so lost.

I step inside the white-on-white interior. Lots of windows. Lots of light. Lots of mirrors. But it's the stark whiteness that makes it seem like I'm in a dream. This place has a spiritual feeling to it. It used to be a church, and some of those angelic spirits remain. And the architecture is so unreal. There's a marble obelisk pointing up at a fifty-five-foot-high dome. That, the rich smell of all the foods, and the fiber-optic lighting, make it seem like an angel should come down with a plate of Chinese or Italian cuisine and take me up to martini heaven.

I put on my business smile and tell the hostess that I'm looking for someone. They have the nicest employees. She lets me go look around. Purse in hand, I take easy steps by the gold-leaf screens surrounding the lounge; all the way bartenders and waiters are smiling and chatting with customers. I'm hoping I don't see Jessica before I see Charles. Don't know what I'd say. Or do.

No sign of Charles.

I take out my cell phone, get ready to call him, and it vibrates. The number from the station shows up.

I answer, "What's wrong?"

"Nothing." It's an assistant. "You had two FedEx packages delivered right after you left. Some sort of black tubes. I signed for them."

"Thanks. Leave them on my desk, please."

"Are you okay?"

That's the real reason for the phone call.

I say, "I'm fine. See you at the plantation tomorrow."

I hang up and get ready to call Charles, but I look up and see one of the hostesses leading a woman over the saintly catwalk that separates the two sides of the building. The woman is dressed in tans and greens, looking designer from head to toe. The hostess leads her to the back wall that has a gigantic mirror. She's shown a small table, then shakes her head like she doesn't like it. Does that like she's been here a thousand times and knows which seats she wants. The hostess leads. She follows.

Beautiful midnight skin. Permed hair hanging over her shoulders.

No matter how hard I stare, she doesn't look down.

The hostess takes her to a private booth that has butterscotch leather curtains tied back.

My heart beats so fast. Fingers dance against my folded arms. Throat is so dry.

Jessica is here, a capella. I feel relieved. Then I think about David Lawrence, wonder why he's not here. I'm glad he's not. That drumbeat still echoes with every step. I'm not sure I can handle seeing him. I feel something, too much, when I think about him.

I should go up there. Have a face-to-face with her. This is a woman thing.

The woman dressed like a model. The peasant girl dressed in blah.

I don't think so.

I head back outside, phone up to my ear, rushing down the steps, calling Charles.

I ask, "Where are you now?"

"Crossing Sawtelle and coming up on National."

"You're not even at the 10 yet. What's taking so long?"

"CHP ran a break and stopped traffic. Looks like an accident."

"Can you get off and take the surface streets?"

"Assholes won't let me get over."

"You using your signal light?"

"Yeah."

"That's why. Never signal if you want to change lanes."

"Don't matter. Surface streets might be just as bad."

I curse. "We were supposed to get here first."

"I know."

"It's ten to six and she's already here."

"She alone?"

"Why?"

"Is she?"

"She's alone."

He lets out a deep sigh. I can't tell if that's a good thing or a disappointment.

I ask, "You want her to not be alone?"

"I hope you didn't expect me and her lunatic husband to sit at the same table."

"She's here. I've fought traffic to get here. She's waiting."

"I'll be there as soon as traffic loosens up."

"Call me when you're getting off the freeway."

"Where you going?"

"Shopping."

Westwood Boulevard is a busy strip that runs into the south end of UCLA. Lots of eateries. Lots of movie theaters. A million places to shop between here and the campus.

Twenty minutes and two hundred dollars later, I'm wearing wide-legged khaki pants and a white form-fitting top. A colorful silk scarf covers my locks. I dump my peasant gear in a bag, then hurry to spend another hundred on a pair of chocolate pointed-toe slingbacks. Then I use the bathroom at Starbucks. Pollution, stress, and sun have my skin feeling icky. Have to wash my face, redo my lipstick, and then put on a touch of makeup to hide my imperfections.

My palms won't stop sweating. Even if this meeting only lasts two minutes, I have to look perfect.

My cell phone rings.

Charles is on Weyburn, about to turn onto Westwood and pull up in front of EuroChow.

His lover, the woman he was going to leave me for, is in the restaurant.

I say, "Don't go in there without me."

Charles waits at valet parking. He sees me in a mix of people, walking up the boulevard, bag in hand, and comes toward me. He's wearing dark shades, has on a dark four-button suit, dark shirt, dark tie.

I say, "Dressed to impress."

"Wore this to the interview."

"How did it go?"

"Right now I'm focusing on moving on with my marriage."

He takes my bag from me.

He says, "That's all I care about right now."

He wants to hug me, I see it in his eyes, but I also see the pain. We've had joint affairs. My lover has humiliated him in more ways than one. His lover is here. This is awkward. So we don't try to embrace each other. I fold my arms, hold myself. He stuffs his hands in his pockets.

I say, "Let's do this."

"We don't have to do this, you know?"

"We have to."

Darkness is moving in, the sun being swallowed by the ocean. Maybe it's the lights, or my eyes, or my restless mood, but this time everything is so overwhelmingly pristine and pure that I'm bum rushed by too many emotions at once.

Charles asks, "Sure you're okay?"

"No."

"You're shaking."

"So are you."

The truth is I'm afraid to see her. She's a criminal. So am I. Our sins are equal. Once is the same as a hundred times.

The restaurant doesn't feel heavenly white anymore. It looks more asylum-white. Everything is too large, too over-done. I'm nervous and I start looking around, thinking that someone is about to come after me with a straitjacket.

I ask, "Why does she want to meet us?"

"You read the e-mail. For resolution."

"No, I mean why us? Why just me and you? Why not her husband?"

"She knows if he was here . . . no telling what I'd do at this point."

I shake my head, my expression saying that this isn't adding up. "Is there something she's going to say that I need to know?"

"No."

"Then there must be something that she's going to say that she doesn't want him to hear."

He shifts, touches his swollen eye, then rubs the edges of his face.

I say, "Don't have me going in there looking like a fool."

The hostess comes toward us and Charles touches my arm, asks the hostess to excuse us, then asks me to step to the side.

I ask, "What's going on, Charles?"

"Come over here."

We move near the rest rooms, hide ourselves in the dim, small space by the pay phones.

He takes his shades off and stands there, face tense, anxiety rising.

He says, "She was pregnant."

That stings my soul. I can't talk for a moment. His confession has sucked the air out of my lungs. I put a hand out, use the wall to hold myself up. Charles puts his hand on my shoulder. I move it away.

I repeat, "Pregnant."

"Was."

"Was?"

He nods. "Was."

"She had an abortion?"

"Miscarriage."

"She miscarried?"

"Yeah."

I ask, "When was this?"

"She called me last Friday."

"Yesterday?"

He pulls his lips in. "Week ago yesterday."

"Damn, Charles."

"She'd gotten into it with him, left as fast as she could,

panicking, didn't have anywhere to go, checked into a hotel, said she was stressed and crying and all kinds of shit. She said her back was hurting too bad for her to drive out to her cousin's in Palm Springs. Then the next day she started cramping real bad, called me at work because she had been up all night, needed me to leave work and take her to the emergency room."

I stand there, absorbing it all, trying to understand. Jessica gets busted, has an all-out fight with her husband on Thursday night, runs out, and David Lawrence assumes she ran to Charles.

I ask, "You sure about that?"

"I was there."

"Where is 'there'?"

"At the emergency room."

"What emergency room?"

"Kaiser."

"And you were there?"

"I talked to the doctor." He nods. "So I know she had a miscarriage."

"Where was I?"

"The station."

He tells me by the time he got off work and went to her hotel, she was doubled over and clotting.

I say, "You waited until you got off work?"

"I didn't know until the middle of the day. I can't just walk out on a class."

I'm perplexed; too much has happened too soon. The journalist in me wants to come to life and ask so many questions, wants to ask if he was sure it was his, if Jessica was sleeping with him and her husband, but I'm not sure if any of these questions are relevant at this point.

I ask, "How far along was she?"

"Few weeks."

"What's a few weeks?"

"She said between thirteen and fifteen weeks."

Again I shut down. People go in and out of the bathrooms. Our expressions are clear. Even if we try to turn our backs, our energy fills the space around us.

I ask, "Is that why you were going to leave me? Because of the baby?"

He struggles with his thoughts, his words are ragged. "I believe in family."

"Give me a break. You had a fucking affair. You're no Ward Cleaver."

"That would've been the right thing. For the baby."

"For the baby."

"I want to have a child, but I don't want to have a bastard child."

"People at your job already knew, didn't they?"

"People talk."

"Teachers are worse than kids when it comes to gossip, Charles."

"Lower your voice."

"Then she miscarried. And you walked away."

"Back when she told me that she was pregnant, that brought things into perspective. I didn't want to be with her. I had wanted to end it a long time ago, but it's not that easy."

I'm not hearing his excuses. I say, "It scared the shit out of you."

"It let me know how I felt about her. And us."

I say, "Whatever you had with Jessica stopped being fun."

"It gave me clarity."

"Where did she go after that?"

"I checked her back into the Best Western."

"Which one?"

He makes a frustrated sound. "In Rowland Heights."

Now I know where their love nest was built, at a hotel near his job.

He says, "She called a cousin to come stay with her."

"Her cousin in Palm Springs."

"Yeah. She was going to drive out as soon as she got off work that evening."

"Did you at least wait for her cousin to get there?"

"Couldn't."

"Why didn't you stay with her?"

He makes a face that says he's a man who had to make a hard, ugly choice. He tells me that it was getting late, that it would take her cousin forever to get from Palm Springs to the hotel in Friday traffic, that he was torn and had to choose between staying at Jessica's bedside and going home to his wife. He had to decide which way he was going to go with his life.

I ask, "Did you tell her that?"

He says, "We had a face-to-face."

I pause and think. The words roll off my tongue, "On Tuesday."

He looks surprised that I know.

I say, "You went to see her on Tuesday."

"How did you know?"

"You lied about being at a movie and you came home with the food from CPK. You stopped to get food so it would look like . . . You covered your tracks. You thought it was all over. You went to see her, she told you her husband knew, but you knew that because he'd come after you at your job, in front of everybody, and since she had miscarried . . . Bet you were pissed, told her you were done with her, walked out on her, and celebrated by bringing me dinner."

"Look, I wasn't celebrating."

He runs his hand over his mane, smooths out his coat, and I read the lines in his face; the thickest one shows his guilt over not staying overnight with his lover. Even with her laying up in a hotel room in pain, the blood of a new death seeping into a cotton pad, he chose to go home.

I say, "The best way for a woman to know how a man feels about her is by getting pregnant."

"Don't say that."

"I'm speaking from experience. A woman gets pregnant, then she finds out who she's dealing with. How her lover really feels about her. If they have a future."

"I'm not going to lie, it was a wake-up call."

"It always is."

He says, "It wasn't meant to be."

"No, you got lucky."

He lets out a strong sigh.

I say, "So careless. You have been so careless."

"I know."

"I can't believe you got another woman pregnant."

He can't say anything.

Finally, I ask, "Anything else, Charles?"

"Nothing."

"You sure?"

He lets out a strong, yet uneven sigh. "Nothing else."

I stand near the pay phones, looking down.

He asks, "What you thinking?"

"I feel sorry for Jessica. You left her. She was scared. Alone."

My voice sounds so very Zen. I'm crying, but there are no tears.

My own abortion from years ago, that feeling of abandonment, that pain haunts me. My teenage lover telling me that he didn't love me, telling me to get over it, as if I could cure being in love overnight. Love is a madman's disease, and I went crazy. Didn't want to live.

Charles knows that.

Women love more profoundly than men. I can only imagine what Jessica went through.

Charles turns to one side, his shoulder against the wall.

He says, "I know it seems like I'm a monster, but I'm not."

"I'm just a woman. You're just a man."

"I was living in the moment and it got out of hand. You get in too deep, things get carried away, and there's no easy way out."

"That's because the heart gets involved, Charles. The heart anchors you."

Forks are clanking against plates; the aroma of well-seasoned foreplay fills my senses. Potential lovers are touching hands, sipping martinis, smiling, and having light and flirty conversations. Words of lust are being sprinkled all over the room.

He asks, "What do you want to do?"

I can't answer. Too many conflicting emotions are tugging at me.

Feels like I'm floating over us, looking down, in another trance. He says my name and I blink a few times, turn and stare at my reflection in the silver part of the pay phone. I touch my locks, try to fix my expression, create one that's strong, one suitable for public display.

I say, "You owe Jessica an apology."

My words stun him.

I tell him, "You should fall on your knees and apologize to her."

He nods. "Can you forgive me?"

I say, "Your inability to see how much an open and honest dialogue between us means to me, and your refusal to acknowledge that I have real feelings for you, makes me sad."

We stop talking when someone walks into the men's room. Then someone comes out of the ladies' room. No one looks at us. Then we're in this prison-sized space, alone again.

This fucks me up. I'm trying to maintain. Trying to understand what is going on. David Lawrence had to know. He had a ton of their correspondences. He didn't tell me about the baby. Gave me the pages he wanted me to see. Used those IMs to get to me. He played me.

"I had sex with her husband, Charles." I'm not saying that to be mean. Those words slip away from me on winds of guilt and surprise me too. "How do you feel about me after that?"

"It hurts like hell. He used you."

"Is that what you choose to believe?"

"Yes."

I make a definite hand motion, one that tells Charles I'm ready to go see the woman he's telling me he lost a child with. The woman he abandoned in some hotel room, before running home and falling into my arms.

20

The hostess leads us up the white staircase. I'm a few steps in front of Charles, trying to control my walk, unable to put my eyes on him right now, so I'm gazing down at the part of the floor that is clear and shows the wine cellar beneath, but as soon as we get to the second level, he takes my hand and leads the way. He used to take my hand and ecstasy would crawl through my veins, my heart would swim in wine. Now the nearness of him creates confusion.

We move across the catwalk and come up on the booths draped with butterscotch leather curtains. The smiling hostess stands to the side and Charles steps up to the opening first. Jessica lowers her cosmopolitan and the expression on her face is hard to describe. She sees my husband and is startled, jerks like she's been shaken from a dream.

She says his name, "Charles . . . ?"

Her surprised expression changes into a wide-eyed smile filled with deep-fried love. She remembers other things and her eyes transform again, become those of a woman done wrong.

Charles slides into the booth in a hurry, and I sit next to him. The hostess leaves.

The booth feels enclosed, like a small cave with beautiful place settings.

Jessica isn't moving. She holds a bewildered expression.

Charles says, "I told her everything. She knows everything."

Then she scowls at me like I'm wearing a mink coat at an animal rights convention.

Jessica asks Charles, "What's this?"

Charles's tone roughens and he tells her that we're here to meet her, just like she asked in the e-mail.

She says, "What e-mail?"

We all fall silent, our gazes going back and forth at each other. At first, I think she's playing a game. And my empathy for her changes into a frown filled with irritation.

I ask her, "Why are you here?"

She gives me that why-are-you-talking-to-me-bitch attitude, and the tone to match. "We're celebrating our anniversary. We're meeting some of DL's friends here."

I understand what's happening. It throws me into a mild panic.

I say, "Charles, come on, we have to go."

Before I can scoot out of the booth, the hostess comes back again, all perky and smiling.

He's right behind her. Dressed in jeans. A white cotton shirt that's open to the middle of his chest. Black leather jacket. Square, yellow-lens sunglasses. His afro is wild and funky, eccentric and off-center. His demeanor is confident, borderline arrogant.

David Lawrence is here, facing all of us.

I look up at him and become aware of my vagina.

I swallow.

Charles stiffens beside me. His body is a wildfire. Then he

loosens his tie and moves against me. He wants me to get out of the way so he can get up.

I'm not moving.

David Lawrence takes off his shades and shows the puffiness under his eyes. He's worn, has had no sleep, no rest, no peace. No one at this table has.

He looks directly at me. A hesitant smile creeps up in the corner of his mouth. I almost smile in return, then I remember that we are at war. I remember the video. I remember to frown. He gazes at his wife. She's shaking now. Then he cuts his eyes at Charles. He's staring at the reds and blacks in Charles's swollen eye as if it's artwork. He nods and almost smiles.

He asks Charles, "How you doing?"

Charles leans in, gives him an intense stare filled with disdain. "What kind of psychological game are you playing?"

David Lawrence says, "I don't want to start any shit, but I love my wife. That's why I'm here. And she loves me. With that said, Jessica has something to say and she wants both of you to hear it. Then you two can go."

"You sent those e-mails out and kids got them. What kind of monster are you?"

"You wrote them. To my wife. What kind of monster are you?"

Charles sucks his teeth. "You went too far."

"No, you went too far."

"This was between us, not the parents and the children at the school."

"Maybe parents need to know what kind of immoral pervert is teaching their kids."

Charles wants to get out of the booth. I want to leave too, because like David Lawrence, I want to be able to control the situation, but I don't move. There is too much volatile tension right now. If I do, nothing will separate him and Charles. I put my hand on Charles's leg, signaling him to wait it out, reminding him that this is what we came here for, our resolution.

I say, "People are watching."

A few people across the room are looking our way with condemning eyes, trying to see what's going on, and Charles backs down. He sits up straight, hands rolled in fists.

David Lawrence sits next to Jessica. He's facing me. Charles is facing Jessica.

Husbands and wives side-by-side. Lovers facing lovers.

I understand. David Lawrence has Jessica's password. He can get into her account. He sent out the e-mail. He's done what he feels he has to do to get his house back in order.

I ask, "What's going on?"

David Lawrence tells me, "I got this idea from your list of questions."

"I figured as much."

"You're a smart woman. Creative and bold. Think I told you that."

Charles's eyes are trained on David Lawrence.

Jessica watches me, perspiration on her eyebrows, her brown eyes so green.

This is unreal. We're all here.

The four of us sit at a table filled with scars and open wounds. Four strong people who have been weak in the flesh. We are linked forever. I look at Jessica and Charles, and I imagine them together, their bodies connected. If I say that I am unable to see them in that way, I'd be lying to myself. It's hard for me to see much more than that. But it's there. If I open my eyes and see what's real, it's easy to see that they are two people who have loved.

And David Lawrence. Since I met him at that deli to discuss our spouses' affairs, every time I close my eyes, he's behind my eyes. I connect to him. We love deeply. If only we had met during calmness and sanity, without our spouses' indiscretions as our bond.

Looking at my hands, I think of Tyra the Tyrant, then raise my head, steeple my hands in front of me, and let my eyes meet him head-on, sound as strong as Tyra does, and tell David Lawrence, "We're here. You have our attention. Make it quick."

We are interrupted. The waiter comes to take our drink order. We all sit back. We all pretend. I ask for water with a slice of lime for me and Charles. David Lawrence orders a mojito for himself, another cosmopolitan with extra cranberry juice for his wife. She's barely sipped the one she has, but he orders her another one anyway.

The waiter leaves.

I put my trembling hands in my lap, dry my damp palms on my khakis.

David Lawrence asks me, "Did your husband answer the questions?"

Charles's voice is deep and firm. "I'm right here. Got something to say, talk to me."

"And like it said in the e-mail," David Lawrence says, looking at Charles, "I don't want any drama. I want all of us here so there will be no misunderstanding as to where we all stand."

Charles says, "I'll tell you where we stand, asshole."

I say, "Charles, don't."

David Lawrence and Charles stare each other down the

way men do in prisons. David Lawrence's gaze remains on Charles as he tells Jessica, "Now, tell him what you told me."

Jessica is shivering. "DL, don't do this."

"Tell him you never loved him."

"DL, don't do this."

She rocks and stares at her cosmopolitan glass.

I say, "What we talked about downstairs. Charles, do you want to say—"

"No."

He refuses to apologize, or show any weakness, in front of David Lawrence.

Jessica rocks and rocks and stares at her cosmopolitan. She seems so vulnerable and small, beautiful and exotic features distorted by the depression in her eyes. She reminds me of a woman who confuses sexual pleasure with true love, or falls in love with the idea of love itself.

After all Charles has told me, a part of me wants to wrap my arms around her and offer sympathy. Not because I like her as a person. I don't like her character. But I feel for her as a woman. She's been traumatized. It's unnatural for your child to go first. Even if it never made it into the world.

I try to be the voice of reason, say that we all want the same thing, to be healed, pain-free.

I say, "Since we're going by my list, we do it the way it's on the list."

Jessica wipes her eyes. "In that case, everyone needs to answer the same questions."

She's talking to me, telling me that we're not as different as I think we are.

Charles says, "She's right."

I say, "I have no problem with that."

David Lawrence shakes his head. "No."

"You painted her, Charles," she snaps. Her eyes are glazed over with jealousy. She sees everyone's expressions, then shakes her head. "I mean DL."

That mistake halts us all.

Jessica brings her hand up to her head, uses her fingers to comb her black hair away from her face, then moves her jittery hand and knocks her cosmopolitan over.

The crimson liquid moves across the white tablecloth toward Charles.

I grab my napkin. Charles grabs his napkin. We both toss them on the river.

Jessica bumbles to get the glass upright. It rolls and falls on her side of the booth. She leaves it on the floor. David Lawrence watches, his jaw tight, eyes wide.

Jessica talks with her hands, says, "DL, sorry. Sweetie, that was an accident."

We live in a strange moment, like when you're making love, when you're in the heat of the moment, and you scream out the wrong name. It stops everything. You lose your rhythm.

We have lost our rhythm.

David Lawrence is still quiet. So is Charles.

The waiter comes back with our drinks. His interruption takes away some of the awkwardness.

Now we can start.

David Lawrence says, "What was mine was stolen. It feels like my dignity was taken. I couldn't find out what was going on. Deception was my only option."

Charles says, "You went too far."

David Lawrence says, "Then I apologize."

They stare. Charles shakes his head, drinks some of his water.

I ask Jessica, "Do you love Charles?"

She shakes her head. "I love DL."

"Then what was all of . . . this . . . about?"

She snaps, "It was about nothing."

I wait a moment.

I ask Charles, "You love Jessica?"

"I fell in love with her. Then I fell out of love with her. But I never stopped loving you."

I pull my lips in. His answer is too real for me. I expected less than the truth.

I say, "Do you have plans to see each other?"

They shake their heads.

Charles asks, "What about you? You were with him less than twenty-four hours ago."

I say, "It was nothing."

"Two nights, and I'm supposed to think it's nothing?"

Jessica stiffens. She didn't know. Her eyes water. Her pain deepens.

I say, "It was revenge sex. It was nothing. I felt nothing."

Now Charles is wide-eyed and shattered. My answer is too real for him.

I remain still, refuse to squirm, or touch my hair, or my nose, or let my voice fluctuate.

Jessica asks David Lawrence "Is that what it was?"

He nods.

Charles speaks with firmness. "Then how do I know it's over?"

I say, "Because I say it is."

No one is looking at anyone else.

David Lawrence tells Charles, "You have a wife who feels deeply."

"And you disrespected her."

"She is very vulnerable. I saw her falling apart, and I took advantage of that. I apologize."

Charles groans, starts tapping his fingers on the table.

David Lawrence says, "No one on that side of the table has any reason to contact anyone on this side of the table. Am I correct?"

Charles snaps, "The same for that side of the table. Remember that."

David Lawrence doesn't challenge Charles, just nods. He's spent. He tells Jessica, "The condom wrapper you left in your ride caused all of this."

Jessica says, "I told you that it wasn't mine. It was my cousin's."

With what Charles just told me, I believe her. We marinate in irony. Someone else's sloppiness led us here, stole my bliss, and took me from joy to pain.

David Lawrence slaps both of his palms down on the table, says, "Then we are done."

Even in the end, he still wants to be in control. He wants to start it, wants to end it.

I say, "One last piece of business. I believe in fairness. I believe in paying my debts. So, if you want us to, Jessica, I need to know how much the hospital bill was, we'll split it."

David Lawrence looks at his wife and asks, "What hospital bill?"

Again, the climate in our four-star cave changes.

Jessica takes his hand. "Nothing."

David Lawrence looks at me, again asking the same question, needing to be led out of the dark.

I say, "We're being honest here, Jessica. All I know is what Charles told me."

She closes her eyes, her lip quivers, and the tears come.

Jessica tells her husband about being pregnant. She tells him about the miscarriage. She tells him that she didn't go to Palm Springs, just hid out in a hotel room. Her cousin never showed up. She was alone the whole time. Her voice is broken and the words don't come easily. Each breath strong enough to blow out a hundred candles. Charles holds my hand, squeezes it as she tells her version of what has happened. She was three months pregnant.

Hearing her admit it fucks me up that much more.

David Lawrence's expression, the new level of confusion and angst, answers my question. I thought he knew. He didn't. He says, "The situation. In the e-mails to him you said something about your 'situation.' Is that the 'situation' you were talking about?"

Jessica nods. "That's not something I wanted to talk about over the computer. That's something you talk about face-to-face."

He struggles with this truth, then asks, "Whose was it?"

Charles tells him, "Mine. It was mine."

I ask, "How do you know, Charles?"

David Lawrence looks to Jessica for a denial. There is none.

All words in this small space fade. All I hear is the chatter and laughter, the sounds of silverware clanking against plates, so much celebration coming from outside our booth.

I wipe my eyes. "We're done."

David Lawrence doesn't move. His warrior's shield, his arrogance, all of it has been destroyed. His pain dethrones him. He looks small. His power diminished.

Jessica has her arms around him, her head on his shoulder, telling him how much she loves him, asking for forgiveness.

I slide out of the booth. Charles slides out too, his movements rugged, like he can't wait to get out of this prison. Nothing more needs to be said. We can all go our separate ways.

But Charles touches his eye when he stands. He tells them, "Happy anniversary."

His last word. His final blow.

He walks away, his bitter stroll moving him deeper into the whiteness of the building.

David Lawrence looks up, top teeth biting his bottom lip, the lights reflecting on his eyes. Tears roll down his face. He leaves them be, remains seated, shaking his head over and over.

I open my mouth. Words want to come up from my heart, but when I see the opaqueness in his eyes, all I can do is swallow and shake my head. I leave them to handle their own affairs. I have to deal with mine.

I don't catch up with Charles until I get outside. He's near valet parking. We're back in the din of the village, back out on crowded streets. College students, yuppies, buppies, muppies, an international crowd of people is out on the boulevard. After being in that booth, the world seems so large now, the air so fresh.

Charles says, "Give me your ticket so I can get our cars and we can get out of here."

I'm emotionally depleted. I give him the ticket. The rest I will deal with later.

I look down at my feet. I see new shoes. New pants. A new blouse.

Outside of my purse, my hands are empty. Charles isn't holding anything.

I ask him, "Wait, where is my bag?"

"What bag?"

The shopping bag that has my jeans and blouse is missing. I struggle to think of where it is, then I remember giving it to Charles before we went into the restaurant. I don't remember him having it in his hand when we went to the booth.

He says, "I must've put it down when we were talking by the pay phones."

Charles hands me the valet tickets and hurries back toward the restaurant. Before he gets inside, the door opens. David Lawrence and Jessica are coming out, but they're not walking together. She's a few feet behind him. They all stop for a moment.

David Lawrence. Jessica. Charles.

It happens too fast. I don't expect it.

David Lawrence opens his leather coat. He takes his gun out.

He points it at Charles.

There are no words, no hesitation, no time for Charles to react before the explosion.

My mouth opens to scream; my body convulses, but the scream won't come.

My husband falls to the pavement, falls slow, but lands hard, then rolls down the steps.

Charles is barely moving. A rag doll in a twisted position, gasping for breath, life leaching out of him.

His blood flows like wine. I want to run to him, put my hand over the red spot. The part of my brain that creates movement has shut down.

No one screams. Everyone stops and looks to see what's going on.

David Lawrence stands under the bright lights of the restaurant, numbness on his face, eyes glazed over, smoking gun in hand.

People see, but they don't react. They're in shock. One by one, they scream. People flee in all directions. A car crashes into another at valet parking.

Jessica stumbles to Charles, falls at his feet. A glassy look is in his wide eyes. Blood foams around his mouth. He's sucking in air, fighting her, as if his nervous system is doing things on its own. Jessica is hysterical, her hand pressing down on his bloody chest, calling her lover's name over and over, crying out for help like a woman gone mad.

David Lawrence follows his wife, then points the gun at her head. His hand is trembling. He hates her. He's trying to pull the trigger. She looks back at him with wide eyes. In that moment, he sees her. Remembers how much he loves her.

He points the gun at his temple.

Panic beats inside my chest. My scream burns out my throat.

I watch the second explosion.

David Lawrence's lifeless body falls to the sidewalk.

21

Cars screech. Horns blow. People dial 911.

So much noise.

Police cars skid to a halt. One officer takes the gun from the ground, the other rushes to David Lawrence, checks for a pulse, then starts CPR.

Jessica falls away from Charles, sits there, bloodied and unmoving.

Another officer runs though the crowd and goes to my husband, presses on his chest. There is so much blood on the pavement. My emotional compass is spinning in circles. My steps toward Charles are jittery. Knees wobble when I look down at his pain.

He's fading.

The first ambulance arrives, its siren wailing until it rolls to a stop. The wail from the second ambulance is right behind them. So many flashing lights. Six medics appear with equipment, racing toward the front of EuroChow. News vans from television stations appear. Cameras record graphic shots that will not air. Spectators are being asked questions—what they heard, what they saw. Curious people create a wall behind a barrier. Yellow police tape is all around me. A child is crying. Normal business in Westwood Village comes to a halt.

My life becomes breaking news.

Jessica sits on the steps of the restaurant that used to be a church, her knees to her chest, fresh horror in her eyes, covered in my husband's blood. David Lawrence lies a few feet away from her. The first set of EMTs goes to him, one talking on his two-way radio.

Male. GSW to head. Entry and exit visible. No pulse. CPR in progress until arrival at hospital.

One of them talks to Jessica. She's falling apart.

I'm not crying. Want to. Can't fall apart right now. Not sure I know how to fall apart.

The second set of EMTs rushes to assess Charles. Two-way radios squawk as they call in my husband's status. *Male victim with GSW to chest, respiratory distress. Difficulty breathing.* He listens with a stethoscope. *Barely visible rising of the chest on one side. Diminished sounds auscultated where bullet entered. Victim has foamy bloody sputum. Indicative of GSW to lung. No breath sounds from the lung involved. Deviated expansion of the chest.*

They keep calling him "victim." He becomes The Victim.

A camera flashes. I turn and see the world watching us. So many people find fascination in the tragedies of others.

Paramedics surround Charles and work on the bloody wound in his chest. Intravenous lines are started in his upper arms. He's hooked up to a machine that flashes an eerie green fluorescent color. One of the EMTs is breathing for him with a bluish object that's shaped like a football. Over and over he squeezes it gently.

I ask, "What are you doing to him?"

"Who are you?"

"I'm his wife."

He asks me medical questions; wants to know if Charles is on medication, if he has allergies, diabetes, heart disease, other things. Arms folded, I answer as quickly as I can. He repeats it all into his two-way so the hospital can get ready to receive him.

The other EMTs rush David Lawrence into the ambulance. Jessica is hysterical; they don't take her with them. Their siren blares as they head up Westwood Boulevard. I know the EMTs can't pronounce him dead. Only a doctor can do that. They're just following procedure.

He's gone. He was gone before his body hit the ground.

Charles's EMT holds gauze to his chest. Blood soaks into the whiteness.

I choke on my words, "Is he going to die?"

"He's lost a lot of blood."

"Don't let him die, please."

"We're doing everything we can, ma'am."

People talk, but all words are incomprehensible, as if everyone is chewing on cotton.

They're applying pressure to his wound, but the blood still flows. He rests in a red river, the same river that covers Jessica's clothing. They work fast, suction all secretions from his mouth, make sure his tongue isn't in the way, then put a breathing tube in his mouth.

I swallow and try to stay out of the way. I'm on autopilot. I know how this works, have seen it countless times. I'm having a hard time breathing. I have to turn around, look down.

Another camera flashes. I want to curse them all.

They give Charles oxygen.

Over and over I ask what's going on, how he's doing. My

voice is too small to be heard. They're busy relaying information, telling the trauma center about blood pressure, pulse, respirations. I stand close, try to listen and understand what the fuck is going on.

The police are interviewing Jessica. I stop rocking and look toward them just as she motions toward where her husband was lying, toward me, then toward Charles.

They strap Charles to a portable gurney, then rush him to the ambulance. I run with them. They help me get inside. Sirens wail as we leave the village.

I look back at them: Jessica, the police officers, the media getting their footage, the spectators with the flashing cameras. Jessica walks forward from the crowd of police officers, arms folded the same way mine were, watching us vanish into the traffic.

Then the EMT says that Charles is crashing and he's advised to proceed with ACLS.

I close my eyes and pray.

Fluorescent lights blind me as I rush inside the hospital.

My shoes click-clack with the frantic pace of the paramedics. The scuff of feet in soft-soled shoes echoes. Doors with pneumatic hinges open and close. The scent of disinfectants replaces the stench of carbon monoxide.

Doctors and nurses take over. A trauma surgeon. A pulmonary physician. A person shows up to draw more blood. They have to X-ray to find out where the bullet is lodged. Ventilators are set up. Breathing machines. They have to give him blood. Get him stabilized. Antibiotics. Tetanus shot. All they say and do gets jumbled in my mind.

I lose all sense of time and place.

It's a hellified and busy night. Plenty of people are in the waiting room, friends and family of other victims. Anxiety and tears surround me.

I blink and I'm out in the hallway, talking to the police.

After that, the *L.A. Times* wants to talk to me. That means the story has hit hard.

I find a television. "Attempted murder-suicide in Westwood" is on every local station.

This tape was shot shortly after . . .

. . . Jessica Lawrence, here in this video footage, covered in blood . . .

Recapping our top story of the day . . .

After having dinner with the victim, the suspect, David Lawrence, shot . . .

Footage of us at the scene, the ambulances, the chaos, it's all there on the tube.

So it goes.

I rub my temples and call my mother. I'm upset. I just saw my husband shot. I just saw a man I slept with kill himself. Still, I tell her as little as I can, then ask her to tell my two sisters, but not before the morning. I call Charles's parents in Slidell. They hear the bad news in my voice as soon as they answer. It's hard to lie to them, but I keep it vague, just that Charles was shot as we left a restaurant, and he's in surgery, and I'll call them back as soon as I hear something.

By then my cell phone is vibrating nonstop. It's driving me crazy. People from the station are calling to check on me. I even get a call from Tyra. She sounds kind. Wants me to call them so they'll know I'm okay so far as injuries are concerned, and wants to know what she can do to help. Friends have seen the news. People from Faithful Central have heard.

* * *

Yvette shows up, running to find me, looking frantic and confused.

I look at my watch. It's after one in the morning.

She hugs me. "Damn, Freckles."

"I'm not having a good day."

Feels like I'm bleeding from the back of my head, but it doesn't hurt. I put my hand on my head, then my neck. The blood isn't blood. It's sweat. I'm hot. Nauseated. I need water.

Yvette asks, "How is Charles?"

"Still in surgery."

"Fuck."

"They say it can take up to eight hours."

"They give you any updates?"

"Critical condition."

"David Lawrence?"

My face says it all. My lover is dead. I don't know what I'm supposed to do, or how I'm supposed to feel. I can't call anyone. I'm angry. Feeling guilty. Confused. Don't understand why this had to get to this point. David Lawrence. That last image fucks me up. And I don't have the right to grieve, no more than Jessica has the right to even think about coming here.

Yvette says, "This shit hit everybody at the station. This was hard to cover."

"What Tyra say? Bet she was having orgasms left and right."

"She was upset. Major upset."

Yvette holds my hand while I babble about everything that happened.

I say, "We were the top story."

"Like a motherfucker."

"Wow. Weird, huh?"

"Weird."

The doctor comes at sunrise, when Yvette has gone to the cafeteria to get us some food. He says my name and I close my eyes in prayer. He looks like Robert Wagner with George Hamilton's tan. We move to the side, away from everyone, so he can talk to me. He takes my hand, pats it like I'm his favorite daughter, and verifies that my husband was shot in the lung.

"The bullet entered at such an angle," he tells me, "it destroyed the vital veins feeding the blood supply to that lung."

My voice trembles. "What does that mean?"

"By the time surgery was started, loss of oxygen and blood had caused the lung tissue to start a process of deterioration."

"Wait. I'm not understanding what you're saying."

"Your husband lost a lung. We had to do a pneumonectomy."

Something hollows inside of me. I'm groaning, shaking my head.

He asks, "Would you like me to give you something?"

"What do you mean?"

"You've witnessed a lot."

"No shit."

"Let me get you something to calm you."

"No, I'm fine."

He motions. "Your other hand."

I look down. Anxiety has my left hand shaking like I have a neurological disorder.

That hollow part of me caves in. My voice breaks. "He lost a lung?"

"Yes."

"Will he need a lung donor or . . . ?"

"You can live with one lung."

"Okay." I take a hard breath and straighten my back. "What now?"

He tells me that they have to clean and cauterize. And Charles will have to have a chest tube to drain the empty cavity of any leftover secretions.

"Is he awake?"

"He was. But he's drugged. A little panicky."

"Because of the last thing he saw."

"Exactly. So he'll be drifting in and out."

"Where is he? When can I see him?"

"As soon as we get him settled in ICU, you'll be allowed to visit."

He starts to leave, but only gets a few feet away before I call him. He comes back.

I ask, "Can you hook me up with something stronger than Valium?"

Yvette holds my hand while we go to ICU.

I don't recognize Charles. His face is scarred, swollen even more from where he fell. They've given him lots of fluid in surgery, so he's bloated like the Pillsbury Doughboy. He has a breathing tube between his lips, held there by a thing that looks like a headband. A ventilator the size of a mini-fridge makes a nonstop hissing and sighing sound. Too many monitors to count. And a slew of IV fluids are hanging at his side.

The nurse comes in. "You're family?"

"I'm his wife."

"Well, rest assured he's in good care."

The nurse's name is Regina Philpot. Nice sister from Augusta. Almond-shaped eyes. Round face. Short waist with long legs. Yvette and Regina make that Southern connection, and do what people from down south do, try to see if they know any of the same people.

I'm looking at Charles. All the tubes. The IVs. The smells. It's too much to digest.

When Regina hears that I have North Cakalaki in my blood, she tells us that her grandfather was from Charlotte. Says she still has family back there. In two minutes we're talking like we're the best of friends. Regina is very positive, good at easing me.

She doesn't ask me what happened. They already know.

I ask, "What should I expect?"

Regina tells me that Charles will be here until he's stable, and then will be sent to a surgical ward. She breaks down some of the rehabilitation that Charles will have to go through, the X rays, how he'll be weak and dependent.

She's very reassuring. I trust her when she says he'll be okay.

I wash my hands. Then I touch my husband. He's warm. He's alive.

He opens his eyes.

I touch his wavy hair and whisper his name.

He closes his eyes.

I ask Regina, "How long will he be here?"

"Barring no complications postoperatively, a week, give or take a day."

I give her my numbers so she can call if anything changes.

Then I leave.

* * *

Yvette takes me down the 405 in her SUV. Sunday morning traffic is light.

I'm on the cellular the whole ride, talking to Charles's family. They call me for updates. I tell them he's in ICU. His parents and siblings are packing so they can get here.

His father demands, "Why won't you tell us what happened? Was it a robbery? Was it some of that gangbanger, carjacking stuff that goes on out there?"

His son almost died. He's upset.

I'm tired. I'm scared. I'm frustrated.

So many lies have come and gone.

I say, "He had an affair. The woman's husband shot him."

"What? We talked to you last Sunday, y'all were leaving church . . . everything was fine."

"And right now I'm struggling to not go over the edge—"

Yvette takes the phone from me and finishes the conversation.

I take one of the happy pills the doctor gave me, swallow it dry. Hope it kicks in fast.

We change freeways, go from the 405 to the 110 to my exit on the 91.

I see people jogging across the street at CSUDH; construction workers are on campus building the soccer stadium. As soon as we turn into my complex, we have to stop at the gate. I don't have a clicker. It's in my car. The guards see me, ask how I'm doing. Neighbors come out. The community knows. Curious people want to ask questions. Everyone wants answers.

Yvette is at my side. She asks them all to let me rest, to respect that.

The garage has a control box outside. I put in the code and the new door whirs up.

We look at the fist-sized holes in the walls, take in all the destruction.

Yvette says, "Wow."

When I come into the house through the garage door, a stack of papers is sitting on the counter. At first I think it's Charles's work, something to do with social studies. It's not. It's the answers to all my questions. They've all been answered in detail. I throw them in the garbage.

22

On the map, Delaware looks like a peninsula between larger states. I don't fly on small planes, so I get a flight into Philadelphia, rent a car that has a navigation system, and use that to find my way south. First Wilmington goes by, and then I pass through Odessa and Smyrna.

Almost two hours later, I find myself in Dover, cruising Route 13.

Magic 98.9 and Angel entertain me for a while, and then I pop in a Tim McGraw CD. Let him give me his blue-eyed blues as I ride. The wind sings through my open window.

I ride the two-lane road to see where David Lawrence lived, stick to the speed limit, checking out the agricultural area, lots of wide-open land, blue skies forever, trailer homes, signs saying you can buy a lot for less than thirty thousand, McDonald's, occasional car dealerships, Warren Electric, Best Western, Dukes Lumber Company, Comfort Inn advertising rooms for $49.95, Collins Custom Homes, Sunrise Motel, Wal*Mart, Sears, Food Lion, Tru Blue Gas, cars broken down in the front yard down near Boyce and Sussex.

This was his world. No high-end cars cluttering the highway. No real traffic. The simple place where David Lawrence grew up. Where they will scatter his ashes.

A big, tall sign that has yellows and creams and reds and browns catches my eye down where Route 13 and Route 42 intersect. Wa Wa Food Market. I slow down and stare at the brown building. Minutes later a smaller sign catches my eye. I signal and pull into the gravel lot at Yodder Overhead Door Company. A Wawa girl worked here. He told me that.

It's time. I turn around and head for Faries Funeral Home.

I get to his memorial service early. There are so many flowers here. Too bad the dead can't smell. I get a program and go to the front, look to make sure my flowers are present. They're a simple arrangement, heartfelt, with my name and 1 Corinthians 13:3–8 on the card.

I take a seat in the middle, on the aisle end of the row, with my purse and alto saxophone case at my feet. I read about David Lawrence over and over.

Someone sits next to me. A woman with red hair. Her black suit is nice. She looks cosmopolitan, stands out from the locals the same way I do. She tells me she saw me at the airport. That we were on the same flight from L.A. to Philly. She came here alone as well.

She asks, "You went to school with him?"

I shake my head. "I met him two weeks ago today."

"Oh."

"He painted me. You?"

"I'm an artist too."

"Oh."

"We did art shows together. We were just in Canada together. Great guy."

I nod. "You dated him?"

"No." She chuckles. She wears a nice wedding ring. "Just

ran in the same circles. Me, him, Woodrow Nash, Bibbs, Gatewood—all of us always ended up at the same spots."

"I saw flowers from Bibbs." I motion toward the front. "By the ones from Dover High."

"Yep. We all run in the same circles."

"Guess the artist community isn't that large."

"The African-American artist community is even smaller."

Her words throw me for a second because I thought she was white.

I say, "He was a great artist."

"You?"

I know what she means. I answer, "We never dated."

I tell her my name.

She tells me her name is Kimberly Chavers. She met David Lawrence a few years ago when she and her husband first moved to Los Angeles. Both were at a seminar at UCLA.

She reads her program. Shakes her head and says how tragic this is.

She says, "Life is so short."

I agree. We both lower our eyes and look at the smiling face on the program. That pauses our conversation, but doesn't stop my thoughts about what she just said. Life is short. All journeys end here, in death. Right now I'm not who I wanna be when this journey ends.

Over time, more people come in and sit. Not many people at first. Then the crowd grows. Pretty soon over two hundred people are here. All the chairs are taken and people have to stand. Everyone knows each other. I feel like an outsider in a simple black skirt and jacket.

There is a commotion, some talking that carries.

People are whispering, searching for answers.

I've looked for answers myself. There are no answers.

There never really are. Questions always outnumber the answers.

The director calls for our attention.

The family is out on Governors Avenue, lining up to come inside.

We stand.

His mother is brought in first. A heavyset woman in a dreary blue dress. Wrists together like she's in handcuffs. A female and a male guard at her side. Her red and gray hair is in long braids. Her face used to be very pretty. Despite the lines and light scars, I can tell she was a beautiful woman. Her walk is a shuffle, as if she's grown used to a prison cadence, or maybe she's in no hurry to get back to her prison. She looks at people, as if she's trying to remember the names of the faces she never thought she'd see again. She sees me and pauses. Her eyes tell me that she wonders who I am. She moves on and sits down. Relatives of all ages come in behind her.

His mother shifts, looks around at the funeral home like she's never seen it before.

I ask Kimberly, "Did you know his wife?"

"Not really. She never really came out to the events we had."

"Wonder where she is."

"You read the article in the *Times*?"

"I read it."

"And the news too?"

"Yeah, I saw it."

"Would you show your face?"

"If I had nothing to be guilty about, yes."

She pats my hand. "Glad you came."

I know she knows who I am. She's kind about it. We leave that at that.

There are prayers and songs.

When it's time for people to speak, quite a few do. They remember him as a boy. As a teenager. As an ambitious young man who lived for his art. They talk about how funny he was. He was a generous boy who loved to fix cars for free. They tell the things I'll never get to know.

I ask if I can play a song for him. They tell me I can. It's original. It's short. It's nice.

His mother watches me with intense curiosity the whole time.

When I'm done, I nod at her.

She blows her nose, wipes the tears away, and nods back.

I gaze at her for a moment, giving her my thoughts and true feelings.

And she smiles. I see the young woman inside her. The woman with so much passion.

She mouths, "Thank you."

I mouth, "You're welcome."

I leave.

Outside in the parking lot, beyond the hearse and family cars, the sun shines down and reflects on chrome. The sparkle calls my attention to a classic Benz that is parked next to the building. A 250SL. Taupe color. Hardtop off.

I walk over to the car. A single passenger is inside.

Jessica.

She wears all black and a hat with a widow's veil. She pulls the veil away from her face when I get close. Sunglasses with rectangular yellow lenses tint her face. She uses a tissue to wipe her nose. Heaviness rests under her teary and bloodshot eyes.

I stare at her. The face of my husband's former lover. The face of my dead lover's wife.

I want to say something to her, but there are no words.

Outside of our dreams, I pray we never see each other again. She lowers her veil and starts the car. Firm grip on the handle of my sax case, I head to my rental. By the time I start my car, the Benz is pulling away from the church. That car gets smaller in my rearview mirror.

On my system, the CD player on repeat, Tim McGraw sings about the cowboy in him.

While I'm riding I-95 back toward Philadelphia, I call and check on Charles. I love him, I care about him, but our universe is different now. We will never be the same. My mother and one of my sisters have been to L.A. and gone back to North Carolina knowing the truth. Charles is recovering and his family is still there, caring for him. His mother and one of his brothers are at the hospital with him right now. He's been discharged, but they have to drive him out to UCLA for his therapy. Other relatives are camping out at our home. In her thick Creole accent, his mother tells me that Charles is alert, eating solid foods, and making progress in therapy.

She says, "He's still in pain, but it's not as bad. He won't be able to lift anything or drive for a while. The medication will have him drowsy. He'll need someone to cook."

I respond, "He's alive. He's out of the woods."

"I'm thankful."

"They say a parent losing a child is the harshest tragedy. Be very thankful."

"You've hardly been here."

"I know. You're doing a great job. Stay with him until he gets better."

"Then what will you do?"

"Then we'll decide what we're going to do about the house."

They know all there is to know about our fifteen minutes of infamy. Between the papers and the news coverage, not much needs to be said. Over a week has gone by and our story, so far as the media is concerned, is old news.

Charles's mother asks me where I am and when I'm coming back.

All I tell her is that I'll be by the house tomorrow. Before I go to the station, I'll come home to talk with Charles. I ask her to call me on my cellular if they need anything, say it all in a gracious and loving tone, blow her a kiss, and send my love to all before I hang up.

We sit out on the patio and talk. Charles pours his heart out, gives me his soul. We know where this is heading. This is our castle in the sand. Each time the tide comes in, it will take away what the wind does not scatter. If I stay, we'll become ghosts of who we used to be and this house will become our tomb. If I stay, the person I am now, he will resent. And if he doesn't resent me, I'll resent his weakness. There is no way for us to get to Paradise. Every day it will be less and less, so I tell him that it's time to take the wedding pictures off the walls and take the rings off our fingers. Put them all in boxes with the cards and letters that we may never read again. The universe has put us in a place where we're forced to make a choice.

Charles says, "But you don't want a divorce?"

"Divorce means nothing to me right now."

"Anything I can say or do to stop you?"

"No. But . . ."

"What?"

"I'm going to need some cash. Traveling money."

"I'm scared of losing you."

"And I'm scared of not finding myself."

I do it face-to-face, holding his hand for the last time, all of my words spoken in love, not anger. I'll leave him loving him, but not being in love with him.

He says, "But we did love each other, didn't we?"

"Once upon a time."

He holds my hand like he never wants to let go. I'll probably almost call him a thousand times. He'll call me and I'll almost answer just as many.

I ask, "Why didn't you apologize to him? He apologized to you."

"I don't know."

I pat his hand. He's a little boy who still has a lot of growing up to do.

He's my husband. We're forever linked. All of us will be.

I'll never forget.

And every time he takes a breath, he'll remember.

Going by work is just a formality. I have a lot of vacation time on the books and I need a lot of time away. I can't do the stress thing right now, don't know if I ever can again.

Tyra says, "Take as much time off as you need. You'll have a job when you come back."

"Thanks."

"Don't know if you've heard, but I'm letting Yvette work on a documentary for the station for Black History Month."

"Let me guess." I chuckle. "Something to do with Eritrea, right?"

"With fairness to all parties involved. Can't misrepresent Ethiopia. Have to keep it balanced, no propaganda, need the facts, above all we have to keep it entertaining."

"Think people will be interested?"

"Doubt it. But she thinks that if we try to tie it in to problems over here, don't really have a strong angle, maybe something about how we've all become so separate."

"The Diaspora. Sounds promising."

"Would love for you to produce it."

"A month ago I would have. But no thank you."

All I want to do is pack up my horns and go out and see what kind of talent I have, find some gigs, get my discipline back on track, and create art through my songs. A new nervousness covers me and I welcome that uncertainty.

I pop into the control room, then talk to the anchors, walk around and holler at a few people at the shop, let all of them see my smiling face so they know I'm doing okay. There are hugs and kisses and thank-yous. Breaking news comes. They all get back to their frantic paces.

I step into Yvette's editing world and she stops working. She stands and hugs me.

She asks, "Know where you're going?"

"Not really. I'll know when I get there."

She says, "Don't forget. I've got an empty condo sitting in the ATL. You need to get away. If you want, go down there and regroup. You'll only be a few hours from your family."

I say, "And Fort Mills."

We laugh a spiraling laugh.

I say, "Maybe I'll pack my Altoids and work on catching up with you."

For a while I may live like Yvette, free to possess and desire in adventure. Maybe I'll create my own sashay, one that rejects all the freedoms denied to a woman.

She tells me, "Wherever you go, call me, and I'm there when you need me."

"I will."

"Now go before I start crying."

"Love you, Yvette."

"Love you too."

I find an empty box and go to my doorless office, to my secondhand desk that sits in a field of open desks, and get ready to pack up a few things. Televisions are on, computer screens are lit up, but no one is in the area right now.

Two huge black tubes with FedEx labels are in my chair. I cut the duct tape off the end of the first tube. The end unscrews. Inside, rolled up, is canvas. I unroll the canvas. The ends keep curling so I use my phone, scissors, discs, and sorority paperweight to anchor each corner.

I stare at the image for a few moments.

Then I hurry to open the second black tube, unroll the second canvas, find more things to use as weights to hold the ends down.

They are the paintings of me. In colorful reds and browns. The first is the likeness of me reading the IMs. That deep expression of lost love so clear in my eyes. *Revelation.* The other is me in an erotic pose, with my breasts exposed, eyes closed, playing my sax. *Sunset.*

My complexion, my locks, breasts, thighs—his vision of me is sexy and beautiful.

I stand between the paintings. In one I'm sad. In the other one I'm happy. I want to be the woman in the happy picture. That's who I am. The woman in the other picture, she's not me. She's the one who broke her neck to make sure her husband was satisfied, broke her neck at a job that stressed her out, broke her neck trying to please everybody but herself.

I'm gonna be the girl in the happy picture.

Attached is a handwritten note.

It reads, simply. "I wish I had met you first. Before we met them."

My heart feels lighter. Tears flow. I whisper the same to the wind.

It's time for me to pack my things and get in my Baby Blue and head up the 101. Maybe go north and find a little nightclub, maybe someplace in the Bay, maybe Seattle, a place where I can play my sax, do what I love, and show people what I feel through my music. Let that be my rehabilitation.

The wind makes my locks dance as I adjust my rearview and look at the face of the woman in the mirror. Her brown skin and cinnamon freckles are coming alive in the sun, letting me see those familiar constellations. Corners of her smile are coming back.

I kiss her sadness good-bye.

Notes from EJD

☺☺☺

It's the 25th of August, 2002, and I'm getting ready to head out to Brasstown Bald with Dr. Melanie Richburg to go hiking up Georgia's highest mountain. I just finished the first draft of the book you're holding in your hand a couple of days ago. The original title was *Restless*, then changed to *Another Man's Wife*, and only God knows what it'll be when it hits the stores. *AMW* might get dropped because I have a close friend down in Florida, Shonda Cheekes, coming out with her first novel, and it has that great title.

As usual, I started out writing a different book, then somehow ended up working on this one. About one hundred pages into whatever I was working on at first (give or take thirty pages) this other idea I had been mulling over sort of took over. That was mid-March 2002. That always happens. Most artists can testify to that. Something bites you on the ass and you spend the next few months scratching until the itch is gone.

The motivation for this one was simple. It's the same enthusiasm from book to book. I'm always trying to do something different. Always trying to get a little better at what I do. I hadn't done a book, top to bottom, first person, female voice, present tense.

I try to keep it gritty and fresh. And fun. I'm always trying to come up with lies so good, you think it happened, and this is that character's journal. That's it in a nutshell.

Once again, here's that good old disclaimer that so many people tend to ignore. This book is fiction. It didn't happen to anyone I know. That goes for all of my books. Thanks for asking. Now stop asking and give it a rest. (Insert gratuitous smile.)

Oh, I took a break and studied Robert McKee's book *Story: Substance, Structure, Style, and the Principles of Screenwriting* as I worked on this. I always read a few books (fiction and nonfiction) while I work, but this one helped me get out of that writer's block I'd slipped into. It was great in getting me back to the basics of storytelling and scene development. His book either reaffirmed or reminded me of a thousand things, but most of all I remembered to focus on that good old "reversal of expectation" when writing each scene. And that there are really no bad guys, not if you get into the character and see the situation from his or her POV, understand that individual's motivation. Every character in a story is human, wants something, and never sees him/herself as an antagonist.

I love creating the characters, the same way an actor loves getting to play a new role. Over the last decade, I've had the opportunity to play "what if" with so many fictional lives. And as a writer, in my own opinion, you have to "become" every character in the book, to some degree, and no matter how small the part, you have to forget who you are and be willing to get inside their skin, see the world from their perspective. That, my friend, if you get it right, is mucho fun. And I'm doing my best.

I love getting their stories right—whether it involves running scams, or a spin on the love triangle theme—and telling it the best I can, and not having someone look at my work and go, "This sure is a lotta pages." Don't get me wrong, I have a great appreciation for constructive criticism (the operative word being constructive, not personal views) and I don't mind having a great fat-trimming session. Trust me; I'm not trying to write something the size of *War and Peace* over here. Hell, I love trees just as much as the next man. Grew up with a few in my backyard. Damn, I miss dem plums.

Before I go on and on till the break of dawn, let me give shout outs to my crew.

Thanks to the hardworking peeps at Dutton (Carole Baron, Audrey LaFehr, Lisa Johnson, Kathleen Matthews-Schmidt, Jennifer Jahner, Betsy DeJesus, et al.). You peeps have been great. Eight years and just as many books have flown by.

Sara Camilli, my agent since I stepped foot on this Yellow Brick Road, thanks for the confidence in my work, regardless of the "genre." You have been a great champion.

And thanks to the people who gave me that honest feedback along the way.

Jennifer McDaniel, thanks for being the voice to this nameless character. You read her well, countless times. She will forever sound like you in my mind.

Tiffany Pace (in Hot Vegas) thanks for pointing out all the (clearing throat) errors. Thanks for being a big part of the team. And I confess, you're one of the best I've met, and shoulda been here since day one. Hope you stick around until I get bucked off this pony.

Travis Hunter (ATL), Jihad Uhuru (ATL), Audrey O. Cooper (L.A.), Bobby Laird (L.A.), thanks for having my back. Victoria Christopher Murray, Kimberla Lawson Roby (and my big brother Will), Lolita Files, thanks for the years of friendship.

Dana Lynn Wimberly (ATL), Brenda Denise Stinson (L.A.), thanks for helping me keep my biz in order. Emil Johnson (L.A.) and Anthony Lyons (L.A.), thanks for all of your input.

And I have to thank the people who gave me insight on a few occupations as I went along. Even though I used bits and pieces of what they shared, and all of my friends are brilliant, this story is in no way about any of them. Don't get it twisted.

Denae Marcel in L.A., thanks 4 letting a bro call ya and ask a zillion Qs about your art.

Olivia Ridgell in Chi-town, Erica Calhoun in ATL, Yvette Hayward in NYC, thanks 4 taking the time out of your schedules to read my work in its rawest form. It amazes me how many times all of you were willing to look at every rewrite, even if it was a one-liner.

Salathia Britt in North Cakalaki, o ye e-mail buddy, many thanks for the Southern Fried info I got from ya on your alma mater and your sorority.

Regina Philpot (RN) in Augusta, GA. Thanks for the medical info!

Natalie A. Godwin, thanks for allowing me to look around both of your jobs. Thanks for answering so many questions, no matter what hour, even in your roughest moments. Stay positive '08.

Gwen Price in Little Rock, my RN friend, thanks for allowing a stranger to call you while you were making dinner. That was really cool of you.

Rahel, my Eritrean pal, thanks for the e-mail. You asked, you got it. 'Nuff said.

And Kevin Colvin, my brother on the Westside (throwing up the W!). Keep your head up.

Now, does anybody 'member what I said at the top? I'm about to bounce out and head up a big hill in Northern Georgia. I'm dropping bread crumbs, but if I don't make it back by the time the next book tour starts, remember I was last seen heading toward the Chattahoochee National Forest with Dr. Richburg. Hope we didn't find Big Foot.

Send help. ☺

Peace and blessings.

ejd